Old Fashioned

Albert Smith's Mystery Thrillers Book 3
Steve Higgs

Contents

Chapter 1

Albert pushed his plate aside, his appetite sated. In Holland for the first time in his life, he felt guilty for the steak and chips he'd ordered. He was supposed to be sampling local delicacies and expanding his palette. Yet his hunger saw steaks being delivered to a duo of women sitting at the table next to his and the decision was made right there and then.

He would explore Dutch dishes tomorrow.

Unusually, Rex's head did not appear at the side of the table the moment Albert stopped eating. For once he wasn't loitering next to his human's chair. He was upstairs in their room, snoozing peacefully on Albert's bed, his belly full of doggy chow from his own dinner an hour ago.

They had arrived by train that afternoon from the Alsace region of France and walked from the station to their accommodation following the map on Albert's phone. For Albert it was the chance to show off some newfound skills, though without anyone to appreciate his brilliance, the only one impressed by his feat of satellite navigation was Albert himself.

Pleasantly surprised to find a restaurant next to his small hotel, he gratefully left Rex in their room to enjoy dinner by himself for once. Not that he disliked his dog's company, but Rex always wanted to share whatever Albert was eating and whatever anyone at the tables around them were eating, and ... well, I'm sure you get the picture. It was relaxing and peaceful not to need to consider Rex for a short while.

The larger than normal German Shepherd came to live with Albert after his career as a police dog came to an abrupt close. He was listed as too difficult to work with, but the truth of it was simpler: he was brighter than most of his handlers.

The waiter arrived, collecting the plate and cutlery with deft, familiar moves.

"Would you like to see the dessert menu?" he asked, balancing Albert's dirty plate on his left hand.

He got a brief shake of Albert's head in reply. "No, thank you. That steak has finished me off. It was quite delicious." The waiter dipped his head to acknowledge the compliment, even though it was aimed at the chef. When he turned to leave, Albert hastily added, "Could I get the bill, please?"

He was in no particular hurry to leave; he had nowhere else that he needed to be, yet his stomach was full enough to border on uncomfortable and he wanted to go for a walk. Rex would appreciate the chance to stretch his legs too.

With only a few months to go until his seventy-ninth birthday, Albert was making the most of whatever time he had left. Having lost his beloved wife the previous year, the haunting memories in their house drove him to get out and explore the world. It started with a culinary tour around the British Isles where he intended to learn to cook many of his favourite dishes. What he mostly learned was that his years of letting Petunia do all the cooking left him rather inept in the cheffing department. However, the desire to learn took a near constant backseat to something he was actually quite good at: investigating crimes.

A long career as a law enforcement officer and numerous promotions that culminated at detective superintendent guaranteed him a pension that was sufficient to support his travels while simultaneously underpinning his confidence as a sleuth. He could find no rhyme or reason behind the constant succession of strange circumstances his journey delivered him into, yet as if guided by the hand of God, everywhere he went, he arrived just in time to stumble into murder, robbery, embezzlement, or just plain criminal enterprise on an industrial scale.

Reflecting on the drama and excitement his culinary tour became, Albert had to admit he held no regrets, yet would state, if asked, that he would be equally happy to enjoy his days with a little less adrenaline coursing through his veins.

The waiter returned with the bill and a card reader, his eyebrows raising when Albert chose to pay in cash as though it was as outmoded as cooking at home. Leaving a generous tip, Albert checked his pockets to be sure he had all his belongings and made his way through the busy tables to the exit.

He felt good about Amsterdam. He'd been here for hours and nothing bad had happened yet. All around were people enjoying themselves, going about their lives without showing the slightest sign they were primed to engage in a murderous rampage. In the morning, he would explore the city, taking Rex for a long walk on a route he'd already mapped out. They would stop for coffee and stroopwafels, a caramel filled sandwich wafer locals warmed over the top of a hot beverage. He'd never had one before and that oversight would be corrected. They would stop for lunch too and if he could get in with Rex, there were museums he wanted to explore.

Smiling to himself, Albert left the restaurant, turned right and almost immediately right again to enter his hotel. Amsterdam was going to be different.

Chapter 2

"**S**how me the list for tomorrow night." Sylvia van Lidth gazed out across the Amsterdam skyline. Her penthouse apartment provided views on all four sides, a feature that convinced her to hand over the exorbitant price the real estate agents placed on it. That was eighteen years ago, back when she was only making a few million Euros a year. Now the price was a drop in the ocean and the value had grown fortyfold.

A sound investment, not least for the impact it had on prospective clients.

She ran a very bespoke business that catered to the superrich. To those who were able to buy anything and therefore wanted nothing. They didn't want things, they had already bought them all, but experiences, the thrill of blood and rage and adrenaline, that was something they would pay for. And Sylvia was very happy to provide it.

Her assistant, a thirty-two-year-old American woman with a law degree from Harvard, handed her a tablet and stood quietly at her side to let Sylvia interrogate the information it displayed.

Using an index finger to scroll, Sylvia looked at the guest list first. It was arguably the most important element. One had to get the right people in. Get that right and the night would go well regardless of how the fights panned out.

Satisfied, she moved on to look at the fights themselves. It took her less than a second to spot the problem.

"Chelsea there is a gap."

Chelsea nodded. "I have people working on it."

Sylvia liked Chelsea. She was efficient and ambitious, two characteristics she admired. She also trusted her, Chelsea had been in her employ for almost four years and was yet to let her down or disappoint, but a hole in the program so close to the event? That wasn't anywhere near good enough.

Wise enough to know more assurance was required, Chelsea continued to talk before her boss could ask the obvious questions.

"The gap is only a few hours old. We had a full lineup until this afternoon."

"What happened?"

"The contender suffered an injury. He was limping."

Sylvia pursed her lips. At least no one was trying to include a subpar contender; that was worse than having no contender at all, but the bout was against a champion from Russia, presented by an oil oligarch. Hardly the kind of person Sylvia wanted to disappoint.

"Who do you have working on a replacement?"

Chelsea sucked in a breath. She was praying they could deliver.

"Everyone."

As answers go it was the best she could have hoped for. Handing back the tablet, Sylvia van Lidth turned her gaze back to the Amsterdam skyline.

"Very well. I want to know as soon as a replacement is found. I will approve him myself."

Chelsea bowed her head and departed, her steps unhurried until she was out of the apartment, then the pace increased. There had been a big build up to this event and it had to go perfectly. Sylvia took the bad news with a startling level of calm; she was better known for her explosive temper.

With so much riding on the next twenty-four hours, Chelsea called to cancel her date for the night and cleared her diary of everything that wasn't to do with solving the inconvenient problem she could not have foreseen.

Chapter 3

T he air was cool but not unpleasantly so. Having come from elevation in France, where it had been snowing and Albert almost caught frostbite, it felt significantly warmer than it otherwise might, but regardless Rex needed a walk, and it was both too early and too pleasant out to retire to their hotel room yet.

"This way, Rex." Albert gave a gentle tug on the lead when he felt Rex had spent quite long enough investigating the scents left on the lamppost he faced.

Rex twitched his head around but kept his paws firmly in place. His human was always trying to go somewhere and showed no appreciation for the 'message board' as Rex liked to think of it. They were somewhere new - a regular occurrence for them - thus he had to learn all he could in a short space of time. There were dogs in the area and it paid dividends to know breed and age and gender and more. Chances are he would run into some of them, possibly the area's alpha, so forewarned was forearmed.

Possessing a powerful olfactory system, Rex could take a sample of street air and find within it a million different smells. Right now he was getting the scents of the city rather than anything specific. He could dial down into it but had no need to do so. The smell of coffee, which would have been stronger earlier in the day was now a background odour. Replacing it, the human need to mask their own smells with perfume sat heavy on the air. It combined with food and alcohol, both of which were in abundance.

There was something else too, a sickly-sweet aroma Rex did not recognise. It tickled his nose, leaving behind a piney, skunky grass scent that left him curious.

Albert clicked his tongue and started walking. Either Rex could elect to follow, or he would find himself dragged away from the lamppost when the lead went taut.

Rex chose to follow; he was finished sampling the 'message board' anyway.

Albert's eyes were on his phone which he was using, once again, to navigate his way from one point to another. The streets of Amsterdam were lively; far more so than Albert anticipated they would be in December, and despite the cool air, people chose to sit outside. The tables and chairs outside eateries lining the street had heaters mounted to ward off the cold, and blankets on hand so patrons could wrap an extra layer over their shoulders if they felt so inclined. It was very different to England where Albert was sure such a tactic would not catch on.

The busy streets, however, were not the optimum venue for his dog to perform that which was necessary before they bunked down for the night. He was heading for a park.

Except he wasn't.

Frowning, Albert stared at his phone. The little blinking dot representing his current location had somehow taken a wrong turn. Leaving the restaurants and crowded pavement behind, he'd been confident in his direction. Except now he was on the other side of the road and moving away from the green area, not toward it.

Was he holding it upside down? Albert inverted his phone, but the screen simply rotated with his hand so it looked exactly as it had.

Standing next to Albert's right leg, Rex sniffed the air. There was nothing new about it provided one discounted the dead pigeon squished into the tarmac ten metres ahead.

Convinced he had it right, Albert continued onward, staring down at the blinking dot as it moved farther and farther from where he wanted to go. Perplexed, he was about to turn around when a new green area edged into the screen. It was directly ahead and since one park was effectively the same as any other, and he just wanted somewhere to let Rex off the lead for a few minutes, he continued onward with an indifferent shrug.

He pressed on, confident he would master navigation by phone if he persisted and content he was no more than a minute from finding that which Rex required.

Ten minutes later, Rex's um, output, was in a bin and they were heading back to the busy street where Albert planned to rest awhile with an aperitif. He wasn't one for staying out late and though he liked a drink, he never had more than a couple to avoid the fogging effect they brought. Plus, he was halfway through a book about a paranormal investigator and was excited to get back to it.

Retracing their steps, the phone now secured in his pocket, Albert spotted two men in the street ahead. They were having some trouble getting into their car. At least, that was Albert's first assumption. That belief changed a heartbeat later when he saw the taller of the pair extend a long, thin steel bar which he proceeded to slide between the window and the frame in which it sat.

They were car thieves.

Years of seeking justice for the victims of crime, Albert knew firsthand the impact it could have. It was just a car, a tool designed to get a person from A to B, but for most people it was also the culmination of many months of saving, or the result of a financial agreement to borrow that which they otherwise could not afford. It was their daily transport, the thing that got them to work, or could even be the centre of their business. Imagine a taxi driver and question what he does to make money when he leaves his house to find his car has been stolen in the night.

Instantly incensed, Albert's lips were curling into a growl when the car's alarm went off. He was fifty metres from the thieves yet close enough for the volume to hurt his ears. Up close it had to be painful, but acting as though unperturbed, the thieves popped the driver's door open.

The shorter man – the lookout, Albert surmised, finally did his job and glanced around to see who might have noticed.

His taller partner was getting in, yelling something Albert could see from the movement of his lips, but not hear over the wailing alarm.

Their eyes locked for a moment, the shorter man staring right at Albert. He was five feet eight inches in old money, the measurements Albert had always worked in, with jet black hair cut short at the sides and spiked on top, he had Asian features. Albert judged his age at something close to twenty-two. He was heavy set and wore black jeans and boots adorned with silver spikes on the toes beneath a thick, crimson coat that bore bold white letters down the right sleeve.

His partner was stick thin and six foot three. Also Asian, Albert was too far away to be sure of their heritage, but was ready to guess Korean. The taller man's hair was likewise jet black, but cut into a mohawk that was bleached on the tips.

Albert absorbed it all in the half second he held the shorter man's eyes. He was good at descriptions, a vital skill for a detective, but realising his error, he jerked his hand to get to his phone. A description was one thing – it was all they had back in his day, but a picture was a thousand times better.

Too late, the Korean kid left standing in the street came to his senses and ran to get around the car to the other side. His partner was behind the wheel, fighting to get the car started and both they and the automobile they sought to liberate from its owner were too far away for Albert to do anything about.

Others might have let it go, but Albert wasn't the kind of person who could sleep at night knowing he'd failed to do all that he could. Maybe he couldn't cover fifty metres in a few seconds, but he knew someone who could.

Albert released the clip connecting the lead to Rex's collar with a bark of command, "Sic 'em, Rex!"

Chapter 4

"**H**uh?"

Rex didn't like the alarm. It was hurting his ears and making him think they should be walking away from it, not getting closer. Focused on that, he wasn't paying attention and missed what the old man had said.

Albert had stopped walking, his right arm extended to point in the direction he expected Rex to go. He stayed in that position for a beat, expecting to see his dog explode into action and tear down the street. Glancing down, his right arm still extended, he found Rex looking up at him.

Rex wagged his tail. "*Hey. What's happening?*"

Albert put his hands on his hips. Typically, he had to battle to keep Rex under control. The dog had a built in sixth sense for detecting criminals, and now that there were two right in front of them he was wagging his tail with a goofy grin on his face.

Trying again, Albert jerked his arm in the direction he wanted him to go, and yelled, "Sic 'em, boy!"

This time he got it, and Rex didn't need to be told twice. Although, he kinda did on this occasion.

With his dog belting down the street, Albert jogged behind at his best pace. He was fit and able, especially for his age, but his knees were mere shadows of their former selves and his ankles, back, and other parts habitually choose to punish him should he ever chose to push his body too hard.

Rex liked running and he really liked running when he was told to chase a human. Humans were so slow and they had so many squidgy bits he could bite when he caught up with them. Or he could just run through their legs. The gangly, two-legged design was incredibly impractical, so with their centre of gravity three feet above the ground, the slightest nudge with a shoulder was generally all it took to topple them.

Then they became a cartwheeling, tumbling jumble of uncoordinated limbs and a joy to watch.

The only concern Rex faced as he set off down the street was that he had not one idea who it was his human expected him to chase. There was no one in the street. He saw the two men getting into their car, but even though he could smell the anxiety in their perspiration, it wasn't enough to make him think they were his target.

Humans get anxious for so many reasons: late for something, made a mistake with something, can't do something … Rex ignored the two young men and powered onward, certain the target would become obvious soon enough.

Albert, now thirty metres from the car, watched his dog fly past it. Exasperated, he threw his arms in the air.

"Rex!"

Rex just kept on going.

"Rex!"

Nothing. The street curved and his dog vanished from sight.

Cursing under his breath, Albert was close enough now to get a proper look at the car. As part of his job, he could tell make and model of any vehicle on the roads thirty years ago, but it was not a skill he'd chosen to maintain after retirement.

It was a Nissan and something high-end, that much he could tell. It was also heavily modified with wide wheels and a low-riding body.

The alarm had been warbling for fifteen seconds, surely alerting the owner along with everyone else in the street. Lights had come on and curtains were twitching but so far no one had burst from their door to see what was occurring.

Trying to make himself heard over the din, Albert yelled, "Hey!" though he knew it to be a futile gesture. Even if he could make himself loud enough, they were inside the car with the door shut.

Nevertheless, when he closed the final metres, he grabbed the door handle and attempted to get in. The windows were tinted black which made it difficult to see inside, but he caught the tall Korean man's shocked face when he turned to look at the old codger outside.

He'd locked the door, but the stupid immobiliser was resisting all his attempts to bypass it. Too long had elapsed and though they were loath to report their failure, it was still the preferred option to getting arrested. They had to go.

Albert yanked at the door handle again, leaning down to snarl through the window. The thieves' tool was still sticking out between the window and door frame, and though he had no clue what he needed to do to make it open the door, he figured it was his best chance at gaining access.

Gripping it with both hands, he pushed down and then up, choking out a gasp when the lock popped open.

Inside the car, the taller man snatched at the lock, shutting the door again. His companion had his hand poised on the handle his side and was yelling their need to abort.

Albert popped the lock again, barking in triumph even though he wasn't fast enough to get to the door handle to open it before the man inside locked it again.

Accepting the inevitable, the thieves chose to bail. Albert had switched to using one hand on the tool so his other could yank the door handle the moment he unlocked it, but the door unlocked itself this time, the door handle yielding so unexpectedly Albert fell backward onto the pavement.

The thieves were going out the other side, the man in the driver's seat clambering over the transmission tunnel to affect his escape.

Albert was almost on his butt, only his hands saving him from sprawling on the ground like a late-night drunk. He scrambled around to get his feet better positioned and was getting back to upright when Rex reappeared.

He'd run all the way back to the end of the street without finding a scent he believed he ought to be chasing. There he reversed course, running just as hard to get back to his human while fearing he might have left him in danger. The command to chase was only given in circumstances of extreme peril, but haring along the pavement, he spotted Albert lying on the ground.

That might have given him cause for alarm, but there was no coppery tang of blood on the air and his human was already getting up.

Seeing Rex, Albert jabbed his arm at the car.

"Here, Rex! Get them!"

The shorter man was already out of the car and his friend was close on his heel when Rex angled his body around the edge of the open door to dive inside. He threw himself into the car just as the taller man fell out the other side. Landing on his back, he saw a vicious set of teeth heading for his face and kicked the door shut.

Rex thumped into the other side, colliding painfully with the glass where he abruptly stopped.

A little out of breath, Albert was back on his feet and perfectly positioned to see the Asian men sprinting away. They spared him a glance over their shoulders before they zipped between the parked cars on the opposite side of the street and cut down an alley.

Frustrated and annoyed, Albert crouched to check on Rex just as an angry shout cut through the air. A man was emerging barefoot and shirtless from a house twenty metres farther down the street. Face contorted with rage, he had a phone to his ear, and when Albert looked his way the man aimed his right hand at the car.

Magically, the alarm shut off, dousing the street in blissful silence.

Chapter 5

"Stealing my car!" the man screamed. A woman in a skimpy silky gown appeared in the doorway behind him. She was trying to use the gown to protect her modesty, but in the cool night air it clung enticingly to all the parts she might wish to cover.

Giving up, she yelled, "Axel! Take this!"

The 'this' in question turned out to be a baseball bat; an object the young lady kept by her front door on a just-in-case basis. Axel was already heading for his car, menace in his stride and a grimace on his face when he flicked his gaze around to see what his girlfriend wanted.

He snatched the bat from her hands and threw her his phone which she juggled and almost dropped as she fought to catch it while simultaneously keeping the two ends of her gown together. When the man faced Albert again he held the bat in both hands, gripping it tightly like he was getting ready to swing for the bleachers.

He stood six feet tall, and was seriously lean, the muscles beneath his untanned white skin underdeveloped but all visible. His hair was shaved close to the skull in a tight crew cut, and he had a full sleeve of tattoos running down his right arm. Bereft of clothing beyond the pair of jeans, he had to be cold, but was too angry to care.

"Now just a minute," Albert protested. The car owner had taken so long to get out into the street – understandably given the near naked state of the couple – that he missed the Asian men running away. Instead, he found Albert next to the open car door which still had the thieves' tool protruding from it. He jumped to a natural conclusion and was now advancing with a murderous glint in his eye.

"Stealing my car!" the car owner repeated.

"Axel, is it?" Albert hoped he'd heard his name correctly. "I was just passing. The thieves ran off just before you came outside." He backed away, keeping some distance between them. If he could calm him down a little, he would be able to explain.

Axel was ten feet away and disinclined to listen.

"The police are on their way, but I think they'll believe you got violent and forced me to protect myself." He started running despite his bare feet, passing the still open car door as he took the bat behind his body and began to swing it. Aiming at Albert's ribs, he came at him with enough force to break bone.

Halfway through its swing the bat stopped abruptly. It was just coming level with Axel's body and beginning to pick up speed.

Axel twisted his head around to find a large German Shepherd glaring at him. The business end of the bat was clamped between the dog's teeth. It's big, pointy, dangerous looking teeth, and it growled in a manner that suggested it could, if it so chose, consume the implement like a woodchipper.

Rex was still in the car when the owner found his way to the street. Hitting his head against the door when it slammed in his face had dazed him for a second. Then he struggled to turn around in the tight space. In the end he'd needed to reverse his back end into the passenger's footwell to get his head facing the right way. He'd done so in time to see his human backing toward the rear of the car pursued by a man with a bat.

That sort of thing simply isn't allowed.

Axel tried to wrench the bat from Rex's teeth.

"Give it back, you stupid mutt!"

Rex's growl doubled in volume and dropped an octave in depth. Name calling wasn't going to lighten his mood. He had the fat end clamped in his jaw and enough strength and weight to hold on no matter what the skinny youth might try to do.

Albert wanted to wade in to help, but the man with the bat was too incensed to listen to reason and likely to swing a punch if he got too close. The danger in that was how Rex might react. The man might be holding a bat, but he was the victim.

It was his car the thieves targeted. If Albert could just get him to listen for a few seconds ...

The whoop of a police siren came to the accompaniment of red and blue strobes as a squad car edged into sight. Responding to a call, the cops could see a half-naked man and figured this was the incident in question.

Axel's girlfriend jumped and waved from her doorstep, making sure the cops knew they were in the right place. The sight of her bouncing, untethered chest would probably have stopped them regardless, if only so they didn't crash into the parked cars.

"That'll do, Rex," Albert commanded, his voice calm and patient.

Unfortunately, the order to desist came at the same time as Axel gave the bat another yank. Rex opened his mouth and the poor car owner fell backward, hitting the pavement where he grazed his elbows and back.

Albert moved in to help him up only to have his hand slapped away.

"He's here!" Axel shouted to draw attention his way. "He's here! Get him!"

His girlfriend was shouting too, gesticulating with urgent motions to get the officers moving. They had stopped their car in the middle of the road, leaving the engine running and the strobes lit while they exited. They appeared to be in no particular hurry and Albert knew why: it was always better to act calm. It helped to instil calm in those around you. There would be times when the situation called for a more dynamic response, but this was not one of them.

"If you would please just listen ..." Albert tried yet again to explain only to abandon what he wanted to say because Axel was getting up, still had hold of the bat, and Rex still saw him as a threat. "No, Rex!" Albert shouted just as the police officers stepped onto the pavement.

Rex snarled a threat, his hackles up and his teeth bared. In an instant the lead officer was on his radio exchanging fast words Albert could not understand. His eyes were locked on Rex though, and Albert knew enough to guess what was being said.

"Rex, to heel, please." Albert was sure to keep his hands visible – he wanted to look as unthreatening as possible. Axel no longer looked like he was going to swing the bat at anyone, not now that the police were present, and mercifully that meant Rex obeyed Albert's command.

Dropping his aggressive stance, Rex let his lower jaw fall open and his tongue loll out. Running and chasing and jumping into cars left him needing to pant. He walked past the half-naked man with the bat, keeping an eye on him lest he choose to make a move, but arrived at Albert's side where he turned around to face the perceived direction of danger and settled his backside onto the ground.

Albert breathed a sigh of relief, but it proved to be short lived. The officers arrived to the sight of a large dog acting aggressively. Their natural reaction was to call for animal services which he felt sure he heard them do, even if he couldn't understand Flemish. However, with the dog now calm, the concern regarding Rex's behaviour ought to have evaporated and it had not.

"This is your dog, sir?" The second officer questioned.

Albert was in the process of clipping Rex's collar back to his lead and had to stop himself from retorting with a snarky response. It would do him no favours to act smart.

"Yes, officer. I sent him to chase away two car thieves. Some confusion arose and the owner," he pointed at Axel, "mistook me for the thief."

Axel used his bat to point at the car. "I saw him using that tool to get it open. I was looking out of the upstairs window. There's bound to be CCTV footage from someone's doorbell." He looked hopefully at the buildings facing the street.

Albert cringed and turned his face to the stars. If the owner looked out at the right time, he would have seen precisely what he claimed. The thieves were both in the car and Albert was trying to get the door open. If he'd then run downstairs to stop the theft, he would have missed the thieves running away. When the car owner came out of his house, he found Albert with the car door open. The conclusions he drew were as natural as they were unavoidable.

The girlfriend stepped out onto the street. She had a coat on now, the majority of her body covered at last, and there were knee-high boots on her feet. She had her boyfriend's jacket in one hand, bringing it so he could cover up.

Axel took it gratefully but didn't put the bat down until he was told to do so.

The police officers were still working as a pair; one on the radio with the other managing the people in the street. They were young – in their mid to late twenties – but old enough to have racked up a few years of law enforcement. They knew what they were doing.

Albert attempted to explain his side of the story, but was instructed to remain silent much as he would have done so many years ago. Shockingly, Axel didn't embellish his version, but it made Albert sound like an evil villain all the same. He listened when he explained how his car was a rare model and had been targeted by thieves. It was usually kept inside a garage behind the fence line of a gated street.

According to Axel, several of his friends' cars had been stolen in recent weeks and he wasn't looking to join their ranks.

A second squad car arrived, parking nose to nose with the first to shower the street with even more strobe lights. Residents hung from their doors or watched through their windows, their gazes when they looked Albert's way not exactly accusatory, but not friendly either.

The cool December air worked its way into Albert's extremities, his hands and feet numbing and becoming painful along with his ears and chin. He was about to ask if he could sit in the back of one of the police cars when the two new officers came his way.

"Hands where we can see them," demanded one.

"Are you carrying any concealed weapons?" asked his partner. Like the first two, they were young men, though one was probably in his early thirties and the other looked to be fresh from the academy.

Albert complied, by raising his hands a few inches away from his body, but he didn't answer the question. Instead, he said, "Are you seriously going to arrest me?" He already knew they were and the question about weapons confirmed it. "I stopped a crime in progress."

The senior man said, "Your fingerprints are on the tool used to open the car, yes?"

"I already explained they are and why."

He got a shrug. "Turn around and place your hands behind your back. My partner is going to frisk you. Is there anything sharp in your pockets that could cause injury?"

Albert shuffled around to face the other way. "No, I have nothing sharp on me," he replied with a weary sigh. Yet again he'd tried to do the right thing only to have it blow up in his face.

Rex twitched his head from left to right, trying to figure out what was happening. The police were a source of comfort generally; they were the good guys, but yet again they had gotten things all mixed up and were looking to arrest his human.

When no one started the frisking or approached with handcuffs, Albert turned back to face the officer. "Now come on, chaps. I've already told you what happened. I'm an old man in Amsterdam on vacation and I know you don't actually believe I was trying to steal that man's car. Why do you feel the need to arrest me?"

"Because car theft has become rife in this city," answered a new voice.

All heads turned to find a woman in a suit and winter coat approaching. She was thirty-three or thereabouts, kept her curly red hair cut so it sat half an inch above her collar, and was close to six feet tall. She wore flat shoes tonight, but would tower above the male officers if she chose to wear heels. Her outfit was more high-end and elegant than most detectives would wear, a sign Albert took to indicate that she was many rungs up the ladder, looking for a promotion, and had one eye on the top spot.

Upon seeing who it was, the cops all reacted by straightening their postures and making sure they looked alert. Albert watched her aim her eyes at the oldest of the uniformed officers. He immediately started walking, moving away from Albert to meet his superior.

They talked while everyone else remained quiet, the senior uniform defending his actions or decisions and gesticulating to elements of the scene: the car, the house of the owner, Albert.

Albert silently stewed.

Thankfully, he didn't have to stew for very long. Once the report was given, the detective aimed her feet directly at him.

She stopped just a couple of feet away, close enough that Rex was sniffing at the air to record her scent. "Okay, Mr Smith," she said, "I need to know exactly what you saw in all the brilliant details I know you can provide."

"You're not arresting me?" Albert chose to confirm what he considered to be a vital point first.

"No, of course not. I'm afraid my officers didn't recognise you, but they ought to have been able to rally enough common sense to know you were not the thief even so."

Feeling a weight lifting from his shoulders, Albert said, "Well, thank you, but I already told your officers all there is to know."

"And now you can tell me." She came forward another foot, withdrawing a gloved hand from inside her coat pocket to reveal a business card. "Inspecteur Daniella Hoeks. I think the equivalent in England is Chief Inspector. You were a detective also, were you not?"

"I was," Albert pocketed her card. "You have a car theft problem here?"

"I will gladly tell you all about it over a terrible cup of coffee at the station, Mr Smith. I promise to keep you no longer than is absolutely necessary, but you will need to kill some time while they process your dog."

Albert blinked. Had he heard that right. "My dog?"

His confusion clear, Chief Inspector Hoeks twisted her head to glare at the uniformed officers.

"You didn't tell him?"

The senior man defended himself. "I was waiting for animal services to arrive." A light beep from a horn brought their eyes to a van now drawing to a stop in the street. "Here they are now."

Albert was angry again. The elegant redhead's arrival had alleviated his worries, but prematurely, it seemed.

"What is it that I don't know?" he demanded, adding a firm, "My dog is not going with animal services."

Chief Inspector Hoeks was decent enough to look apologetic when she explained, "I'm afraid he must, Mr Smith. There was a policy change last year, brought about by a spate of dangerous dog attacks. Now, any dog demonstrating aggressive behaviour must be registered, processed, assessed. Please don't fret," she added quickly when Albert opened his mouth to protest, "it's a formality only and will not take long."

Albert narrowed his eyes and held Rex close. "And what happens to the dogs that fail the assessment?"

Chief Inspector Hoeks didn't answer. There was no need.

Rex angled his head up to look at Albert. "*What's happening?*"

Albert gave him a smile and came down to one knee. The animal services team were approaching. A duo of men in their late forties, both balding and badly overweight, their bellies testing the poppers at the front of the coveralls.

"You're going to go with these nice men," Albert coached, his voice upbeat and enthusiastic. "They are going to take good care of you. I expect there will be treats."

Rex raised his right eyebrow. "*You must think I'm stupid.*"

Chapter 6

Three miles from Albert's location, Lee Yoo stared at his phone. It was going to ring any second. His uncle always called around this time of the day for an update. Not about his health or general wellbeing, but about the order.

The order Lee Yoo assured his uncle he could fulfil. The order that was going to net Lee close to half a million Euros. The order that was due in two days.

The order that wasn't ready.

Growing up in Busan in South Korea, Lee had seen his uncle as the rich member of the family. Uncle Kim always drove a sports car, sometimes a Ferrari, other times an Aston Martin. One time he even arrived in a Rolls Royce. Lee got to see him only once or twice a year, but they were some of his fondest memories because Uncle Kim always came bearing gifts.

Lee's father worked in a factory making plastic machine parts to be sold in America. He earned enough money to ensure there was always food on the table, and Lee's mother had a job at a school where she did some secretarial work, helped serving lunch to the kids, and supervised playtimes outside. It was minimum wage stuff, and Lee couldn't understand why his parents were so poor and his mother's brother was so rich.

Lee's father wanted his brother-in-law to stop. Not just stop with the toys and gifts, but to stop visiting altogether. Uncle Kim hit Lee's father and in his infantile way, Lee was glad. His father couldn't afford to buy the things he wanted, so why should he care if Uncle Kim provided them.

When he grew too old for the wonderful toys his uncle provided, the gifts became games systems and music players then concert tickets and, when he was old enough, a car. By then Lee understood why his mother and father were so disapproving of his uncle's generosity.

Uncle Kim was a criminal.

That was the big secret his parents never talked about. His money was dirty, gained through criminal enterprises and in his parents' eyes that meant everything he gave their child was tainted.

Lee didn't see it that way. He was a poor kid born to poor parents, but he didn't have to stay that way. He rebelled in his late teens and when his parents fought back with punitive measures designed to curb his behaviour, he walked out.

At seventeen he joined his uncle and by nineteen he had money of his own and a crew to run. Now he was twenty-six and living in Amsterdam because the 'family' had aspirations far beyond South Korea. His Uncle wasn't the big boss, but a close lieutenant of the man sitting at the top. Uncle Kim saw to it that things got done. He was a ruthless enforcer known for making people vanish when they failed to deliver that which they had promised.

Lee Yoo had promised an order of cars and he was two days away from failing to deliver. The list of cars comprised more than fifty rare models including some Italian sports cars, Maybachs, a Bristol Fighter, which he'd needed to send people to England to obtain, and twelve high-end modified Japanese cars. Lee had no idea who would order such cars, not that it made a difference who wanted them, his job was to locate and liberate.

Amsterdam was long associated with street racing; more so than most European cities, which made it easier to find the modified cars than it probably would have been elsewhere, but he was still short by one of the twelve, plus the Maybach, a particular model of Range Rover that retailed at over two hundred and fifty thousand Euros, and a Ferrari F40 though he did have a location for that one.

He had three teams out tonight, each with an address where they would find one of the cars on his list.

Lee Yoo checked his watch and stared at his phone. His uncle was going to call any minute and he wanted to be able to state he had reduced the items missing from the list by fifty percent. Two days would be enough to find and steal whatever remained.

It would have to be.

The sound of a door opening pulled his head and eyes up. One of his crews was returning. He was in a warehouse-sized lockup in Westpoort where the cars would have their engine and chassis numbers replaced before being shipped. Peering into the gloom, he saw Park flick on the lights.

Relief flooded through him, a soupçon of the tension he felt fading away. If Park was here, it meant Song was right behind him with the car. They had gone after one of the rarest marques, a Nissan GTR. Highly modifiable, they were a street racer's dream and the one they needed had more than a hundred thousand Euros of aftermarket gear added.

However, Song followed Park through the door, confusing Lee. Why wasn't Park opening the roller doors so Song could drive the car in? He rapped on the glass, banging it with his knuckles to get their attention. When they looked his way, they made 'What can we tell you?' gestures with their arms.

They didn't have the car. They weren't supposed to come back without it.

On the desk behind Lee, his phone began to ring.

Chapter 7

"Thank you, Albert." Chief Inspector Danielle Hoeks pushed back her chair and made to rise. She had kept him longer than she intended but wasn't about to feel bad about it.

Park Ji Hoon and Song Bin were petty criminals with long rap sheets. They were South Korean and were yet to do anything heinous enough to make them worthy of attention. Car theft wasn't going to get the courts or papers excited, but if they were involved at an industrial scale ... Among other things, Hoeks was investigating a recent spate of high price tag car thefts. Under pressure to deliver, she wondered if Albert's thieves were part of it.

It felt like a long shot, but if the thefts could be traced back to a Korean gang known to be operating in the city, she could make a dozen or more arrests, retrieve a stack of stolen property worth millions, and score a big win for the department.

Taking up Albert's time had been most worthwhile.

Albert dipped his head to acknowledge her thanks and kept his thoughts to himself. He was being civically responsible; if no one ever helped the police with their enquiries, the world would be overrun with criminals in no time at all. However, while he drank terrible coffee and looked through mugshots, his dog was goodness knows where thinking goodness knows what and Albert was furious about it.

He didn't give a stuff about their policies or what might have happened in the past to make them necessary, Rex was his companion and best pal. Separating them was unnecessary and now that he was done helping the chief inspector, he was going to get him back.

"I can go?" He got to his feet rather than wait for an answer.

"You absolutely can. I will show you out." Changing her mind, Chief Inspector Hoeks picked up her coat. "In fact, I'll drop you at the animal services centre. It's only a short walk from here, but it's tricky to find and not in the best area." She had a dozen things to do now that she had the first decent lead in the car thief case in more than a week, but she had a personal interest in Albert Smith and his dog.

She was playing a hunch. One she could not reveal to anyone. She could have stopped animal services from taking Albert's dog. They would have backed off if she told them to, but she had another case, a case that was deeply personal and completely off the books.

If she was right, Albert Smith would prove to be her way to get it sanctioned.

Albert didn't want to spend any more time in her company, not that she was unpleasant or demanding, but he felt captive in some intangible way, as if as long as he was with her, he wasn't free to do as he chose. Despite that, he accepted her offer graciously; far better to be delivered than have to find it for himself.

The short walk was an even quicker car ride, Hoeks stopping right outside the doors with the engine running to let him out. She offered her hand to shake and thanked him once again for his help.

"You're perfectly welcome," Albert managed a tight-lipped smile. He paused for a second, questioning if there was something else he wanted to say. She reminded him of his daughter in many ways and he felt an almost paternal need to make a supportive comment.

The moment passed and he felt for the door handle, exchanging the warmth of her car for the increasingly cold air outside.

His watch told him almost three hours had passed; surely long enough for Rex to be ready for release. He would wait if he had to but wasn't leaving without him. He had the card Hoeks gave him still, so if there was any resistance to handing back his dog, she was going to get involved whether she wanted to or not.

The animal services building was a squat two storey brick building with barbwire topped chain link fencing on all sides. The door didn't yield when Albert pushed it and a second attempt with greater force brought about a search for an intercom when the door refused to budge. There were lights behind it and occasional barking noises coming from a yard at the back.

The intercom was at chest height to the left of the door. Albert had to bend to get his mouth near the speaker when he pressed the button.

"Vermeld uw bedrijf."

"Um, hello," Albert replied, unsure what question might have been asked.

The voice switched to English. "State your business."

"I have come to collect my dog. I have the form they gave me when they took him."

The voice didn't reply, but a buzzing noise and a click accompanied the door opening a fraction of an inch when the electronic lock shut off. Albert grabbed the handle and escaped the cold to find it pleasantly warm again inside.

Expecting to see a reception area, he was surprised to find himself in a corridor. There were information posters on the walls and a plain A4 piece of paper with a hand drawn arrow pointing to his right. Beneath the arrow it said, 'Reception this way' in Flemish, German, and English.

Albert followed it to the end where he turned left and then right before finally finding some humans.

A man and a woman stood behind a wide counter that separated the room into two halves. Albert's half contained four dilapidated, mismatched chairs, a small coffee table on which a stack of tatty, old magazines sat, an overgrown, half dead yucca plant, and a box of kids' toys that had seen better days. Beyond the counter, the back wall was lined with filing cabinets upon which sat filing trays, most of which contained forms waiting to be filled out.

There were two computer screens with keyboards on the counter, the man and the woman each positioned behind one of them.

They both continued to stare at their screen until Albert was at the counter. He aimed for the woman, as it was a man's voice coming over the intercom and he hoped she might be a little more pleasant to deal with.

"I've come to collect my dog," Albert stated.

"You'll need to fill in a form." The terse, impatient response came over her shoulder with a sigh as she walked the two paces to the filing trays to collect an

A4 sheet. It was a light blue colour. She placed it on the counter and went back to what she was doing.

Albert peered at the sheet, fished out his reading glasses and tried again.

"I can't read this," he pointed out.

Without looking up, the woman angled a hand at the counter. "There is a guide to your left."

Following where she pointed Albert found a laminated blue form beneath a piece of thin Perspex. There were other forms around it, each one filled out with an English explanation for what went in the various boxes.

Albert clenched his fists, bit down his rising bile, and started to fill in the form. It took ten minutes and he had to fight an urge to stuff it in the rude woman's mouth when it was complete.

She sighed again when she had to take her eyes away from her screen to check the form. It got about a two second glance before she dumped it in a different filing tray and came back to her keyboard.

"Breed of animal?"

"German Shepherd," Albert dutifully replied, hopeful that things might now move forward.

"Date when he came in?"

"Today." Albert frowned. "About three hours ago."

The woman went back to the filing tray, checked something, and returned to her keyboard. Worry lines had appeared around her eyes and her forehead had crinkled in question. Something wasn't right.

"Derek?" she called her coworker across. Shuffling a little to the side, she made space for him and pointed to the screen.

"Is there an issue?" Albert asked, his impatience no longer able to stand the black hole of information.

"One moment, please," Derek muttered, his eyes never leaving the screen. Then to his colleague, he said, "I'll have to check." With that he departed through a door to their right leaving the woman alone with Albert.

"What is going on?"

"Just a clerical error, I'm sure."

"What is a clerical error?"

The woman didn't answer. Instead, she offered a weak smile though whether it was supposed to convey apology or just confuse him, Albert could not tell.

Derek came back through the door and there was no mistaking the concern on his face.

Albert's stern expression bored into him. "What? What have you got to tell me? Where is my dog?"

Derek's hands clung to each other as he began to explain the terrible truth. Albert heard the words, but they washed over him. He felt like he was underwater, or dreaming perhaps. Rex was gone, that was the big news they didn't want to share. It was an error on their part, Rex becoming mixed up with another shepherd scheduled for termination.

The reason behind it mattered not one bit for the end result was the same. Albert felt empty. Hollow. When he found himself back outside the animal services building, he could not recall making the decision to leave.

The cold air bit at his skin; it had dropped another few degrees, but Albert didn't notice. Somewhere deep inside his head he knew he ought to be heading back to his hotel, but it all seemed so pointless. What did warmth matter now?

Chapter 8

Rex looked about his cage in the back of the van. There was enough room to get up and turn around, but no more than that. He sniffed the air, hoping he might find some trace of his human. That he found none did not come as a shock. He didn't know where he was, but it certainly wasn't the animal services centre.

When they led him into the back of their van, the two fat men had stood and stared at him. One pointed at his shoulders and came forward to grip them on either side. The other nodded and said something in reply. It felt as though they were sizing him up for something.

They drove him to the animal services place, he could smell it even from inside the van: the fear, the stink of medicinal wipes, and the chemicals they use to sterilise the place. It combined with the scent of dogs and other animals to produce a stench Rex had hoped he would never smell again.

Strangely, when the back of the van opened and he expected to be taken out, they came at him with a machine instead.

"Let's just take care of that tracking chip, shall we?" muttered one of the fat men, talking to himself.

The machine made a beep that prompted the second man to grab a handful of the fur around Rex's neck. There followed a sharp sting of pain that made Rex buck and twist though it was over and done already. He could smell his own blood and saw the first fat man holding something bloody on the tip of his right index finger.

They had cut it from his flesh.

Without sparing him a second glance, they went back inside, returning a short while later. They shut the back doors, clambered into the front, and the van started to move again. Rex was happy to avoid all the horror and undignified treatment being taken inside would guarantee, but things were not as they ought to be, and it had him worried.

He continued to sniff the air, recording the smell of the fat men from animal services. One had been eating onions and cheese, the odours lay heavy on his breath. The other chewed spearmint gum and needed to change his socks. He could also hear them talking through the grill that separated them from the cages in the back, but as before they were talking in a language Rex couldn't understand.

Rex laid his head down and waited to see where they took him. He hoped it would be back to his human, wherever the old man had gone, but it wasn't. The sound inside the van changed, taking on an echoey tone that told Rex they were inside a building. He couldn't see from inside the cage in the back of the van, but it slowed and stopped and shortly thereafter the back doors opened.

They were inside a large warehouse if Rex's nose was to be believed. The air had a slightly musty, damp quality with a tinge of earth mixed in. He couldn't see much from his angle, yet his nose provided plenty of information. There were dogs here. Wherever here was. In a single sample of air he found multiple breeds, all large animals and exclusively male. The scent came with a sense of forlornness, like the dogs here had all accepted their fate and given up hope of happiness.

It sent a chill up Rex's spine.

The sound of footsteps brought his head around to see a man approaching. He wore a dark suit and was twice the width of Albert. He was white, hugely muscular, had a bald head, and a tattoo that started by his left eyebrow and went around the side of his head.

He addressed the fat men as Rutger and Claude, though Rex didn't know which was which. They called him Ivan and displayed submissive behaviour as a lesser dog might to an alpha. He asked questions and they answered, the discussion ending with a wad of cash passing from Ivan to the one with the foot odour problem.

It seemed to please the fat men, their faces lighting up as the one holding the money swiftly stuffed it into a pocket. They came for Rex then, taking his lead from a rack inside the van before unlatching his cage.

He refused to flinch when the one smelling of onion and cheese slid a hand through his collar and gave it a twist. The thick leather crushed against his throat making him want to lunge and bite. It wasn't time for that though. At least he didn't think it was. He needed to know a little more first.

They pulled him from the cage and out of the van, not that he resisted much. Once on the warehouse floor of polished concrete, he was able to look around. The space was bigger than he'd expected. Much bigger. Thick concrete columns supported a web of steel beams constructed to hold the ceiling in place. Spaced ten metres apart, there were five of them across and had to be more than ten in the other direction. Not that Rex could see the whole floor.

There were cars and vans, all newish and clean, parked at one end near the roller doors, and one whole side of the warehouse space was fenced off with a makeshift wall. Constructed from premade plastic panels linked together to create an opaque barrier, it rose more than six feet into the air. Rex couldn't see what was on the other side, but he could smell it right enough. It was where the dogs were housed.

Claude and Rutger closed the van's rear doors, one taking the left door, the other taking the right to meet in the middle. Rex watched them high five and cross over as they walked around to get to the seats in the front.

His lead was now in the hand of the man with the tattooed head. The animal services men were leaving, and Rex was staying.

Rex didn't know why or what but was bright enough to know nothing good was happening. His human wasn't here and never had been. It was only the possibility that Albert would come here to fetch him that made Rex allow Ivan to walk him across the warehouse and around a break in the wall.

On the other side, Rex saw the cages. Not much different from the one he'd just been in, they were six feet by about eight and perhaps four feet high. There were no small dogs in them, just a variety of bullish breeds. He saw Pitbulls, Rottweilers, Dobermans, Bullmastiffs, Siberian Huskies, and Alaskan Malamutes among others. A few raised their heads when he was led by, but most were either asleep or so disinterested in the world beyond their cage that they refused to even look.

Ivan arrived at an empty cage and opened the door.

"In you go," he instructed.

The cage had a bowl of stale water jammed into the corner and a dirty blanket to soften the cage bars a little so that he might lay down and hope to get some sleep.

Rex tensed his muscles. "*How's about a big fat, no?*"

He was going to make a break for it, but Ivan produced a giant dog biscuit from a pocket. Rex had been too preoccupied to even notice he had food about his person. The man tossed it through the cage door and when Rex inevitably lunged for it, his back end received a nudge and the cage door swung shut.

Ivan crouched, keeping both knees off the floor when he addressed Rex.

"My, you really are a big brute, aren't you. Those two idiots actually came through. Just wait until I tell Sylvia. You will make an excellent contender for the main bout. The crowd always likes someone unknown, and with your size they might think you have a chance."

Confused, Rex barked in his face again, threatening death just as soon as he got free.

The man simply smiled.

"That's it. Work on that aggression. The crowd will love it." He rose to his feet, patted the top of the cage, and walked away.

When the sound of his footfall faded and disappeared, Rex looked about his cage. It was a solid construction and his teeth would wear out long before he was able to chew through the steel. He nudged the door with his head, testing it to see how strong the lock was. Hinged on one side and held in place with a latch, it had to be the cage's weakest point.

"*Don't bother*," said a defeated voice.

Rex turned to find the sleeping form in the next cage was, in fact, awake. It was a Bullmastiff, a large male perhaps three or four years old and unneutered. He made no attempt to get up, but his eyes were open.

"The cages are escape-proof."

"I highly doubt that."

"Well, no one has ever managed to get out so far and plenty of us have tried, believe me."

Rex gave the door another nudge with his head. The door shifted slightly, but didn't flex. If he was going to get out, he needed to undo the latch and that would be a tricky proposition with a paw even if he was outside. From the inside it was impossible.

"What is this place?"

"Holding."

"Holding? Holding for what?"

"Dog fights. We will be pitched against each other or against other dogs brought in from outside. If you don't fight back ... well, I'm sure you can guess what happens then. The humans bet money on the outcome of each fight and have a real old party while we entertain them. Sometimes it's more than one on one. They stick a whole load of dogs in together and see who is standing at the end. Or they bring in something that isn't a dog. They had hyenas at the last one."

"How do you know all this?"

"I was supposed to fight at the last meeting, but my opponent didn't show up. I guess you could say I got a reprieve. Not that I am thankful for it."

The bullmastiff's tone was morose. It was as though he had already accepted his fate and chose to do nothing other than wait for its arrival.

"How long have you been in here?"

"A moon cycle or so. The fight was half a moon cycle ago." He lifted his head when he spoke and Rex caught a flash of something red.

Thinking it might be food, he asked, "*What have you got there?*"

The Bullmastiff ducked his head back between his front legs, lifting it again to show Rex what he had. It was a small teddy bear.

He dropped it again and trapped it under a paw. "*That's Mr Bowbows. The humans don't know I have him. I hide him in my mouth when they come around to check on us. My human gave it to me.*"

Rex got it. He'd known other dogs with a favourite toy they carried around, though he'd never had one himself.

The giant in the next cage was no fighting dog. He was domesticated and kind and somewhere out there was a human who probably missed him very much. Rex didn't need any further motivation, but he had it anyway. He looked back at the cage door, then around the walls and floor and roof, checking there were no other weak points.

He wasn't sure how he was going to do it, but he was breaking out of his cage. Then he was getting everyone else out and they were all going to escape from the warehouse. Rex knew some humans were capable of terrible crimes, but he wondered if perhaps this was the worst he had ever encountered. In many ways he hoped they ran into some opposition on the way out. It would be nice to hand out a little payback.

Chapter 9

At some point Albert had started walking. He couldn't remember doing so and when he registered that he was moving, he looked about to realise he had no idea where he was.

The cold was in his bones, numbness creeping into his hands and feet again. He needed to get somewhere warm before it became a problem, but the energy to push on wasn't there.

He kept thinking he could just call 'Rex!' and his dog would appear from around the corner or out of a shadow in which he had been hidden. He almost opened his mouth to do so a few times, only to let the idea die on his lips.

So engrossed in his misery, he failed to notice the form lurking in the alley when he passed it.

"Hey, old man."

Albert stopped and turned.

Two teenagers stepped out into the street behind him. One smoked a cigarette, the end glowing bright orange right in front of his face before he exhaled the noxious smoke into the night air.

"Wallet and watch," the smoker said. There was no threat in the voice, just an assured belief that Albert would comply.

"And your phone," his partner added.

Albert felt his hands curl into fists. He was in pain. His heart was heavier than when he lost Petunia, which seemed not only ridiculous, but perverse. Yet he'd known he was losing Petunia. In the end it became a matter of time – she didn't have enough of it left. And when she went, it was a peaceful final act. Rex had been torn from him and it left a hole in his heart that could never be filled.

"I said, wallet and watch, old man. Do you really want me to take them?"

Albert reached around to his back pocket using his right arm and took a step toward the youths. He estimated their ages to be eighteen or nineteen. They had acne on their chins and cheeks, fluff instead of stubble where they hadn't bothered to shave, and they possessed the wiry, skinniness that would become either fat or muscle over the next few years depending on how they chose to treat their bodies.

The smoker lifted his cigarette to his lips once more, a smile playing across his lips. He thought he was winning at life.

Albert punched him straight in the face. His knuckles connected with the burning end of the cigarette, crushing it into the tip of the kid's nose which was squashed flat by the blow.

He'd pretended to reach for his wallet, then thrown a haymaker knowing it would not be expected and that the stupid kid wouldn't be able to see anything much beyond the glow of his cigarette.

The punch was a sweet one, catching lips and nose in one go. Albert knew there wasn't much power to it, not like he could have generated a decade or more ago, but it was still enough to rock the kid's head back and send him reeling.

Following up with his left, Albert swung a cross at the smoker's partner. He was gawping at the space where his friend had stood a half second earlier, his mouth open in shock.

Albert's punch almost missed when momentary shock wore off and mugger number two tried to duck. Instead of hitting the second kid in the mouth, he caught his chin which proved to be a better spot anyway. The smoker's partner was ducking backward, his centre of gravity somewhere behind his feet when the blow landed.

Overbalanced, he flailed his arms and fell, tipping backward and twisting to get his hands beneath his body.

Incandescent with rage, Albert knew his actions came at the hands of the red mist which was descending over his eyes, but he did nothing to fight it. They were just kids, but they knew right from wrong and were prepared to rob an old man for his few meagre possessions.

The smoker was just recovering from his punch to the face when Albert hit him again. His partner was scrambling to get up, but retaliation wasn't on his mind, only escape.

He yelled something at his friend, the smoker, as he came off the ground like a sprinter rising from the blocks. So frantic to get away, his feet were hardly able to grip the ground, he slipped and fell again before getting his body upright.

Albert aimed a boot at the smoker's backside when he likewise turned and fled. Surprising even himself, he then chased the pair of youths shouting obscenities at their backs. They outpaced him in an instant; there was never any danger that he might catch them. Yet when they reached the end of the road and raced across it with a glance to check if the deranged pensioner was still following, he continued to give chase.

Until they both almost died.

A blare of horns and screeching tyres filled the air, headlights illuminating the fear etched on the youths' faces. Had they not checked to see if he was following, they might have seen the cars coming. As it was, the cars stopped in time, or managed to swerve out of the way. In the confusion, the teenage muggers reached the other side of the street to vanish into the darkness of an alley between buildings.

Slowing to a walk, Albert huffed and puffed to the end of the street where four cars were now parked at crazy angles, the drivers looking every bit as stunned as the kids they almost ran over.

Albert wanted to check everyone was okay. The near miss was enough to quell his rage and the hopelessness was yet to return. Reaching the corner ten seconds after the youths, Albert was about to call out to the drivers when a voice interrupted his train of thought.

"You have got to be kidding me."

The statement came from a young man who was halfway out his car when Albert's eyes tracked around to locate him. He choked a gasp and stared disbelievingly at Axel, the young man who almost lost his car to thieves a few hours ago.

Chapter 10

"Why aren't you in jail?" Axel demanded, reaching back inside the open door of his car to retrieve a familiar looking baseball bat.

The other drivers were exiting their cars, all of which were souped-up, modified versions of standard road cars. Two more were men, both in their late twenties much like Axel. The third was Axel's girlfriend. Albert recognised her even with her clothes on.

"This is the old man I was telling you about," Axel reported, coming around his car with the bat clutched purposefully in one hand. "The one who tried to steal my car. Now he's managed to wheedle his way out of custody."

The four drivers all turned his way, their eyes resentful.

"Maybe he knows what happened to Teagan's Evo," suggested the woman.

"Or Jerome's Skyline," offered one of the men.

"Yeah," agreed Axel, swinging the club around as he came closer. "I bet he knows all about all of them."

There were headlights coming from the right, a whole convoy of them. Their arrival might convince the drivers to calm down and not pursue a violent solution, but Albert could see they were not going to arrive swiftly enough to stop Axel getting a few hits in if that was really what he intended.

Raising his arms, which were warm now that the blood had been caused to flow again, Albert made it clear he was surrendering.

"Please, I can promise you, I was not trying to steal your car. I wouldn't know how and haven't driven in years. I saw two men trying to break into it and got my dog to scare them off, just like I explained earlier."

Axel pointed the tip of the bat at Albert's face.

"I saw you using the tool to open the door."

"Yes, because they were inside and I was trying to stop them making off with it."

Axel's face contorted into a snarl. He was about to shout a retort when the man who was yet to speak finally opened his mouth.

"You're Albert Smith, aren't you?"

Albert was well aware that people could recognise him. His face had graced the front cover of more than half the newspapers in the world. His kids had tried to keep track of it all, buying copies from all over the place to make a scrap book. It didn't make him happy. He didn't want the fame though perhaps infamy was a better term. Seeking to evade the constant selfies and questions was one of the major drivers for leaving his home in England, but here in Amsterdam he was still too recognisable.

However, on this occasion, he believed it was going to work in his favour.

Facing the man, he said, "Yes, I am." His voice came out with all the heart-heavy pain he could not currently escape.

Axel snarled, "Shaggy, who the heck is Albert Smith?"

By comparison, the name was all his friends needed to have their memories jogged.

"Holy cow," the woman gasped. "It is Albert Smith. Axel, this dude is some famous sleuth, man. He saved a whole bunch of people from a cave or something. There's no way he was trying to steal your car."

The corners of Albert's mouth twitched into a sad smile.

"Hey, man, where's that cool dog of yours?" The question came from Shaggy, the man who identified him. He was six feet tall, broad across the shoulders, with shaggy hair that made him look like Tarzan. He wore black workman style boots that matched his black jeans and a denim jacket onto which patches displaying motor racing brands had been stitched. He looked around for the dog that was never coming and that was enough to kill any hint of a smile on Albert's face.

He slumped to his side, using the wall to keep himself upright, though as the blackness returned to swallow him whole, he wasn't sure he cared about staying on his feet.

"Yeah, where's the dog?" asked Axel. He was looking around as well, but his eyes held concern rather than interest. There were still teeth marks in the bat where the dog bit it and Axel was rightly worried it might be his flesh next time.

"Gone," mumbled Albert. "Rex is gone."

The woman frowned, perplexed. "Gone. What does that mean? Axel said it was with you earlier. In fact, you said that yourself a minute ago. You said you used the dog to scare off the thieves."

"He's gone, okay!" Albert raged, unable to control his emotions. "He was taken away by animal services, and when I went to collect him they had already put him to sleep."

Chapter 11

R ex poked his tongue through the bars of his cage, right under the latch. He had tried getting his claws onto it, but they were neither long enough nor sufficiently dexterous for the task. He doubted his tongue would fare any better, but gave it ten minutes of effort before sitting back onto his haunches to think.

"*I wouldn't waste your time*," murmured the Bullmastiff. "*You're not getting that cage door open until the humans come back.*"

Rex 's stomach rumbled. "*They feed us here, right?*"

The Bullmastiff snorted a sad sigh. "*That's about the only good thing we have going for us. They want us strong, so they feed us plenty. Can't have any of the contenders looking malnourished.*"

"*I'm Rex,*" said Rex. "*What's your name?*"

The Bullmastiff had his eyes closed and didn't bother to open them when he muttered, "*I used to be called Kevin, back when I had humans to live with.*"

"*Used to be? What do they call you now?*"

The bullmastiff opened his eyes. "*I'm Dreadnought on account of my size. All the dogs are given fighting names. You'll get one too. I guess the humans don't want to announce a bout between Shirley and Candy. They would rather it was Skull Biter versus Death Punch.*"

Rex's attention was on the challenge of escape, not on what the dog in the next cage was saying, but he managed to mumble, "*I guess that makes sense.*"

Pressing the side of his face against the bars, Rex tried to see the latch. It was impossible. He could get his eye at an angle where it was in sight, but he was so close to it by then that it went out of focus.

"Hey, does the latch lift up or does it slide across?"

Kevin had laid his head down again. His eyes were closed, and he sounded dreamy and sleepy when he said, *"Up, I think."*

Rex sucked in a deep breath and let it out slow. Kevin was trying hard to ignore the dog in the cage next to his, while at the same time trying to avoid being rude. The new arrivals always found it hard, not least because no one could be bothered to be friendly to them. Why do that when you might be fighting them in a few days?

However, when he heard Rex's grunt of effort, he flicked one eyelid open and did so just in time to see the German Shepherd launch himself across his cage. The interior space was too small to do more than get up and turn around, so the sight of Rex driving off his back legs with such force snapped Kevin's head up.

Rex had an idea. He suspected it might be a stupid one, but there was no chance he was going to sit meekly in his cage waiting for the future to happen.

Leaping at the cage's front panel, his aim was not to ram the door open using his body weight as Kevin imagined, but to make the whole thing flip. To do that he couldn't have any part of his body on the cage floor and had to strike the front panel as high up as he could – not easy in such a small space.

He slammed into it with his shoulder high up on the panel near the roof. The cage shunted forward two feet and the back end lifted off the floor. It clattered back down again, just as it had been although no longer in line with the other cages.

The sound was enough to wake most of the dogs though only a dozen of them lifted their heads to see what was happening. Most did so just in time to see Rex's water bowl hit him on the back of his head. It did so with a comical 'dong!' sound, emptying its contents down his coat.

The dogs laughed, amused by the latest arrival's futile efforts.

One was a Husky to the other side of Kevin. His name was Bruiser, but the men holding him had changed it to Bone Shaker.

"*Here, what's he doing?*" Bruiser asked.

Kevin shrugged. "*Beats me. Trying to escape, I think.*"

Bruiser laid his head back down. He'd spent hours trying to find a way out of his cage and knew the futility of the endeavour. Besides, even if a dog could get out of their cage, they were trapped in a building with humans who would catch them.

Fifty metres away in an area the men left to guard and manage the dogs had set up for their comfort, Levi looked at Hans.

"Did you hear something?"

"Only you talking during the football match." He picked up a slice of his pizza. It came from Don Giovani's, the best pizza place in the whole city. Ivan had brought it with him when he came to check the new dog.

Levi frowned. "I think I heard something."

Hans huffed, "So go check it out then if you are so worried." He saw himself as the senior of the pair, largely because Levi was short and slight and a ball of nervous energy who needed approval before he did anything.

In contrast, Hans was big boned and tall at six feet three inches. His beard and hair made him look like Chris Hemsworth (in his head at least), and he thought of himself as a take charge kind of guy. Why get up and do things when you could make someone else do them instead?

He pushed the rest of the slice into his mouth, wiped his fingers on a napkin and grabbed another, deliberately not checking to see whether Levi was going to check on the dogs or not.

Rex shook his head to clear it and stared at the front panel. It hadn't budged an inch, but then he hadn't expected it to. That wasn't the aim, but the floor had lifted, and he'd felt the cage tilt. Whether he could tilt it enough was another thing, but in the name of perseverance, he backed up to the far end of the cage and tried again.

With the exact same result.

The cage was now sticking out more than four feet from the line and more of the dogs were sitting up to watch. It wasn't as though they had any other entertainment.

"I definitely heard something," Levi went to grab the remote only to have his hand slapped away.

"Hey, I'm watching. I've got money on this game." Ajax against Bayern Munich was a big deal and he wasn't planning to miss a moment of the coverage.

"What if the dogs are getting out? Shouldn't we tell Ivan?"

Hans shot him a look of disbelief. "The dogs can't get out, dummy. How many dogs have ever managed to escape their cage?"

"One," Levi replied with bold assurance.

"Yes, because you left the cage open."

"I did not!"

"Mm-hmm. So you keep saying, but I reckon that's exactly what happened. If you want to go check them, have at it, but stop interrupting the game."

The ref blew his whistle, pausing the game for some infraction Hans had just missed. He glared at his companion.

"Now, you made me miss what happened."

"It's just a foul. He's giving a free kick."

"Yes, but I didn't see it, did I?" Hans focused on the game. "Don't go bothering Ivan. He will not thank you for it."

On his third attempt, Rex increased his effort, this time trying to grip the rungs of the front panel with his claws so he might hold on if only for a second. However, they were not designed to do that, so he crashed to the ground with a cacophony of amused howls from his canine audience. Rex picked himself up and looked around to find a dog now visible in every single cage. They were lined up to watch the spectacle.

In turning around to look at them he got his first proper sight of the latches holding each cage shut. It hinged from the top to fold down over a horizontal eye. Through the eye a small peg kept the latch closed. As he suspected, the humans didn't feel padlocks were necessary.

The dogs were laughing and egging him on. They wanted to see him try again because they found it amusing to watch him leap and slam and crash to the floor time after time. Some were yet to see the show for the first time and since they didn't want to miss out, Rex chose to oblige them.

His fourth leap was the most powerful yet as though he were doing it for the baying crowd. He thrust off his back legs, hit the front of the cage, shunted it forward a good two feet, and fell to earth before the back end could get more than a few inches off the floor. It was going to be the same result every time; he was never going to topple it.

Not end over end. But side over side was a different matter entirely.

Rex picked himself up, checked his cage was now clear of the row and leaned against the side nearest to Kevin. All around and above him the rows of dogs were laughing and joking, having a great old time watching the new guy throw himself around like a rabid stunt dog.

Pressing his whole body against the side panel, leaning back into the middle and then more or less falling to the side lifted the base upward as the entire cage pivoted off one edge. It hung in the air for a half second, caught at the point of balance until gravity chose the lesser option.

The cage flopped down onto its side, silencing Rex's audience as instantly as someone flicking a switch. Rex performed the same manoeuvre one more time so the cage was now upside down and watched with great relief when the peg fell out. The dogs around him were all pressed against the front of their cages, their mouths open in stark disbelief.

Rex sat back on his haunches in the middle of his cage, looked around at the faces staring his way and lifted one front paw. With a nonchalant tap, he nudged the front panel and watched the latch fall out of the way. A second nudge caused the door to swing open and he walked out through it to rapturous silence.

Chapter 12

Albert drew in a ragged breath, tears threatening to fall from the tsunami of emotions washing over his body. It was less than thirty minutes since he discovered his best pal had been taken from him and though he felt completely numb to almost all external inputs, he'd attacked two teenagers when they threatened him, then chased and almost caused their deaths.

He was adrift, unsure where to go or what to do and certain it mattered not one bit if he chose to simply lie in the gutter and slowly freeze to death.

"Um," ventured the shaggy haired man who first identified Albert, "your dog is kinda big, isn't he?"

"Was," mumbled Albert. "Yes, he was a big fellow." There was no reason to continue talking to Axel and his friends and no reason to stay where he was. Equally, he had no reason to go anywhere, but the other cars heading their way were just starting to arrive and Albert was not in the mood to answer questions or explain things again.

He turned away and began to walk.

"Hey!" called Shaggy.

Albert didn't so much as twitch, he just kept on walking.

"Hey, man, your dog might not be dead."

Albert's feet stopped. He was facing away from them, heading back the way he'd chased the teenage muggers. Conversation was sparking to life, the street racers' friends leaving their cars with predictable enquiries about the result of the race and the identity of the old man.

He didn't turn around, taking a moment to argue with himself. He wanted nothing more than to find out Rex was still alive, but how could that be? The animal services department apologised for his accidental euthanasia. They had the paperwork to show he had been put to sleep. Going back to ask the shaggy-haired man what he might know was tantamount to inviting hope into his life. Hope that would ultimately be replaced by the same burning heartache he already felt. Hope would banish it, but not for long enough to make it worthwhile.

He almost started walking again, but what if the shaggy-haired man was right? If there was the slightest possibility Rex was alive, Albert had to pursue it.

There were footsteps coming his way and he rotated to find Shaggy, Axel, and more coming toward him.

"Seriously, man, there's a chance he could be alive," Shaggy repeated his claim.

Albert felt anger tugging at his tongue. Were they yanking his chain?

With the muscles in his jaw tightening, he asked, "How?"

Shaggy half turned to look back into the small crowd of dedicated street racers filling the pavement behind.

"Where's Fishman?" he called loud enough to be heard by everyone present.

A tall, almost lanky man began to weave through the press of bodies. Albert put his age at somewhere around thirty, making him one of the older racers present. He wore ripped jeans and box-fresh high-top sports shoes beneath a jacket emblazoned with Subaru logos. Around his neck a thick gold necklace led to another Subaru logo, also in gold and Albert guessed there would be a Subaru key in his pocket. His hair was pushed up and held in place with product about an inch above his skull to make him appear even taller than his six-foot three-inch frame.

"Whassup, Shaggy?" asked Fishman.

Shaggy – Albert figured that probably wasn't his real name, but as a nickname it suited him – jerked a thumb at Albert.

"Tell him about your dog and how he wasn't dead."

The instruction piqued Albert's interest, but he refused to let his hope swell. He was about to hear a real-world example, but that was no reason to get excited. It would have no bearing on his situation with Rex.

Fishman looked at Shaggy, across to Albert, and back to Shaggy as though to confirm he was really expected to have to tell the story. Then, with a shrug, he opened his mouth.

"I thought he was dead, but he wasn't."

Albert waited for more, but silence followed.

Shaggy rolled his eyes. "Yes, Fishman, but with a bit more detail. Like why you thought he was dead in the first place."

"Oh." A little colour rose in Fishman's cheeks. "Well, the animal services people told me he was. Raymond is a ridgeback and he got away from me one day. I was at the park, and I think he saw a rabbit. Anyway, by the time I found him the animal services people had rounded him up and were taking him away. I begged them to let him go, but you know how hot they are on dangerous dogs these days. I went to the depot to get him back the next day – they said I had to wait for him to be processed. Well, they apologised but said he had been put down by mistake.

Albert leaned forward, his whole body reacting to the story. It was too similar to his tale, too alike for him to write it off as coincidence.

"But you got him back?" he asked, not daring to believe the same could be true for Rex.

"Yeah," Fishman beamed. "Only, not right away. It was about a week later and he turned up on my doorstep. I opened the door to go to work and he was curled up on the mat outside. He was in a terrible state though with wounds to his head and neck and flank. They weren't life threatening, but when I rushed him to the vet, they called the police and I got arrested."

Albert blinked in confusion. "Arrested? What for?" Had he missed an important part of the story somehow?

"For dog fighting. The police accused me of entering her into a dog fighting ring. They grilled me for hours. I told them I had no idea what they were talking about and in the end I convinced them, but they didn't believe the part about animal services."

"What do you mean?" Albert had to know all the details. He was clinging to every word the man said, and despite himself was beginning to let hope creep in.

"I mean they denied all knowledge. They claimed to know nothing about my dog. There was no paperwork to support my claim and the CCTV footage at the shelter had been swapped out somehow so it looked like I had never visited them. They took my dog, told me he had been destroyed, and covered it up. They got away with it too." He sounded as angry as he ought to feel and told the story with utter conviction. More importantly, Albert believed him.

He dared to believe.

Taking a grip of his emotions before they could begin to soar, Albert checked his understanding.

"You think there is a dog fighting ring operating in this city and that my dog could have been taken specifically to compete in it?"

Fishman shrugged. "I don't know anything about that, man. I'm just saying what happened to me. But the dog fighting ring thing … yeah, I think there is."

"For definite, man," agreed Shaggy. "But it must be high end or something."

"Why do you say that?"

"Because none of us know anything about it."

"Hey, um, I know something about it," volunteered a new voice.

Heads turned and the gathering of street racers parted to let a raven-haired beauty get to the front.

She waved at Albert. "Hi, I'm Caprice," she said. Dressed like most of the women present, which is to say inappropriately for the conditions in her crop top, and figure-hugging trousers beneath a leather jacket she felt no need to zip up, she attracted looks from the men as she passed.

"You know about this dog fighting ring?" he questioned.

"Only through an old boyfriend. We split up more than a year ago, but he keeps coming around trying to get me to go back out with him. He's got money now and thinks that should make a difference. Anyway, he turned up a couple of weeks ago, high as a kite on painkillers because he'd been bitten by a dog. I asked if it was rabid, and he laughed and told me it was trained to fight. I think that is where the money is coming from." She looked at the racers around her. "He has got this sweet Mercedes that is just begging to be modified."

Albert pressed her for more. "You think he is running the dog fights?"

She made a noise like, "Pfft!" and laughed. "That idiot? No, he's nice to look at and all, but he's not got the brains to think something like that up. Ivan is the kind of guy who gets things done, but only if he's told what to do. Whoever he's working for, that's who you want."

Albert's eyes narrowed. The sense of pointless despair was gone, swept away by a new emotion: justice. He gave in to the hope he wanted so badly to feel. Rex was not only still alive, he was being held by people ... animals who wanted to use him for his size and natural aggression. They would pitch him against another dog, and neither would win for they would both come away injured.

Well, the people behind it, whoever they were, had a problem coming their way, a problem in the form of righteous justice personified.

Albert Smith was going to find them, and he was going to get them.

He was going to get them good.

Chapter 13

With the pack of fighting dogs watching, Rex performed his full stretching routine, the one he usually reserved for after he'd enjoyed a particularly deep sleep following a large meal. The captive audience was yet to speak following his escape and Rex knew to revel in their attention for a few moments before addressing them.

They might be fighting dogs. They might be tough individuals capable of beating him if they went head-to-head, but they lacked the confidence to do anything much about their situation. Held captive by humans they didn't know, each and every dog present had chosen to accept their fate. Like Kevin in the cage next door, the fighting dogs believed there was no escape. They would be forced to fight, and win or lose they would then be forced to fight again and again until they could no longer fight or were killed.

What they needed more than anything, what they needed more than hope, was a leader.

An Alpha.

Rex finished his exaggerated stretching routine and looked around at the rows of cages. He stayed quiet, making eye contact with as many dogs as possible. Their faces were pressed against the front of their cages, every last one of them awake and alert.

"*I'm getting out of here,*" Rex announced. "*And I'm taking all of you with me.*" He paused to give them a chance to respond. When no one said anything, he added, "*Or perhaps you don't want to escape this place.*"

His comment jolted the dogs into motion, barking their eagerness to get out of their cages.

Twenty metres away, Levi was already halfway to the dogs when Hans whooped with excitement. The noise from the TV as the crowd went wild made it clear a goal had just been scored. It proved enough to stay Levi's feet for a few more seconds.

The dogs were going nuts about something, but that hardly compared to Ajax scoring against Bayern Munich.

Knowing he'd preened for long enough and that it was time for action, Rex ran back to the cages. There were twenty-eight of them; not that Rex stopped to count or even had the ability to conceive a number greater than 'lots'.

"I'm going to get Kevin out," he called to the other dogs, keeping his voice at a volume only they would hear. If he wanted to get them all out, he was going to have to do it quietly. *"Once he's free, we'll both free someone else, then there will be four of us to free the next four. Just be patient, okay?"*

He started at Kevin's cage, gripping the front with his teeth and giving it a yank. He had to get it out of the line so he would have the space to roll it side over side. They were packed tight in against each other and backed up against the makeshift wall.

Kevin barked his encouragement, his entire character shifting from morose and defeated to jubilant and enthused now that he had reason to believe he might get free.

"Shhh!" Rex hissed through his teeth. *"You'll bring the humans."* He was right and his advice was enough to calm Kevin. However, Kevin wasn't the only one making noise and while Rex was helping to get the Bullmastiff's cage moving, many of the other dogs were too impatient to wait to be helped.

"Hey, you're not in charge here!" snapped a Pitbull. *"They don't need a new alpha."*

Rex shot a glance his way, but went immediately back to his task. There was always going to be an alpha, so it came as no shock. It was something to worry about later.

Or it might be if the Pitbull wasn't egging everyone on. With him barking instructions and encouragement, the dogs were copying Rex's method, throwing themselves at the front panel of their cages to make them move. They wanted to break out and now they knew how they were going for it.

"*Shhhh*" Rex begged, but no one listened. "*You're making too much noise!*"

The noise from the TV died down, the crowd falling quiet once more as the ball came back to the centre spot and the game was restarted.

A cage crashed over onto its side, the Rottweiler inside tumbling with it joyously.

Hans' head shot around, his eyes wide as they took in Levi's panicked expression.

"I told you I heard something!" Levi shouted to be heard as the sound of clattering cages filled the air.

Hans jumped to his feet, his whole body spasming with indecision – he wanted to pause the game, but did he really have time to go for the remote? It sounded like the dogs were escaping, even though that was completely impossible.

The Rottweiler broke free of his cage with a triumphant bark. It was quickly followed by more jubilation when a Pitbull broke free. They were all doing it, one after another rolling their cages until they were upside down and the pegs fell out.

That was good, but Rex was having trouble getting Kevin's cage to roll. He was just so darned heavy. At least fifty percent bigger than Rex, he had less room in his cage than any of the others. Too little, it seemed, to be able to make his cage topple.

"*Hey! I need a hand over here!*" Rex barked quietly. He was glancing around to get someone's attention and therefore looking in the right direction to see it was already too late.

Hans and Levi burst into sight, careening around the makeshift wall with their guns drawn. They expected to find people. Surely the noise coming from the dogs was due to human activity. Someone was breaking them out, that's what they expected to see, so the canine faces that twisted around to look their way came as a big surprise.

Seeing the humans, Rex discarded any thoughts of stealth. "*New plan!*" he barked at the top of his lungs. "*Everyone, take down the humans!*"

It was a solid plan and might have worked. They had the element of surprise and they outnumbered the duo of bewildered looking men by five to one. Unfortunately, generations of behavioural control killed the idea before any of the other dogs could give it a second thought. Dogs don't bite humans. It's not acceptable to do so under any circumstances.

Rex knew better, but that came down to training. As a police dog he was expected to wrestle people to the ground. He got good at it, and it was a skill he retained.

For a heartbeat, the area in front of the line of cages was a frozen plateau. No one moved. No one made a sound. The dogs stared at the humans and vice versa. When the heartbeat passed it was the dogs who moved first.

The Rottweiler barked, "*Leg it!*" an instruction everyone could get behind.

Except it wasn't everyone. Only ten of the dogs had managed to get free. The others were still working on it, many of them trapped in place by the cages that were already strewn across the floor.

Scrambling paws slipped on the polished concrete, found purchase, and the dogs took off. It sparked Hans and Levi who both broke free of their stunned state at the same time.

"I told you I heard something!" Levi bellowed to be heard above the barking dogs still trapped in their cages.

Kevin pushed his head against the bars of his cage. "*Rex you've got to go!*" The tremor in his voice betrayed the pain he felt. His chance for freedom had slipped through his fingers. He didn't want Rex to go, but recognised it was too late to change his own situation. "*Save yourself!*"

Rex growled his frustration and turned to face the two men. He wasn't about to abandon his new friend.

Levi and Hans had no clue what to do. The dogs were all over the place. Armed with handguns, they had the option to start shooting. The sound might penetrate beyond the confines of the warehouse, but it was far enough from everywhere else to believe no one would hear it.

The dogs were assets though. If they killed even one of the fighting dogs so close to the next big event, they would need an ironclad reason why there was no other choice. Even then, the boss lady wasn't known for her compassion or understanding. She was as likely to enter them in the next dog fight as some gruesome new feature as she was to accept their excuses.

The bulk of the dogs already out of their cages had bolted in the two seconds since Levi and Hans interrupted the 'great escape'. It left Rex facing them alone and he knew what their guns represented.

He could charge them. There was a chance they would both freeze, but he thought it more likely he would startle them into firing. Even if they didn't shoot straight away, Rex couldn't tackle them both at the same time, so whoever he left standing was bound to react to save the other.

"*Go, Rex!*" Kevin barked loud enough to jolt Rex into action.

He hated that he was given no choice, but if he left now he could catch up to the other dogs and together they would return.

Pushing his face up to the bars of Kevin's cage, Rex growled through his frustration, "*I'm coming back for you, okay? Just hang on until I return!*"

The humans were moving again, over their initial shock. The taller one was coming for Rex, his mouth set in an angry grimace.

Rex barked his defiance. He wanted to bite someone. They'd taken him away from his human and that was justification enough, but it wasn't just him and while that made it worse, it was what the humans had planned for their captive canines that bothered him most.

He'd been in a few scraps in his life, facing off against another dog when territory or food were on the line, but this was different. That dogs would be made to fight for the entertainment of humans was twisted and Rex was going to find a way to stop it from happening.

A hundred metres away at the far end of the warehouse, the escaped dogs were trapped. Their flight from the bank of cages had not been made with forethought. They had no clue how to get out of the building, their minds filled only with the desire to be somewhere else.

Rex could hear their panicked barks, as could the two humans left behind to guard them. The shorter one had stowed his gun in favour of a control pole – a long stick with a noose at the far end.

With Rex watching, he took a second from a shelf above the cages.

"Here, use this!" Levi shouted to Hans, throwing the pole for his colleague to catch.

Rex recognised the device; he'd been trapped with one before and wasn't about to let it happen again. Not ever if he could help it.

Giving Kevin a final apologetic glance, he spun off his back paws to reverse direction. Now facing the panicking dogs massing by the doors at the far end of the warehouse, he took off.

Hans swung the noose of the control pole through the air Rex's head occupied until a half second earlier, caught nothing, and sputtered an expletive of disbelief.

"Don't sweat it," Levi sniggered. "They're trapped at the doors. We can round them up and put them back in their cages and no one will ever know they got out."

"Oh, yeah? What about the fact that so many of them got out? We need to fix the cages so they don't get out again."

Levi shrugged, unbothered by the unexpected challenge. "I'll buy some padlocks. I don't think they'll be able to pick their way out once those are in place." He liked that Hans was thrown by the mass escape. He pretended to be so calm and in control all the time. It was nice to see him looking flustered.

Dismissing him, Levi used a foot to push some of the cages back into line, smiling when the dogs trapped inside stumbled and fell. The German shepherd was almost to the doors at the far end now, but he wasn't worried about him. The dog would go as far as he could only to find there was no way to go any farther. They could round them up at their leisure.

A few paces down the line of cages, a rotund bulldog made yet another attempt to roll his cage over. He'd managed to shunt it out from between the cages to his left and right, both of which were already empty, but was having no luck furthering his escape.

Levi kicked it back against the wall with a smirk at the heartbroken creature inside and was bending down to deliver a snarky comment when Hans spoke.

"Hey, where's he going?"

Levi twitched his head around and up, lifting it slightly to look over the bank of cages. His mouth opened to question who Hans was referring to, but no words came out. He could see it too, though he wanted to question his eyes.

When Rex left the cages, he was heading roughly in the direction of the escaped dogs.

Roughly.

They were massed at the base of a roller door. Open a crack at the bottom, the dogs could all smell freedom beyond, but with no idea how to open it and no opposable thumbs even if they knew how to operate the switch, they could go no farther.

Rex didn't waste time questioning how to make the roller door move. Instead, he aimed at the emergency exit five metres to the left.

"*Hey!*" he barked at the worried collection of hounds. "*If you want to get out of here, come with me!*"

At the emergency exit, a standard width door with a bar in the centre for ease of egress, he jumped onto his back legs and slammed into it. The bar depressed, opening the door to let fresh, cold air flood in. Using his body to hold it open, he barked again. Some of the escaped fighting dogs had looked his way, but the rest were too frantic to pay attention. Three were trying to dig their way under the door, scraping their claws against the steel of the door or the smooth concrete floor it met.

However, the message passed in a heartbeat and the scent of the night told them everything they needed to know.

Levi dropped his control pole and yanked his gun back out of its underarm holster. Too late though, he fired at the final departing tail just as it whipped through the door.

Rex narrowed his eyes at the humans, memorising their faces as well as their scents. He had no idea where he was. He had no clue what might have befallen his human or how to find him, but whatever else he did, he was coming back to rescue Kevin and the rest of the dogs still trapped in their cages.

And when he did, he was going to get the humans who took him.

He was going to get them good.

Chapter 14

His mind working at a feverish pace, Albert snatched his phone from inside his coat, pulled up the app linked to Rex's tracking chip and pinged it. If his dog was anywhere within twenty miles of his current position, it would show him.

Except it didn't. It didn't do anything.

If he'd been euthanised as the animal services people claimed, it would still ping, so the result was confusing. But only for as long as it took Albert to guess what the nil result meant. Someone was blocking the signal or had removed the chip so Rex wouldn't be found.

Telling himself it was good news even if it felt bad, Albert tucked his phone away and stared at the car club members surrounding him. There was more than thirty of them, all young people in their twenties or very early thirties. He had nothing to offer them and no reason to expect their help, but he needed it. All alone in Amsterdam, he was going to have a tough time trying to find Rex by himself. But with these street-savvy kids …

"They have my dog …" he started, his lips stopping abruptly when Axel held up a hand to silence him.

"You're about to ask us to get involved, aren't you?"

Albert met his gaze with piercing eyes. "No. I'm about to offer you an opportunity to get back the cars that were stolen."

All around Albert, the street racers were paying attention, but most of them had smirks on their faces. He understood what drove their doubt; to them he was just an old man.

He nodded his head toward the cars, took a deep breath, and tried to recall some of the knowledge he'd learned from his previous encounter with a modified car expert.

"You guys are all about four-core intercoolers and direct port nitrous injection."

Eyebrows climbed foreheads. He was speaking their language and getting it right.

"Now, I don't claim to know a whole lot about ball-bearing turbos or titanium valve springs, but I do know a thing or two about catching crooks."

"Oh, yeah?" sneered a man with a leather jacket and a flat top hair do. He wore sunglasses even though the sun went down hours ago. "And how exactly are you going to find them, eh? The police don't know who's behind it and I bet you don't even speak Dutch."

"Those are good points," Albert acknowledged. "Except they are wrong."

Foreheads wrinkled with confusion as the street racers listened for what the crazy old man was going to say next.

"The cars were stolen by an organised gang of Korean criminals. Most likely they are targeting specific cars since," he aimed his eyes at Axel, "the car they tried to get earlier this evening is a high spec model. I assume it is also rare," he prompted Axel to confirm.

"It's worth a lot too," Axel replied. "There's more than fifty thousand Euros under the bonnet alone."

Staggered by the sum and finding that he wanted to know how much the people around him had each invested in their cars, Albert fought to stay on topic.

"I was able to identify two of the gang members with the help of the police. Song Bin and Park Ji Hoon are their names. If we can find them, we can find the gang. If we can find the gang, we can retrieve your cars."

The idiot still wearing his sunglasses voiced his doubt. "How do you know all this, old man? Why should we believe anything you say?"

"Because catching criminals is what I have done with my life and over the years I have become quite good at it. Use your phones to look me up," he encouraged.

"My name is Albert Smith." For once the newspaper coverage of his life was going to work in his favour.

A bunch of the street racers were doing exactly as he suggested, others crowding around them to see what they found. He gave them a moment to absorb the information before continuing.

"They will ship the stolen cars out of the country, but will likely store them somewhere secure until they have enough to move in one go."

"Why?" challenged the woman standing next to Axel. "Why not get them out of the country straight away?"

"Economy. Every time they want to smuggle cars out they need to bribe customs officials or port security guards. They have to secure space on a ship and organise people to move the cars. They will want to do that as few times as possible and not just because it will cost less that way but because each time they move the cars they expose themselves. They will do it once and since they were still trying to steal this gentleman's car this evening," he nodded his head toward Axel, "I think it safe to assume there are still vehicles on their list."

Albert laid out his view of the Korean crime gang's operation in confident terms, explaining how they would handle and ship the stolen cars with enough detail to convince the assembled street racers he knew precisely what he was talking about. While doing so he hoped to goodness none of them challenged his thoughts with a counter theory of their own because he was making the whole thing up.

He had no experience of car smuggling rings. They existed, he knew that much, but crimes of that nature never came under his purview as a police detective. The street racers didn't know that though and his confidence was winning them over.

Albert looked about. The street racers were talking among themselves, whispering questions or thoughts to the person or people standing close enough to hear. Most of them were unaffected by the car thefts, but three of their number had lost their vehicles and were vocal about their desire to let the old man lend a hand.

With the group seeming to teeter on the edge, Albert gave them a gentle nudge.

"I need your help to get my dog back. In exchange I will lend my detective skills to catching the crooks that took your cars and prevent them from coming after them again. Do we have a deal?"

Chapter 15

C hief Inspector Daniella Hoeks drummed her fingers on the edge of her desk and sucked air through her teeth. She felt bad about setting Albert up, but the gamble was paying off.

"Are you going to arrest them?"

Hoeks looked up at the man perched on the edge of her desk. DCI Adam Garfield was too pretty for his own good. It was why she had been unable to resist having a torrid fling with him not once, but twice in the last two years. She had been the one to break it off on both occasions, yet feeling vulnerable and alone she found herself contemplating what he might say if she invited him home.

She couldn't though. Or, more accurately, he couldn't say yes even if she worked up the courage to ask. Assigned to a cross-border multi-jurisdictional taskforce tracking drugs moving out of Amsterdam, he needed to return to his team before they noticed his absence. He was in Hoeks' office because she'd called asking what he was doing and despite the fact that he would be missed, she had a favour to ask.

He'd hoped that meant she was ready to finally acknowledge her feelings, but alas she wanted to talk about work instead. Garfield hid his disappointment; an easy thing to do because he was glad just to get to see her again. To hear her voice. To remind her that he existed. They were no longer together because she favoured her career over their relationship, but he knew there were ways he could make it work.

Hoeks shook her head. "No, that would be counterproductive."

"Because you want to catch the bigger fish?"

"Yes, but more because I don't know who the bigger fish is. If I arrest two lowly animal services workers for supplying dogs to whoever is behind it all, it's likely they won't even know who to point the finger at or even where they can be found. For that matter, while I know they made Albert Smith's dog disappear, I don't know who at the shelter is on the take and who is not. If I arrest the wrong ones, I get nothing, and if I arrest them all I demonstrate how little I know." She sighed and thought about the bottle of vodka lurking behind the files in her bottom drawer.

"But someone in there knows the next person in the chain. You have to work your way up, Dani."

She frowned at her former lover.

"Sorry," he held up his hands. "You know what you are doing." They were the same rank and she was every bit his equal in ability and experience.

She sighed again. "I wouldn't go that far. I just sent a dog to animal services for no good reason other than the hope that his owner would do the work I am not allowed to."

There was no budget to look into dog theft. Not in Amsterdam. Not when they had murderers, organised criminals, and drug gangs to worry about. Her bosses weren't even convinced there was a dog fight ring in operation, and that would remain the case until she could prove otherwise.

And therein lay the paradox.

In order to get an investigation off the ground, she had to first prove there was something to investigate by investigating it.

It was a perfect catch twenty-two and she had been trying to find a way around it ever since her own dog was grabbed almost a month ago. Taken in broad daylight by two men in a panel van, her dogwalker watched the entire event with abject shock. She didn't film it though; the theft too fast for her to think to take out her phone.

There were other reported incidents of the same crime spread out over several years, but it was dogs not kids and the cursory effort put into tracking the people responsible bore no fruit and fell swiftly to the wayside when more serious crimes took priority.

Then Albert Smith presented her with an opportunity too good to dismiss. She felt bad about using him the way she was, but if he was the man the papers made him out to be, the dog theft case was about to be blown wide open.

With no budget and certain using her officers to pursue the case would get her chewed out by the commissioner, she chose to do so anyway. Just for a little while and very much off the books. She had a good relationship with most of her subordinates, so much so that she was able to call on two of them to tail Albert when he left the station.

That was a temporary fix though. They both had family or partners of their own to get home to and it left her with a conundrum – what to do in a few hours when Albert's voluntary, out-of-work-hours shadows needed to abandon him.

She could take over herself, watching him until he retired to bed for the night, or even stick with him all the way through if the wily old English sleuth refused to give up his search for Rex. But she didn't like the possibility that he might spot her.

A man hanging out on a street corner at night was less likely to attract attention than a woman. Especially a woman with her figure. If she dressed the part, people would assume she was just another prostitute; the city had enough of those for one more to go unnoticed, but it introduced the probability of unwanted attention.

Besides, she had a better idea. Call it an old favour from an old lover.

Chapter 16

W hen the dogs burst through the emergency exit and into the night beyond, the first of them ran toward the lights of the city and everyone else simply followed, assuming the dogs in front knew where they were going.

They did not.

Rex discovered this half a mile later when they finally slowed down enough for him to get to the front.

Heart racing and panting hard despite the cold air, he convinced the Doberman leading the pack to cut his pace and stop.

"There's no one behind us. We got away safely."

The Doberman risked a glance over his left shoulder. There were dogs behind him, but no humans and no headlights or engine sounds to suggest they were being chased. Leaving the building, he gave no thought to where he was going. It really didn't matter so long as he was putting distance between himself and the awful cage he'd been living in. Only when the effort of running flat out began to creep into his muscles had his pace begun to dip.

He let it drop off now, cruising to a walk and then stopping, his tongue lolling from the right side of his mouth as he fought to cool his body.

The dogs to his rear caught up, their breath condensing in foggy, billowing clouds over their heads. No one spoke for more than half a minute as they all fought to get their breath back.

"How about some introductions?" Rex asked. *"I'm Rex Harrison."*

The Pitbull sniggered. *"That will strike fear into the hearts of your opponents."*

The Afghan Hound said, *"He's not been given a fighting name yet, Brain Scar."*

"Brain Scar?" Rex sought to confirm he had the Pitbull's name right. *"And who else do we have?"* He looked around at the gaggle of dogs.

"I'm Shadow Fang," said the Afghan Hound.

"Battle Tank," said the Rottweiler.

The Doberman was Bite Knight, there was a ridgeback called Ball Biter – Rex hoped that wasn't alluding to a tactic he employed. Then there was a Boxer called South Jaw, a mixed breed called Mental Mongrel, an Alaskan Malamute using the fight name Snow Beast and several more. There were twelve dogs in total, all different breeds and all thankful that Rex helped them escape.

The casual round of introductions ended when the Pitbull terrier asked, *"Where the heck are we?"* The question was aimed at the dogs around him, but the reply he expected didn't come. *"Surely someone must know,"* he snapped in a tone that reminded Rex the Pitbull believed he was the alpha.

"Amsterdam," said Rex, sniffing the air. *"At least, that's where I was when they took me, and I can still smell the river."*

"Amsterdam?" More than one of the dogs questioned.

"You're not from here?" Rex couldn't hide his confusion. His expectation was that the captive dogs were all locals.

"Nah, I'm from Rotterdam," growled the Doberman angrily.

"I live in Leiden," said the Rottweiler.

"Hoofddorp," supplied someone else.

"I'm from Amsterdam," volunteered a voice belonging to an Afghan hound as it made its way through the pack. *"But I don't know where we are. Nothing much smells familiar except for the river."*

The dogs had been taken from towns and cities across the country. They were all unneutered males aged between two and five and all from breeds known for their natural aggression. They were all well fed and healthy, and with the exception of two, not including Rex, had been held captive for more than a week.

Three had witnessed the previous fights. Held two weeks ago, the dogs were not able to gauge time with such accuracy or in those terms. The sun rose and set and the moon cycled through its stages from full to nothing to full again. Kevin had said he was supposed to be in the previous fight which was half a moon cycle ago.

"*Anyone know when the next fight is supposed to take place?*" He aimed the question at everyone.

The Pitbull sneered, "*Who cares?*"

"*It's tomorrow night,*" supplied Shadow Fang.

"*Hey!*" barked the Pitbull, making the Afghan recoil. "*Focus. We're out now so we don't need to worry about when the next fight is. What we are going to do now is find somewhere warm to sleep for the night and never think about it again.*" He turned to face away from the dogs and was about to start walking when Rex got in his way.

"*What about the others?*"

"*What others?*"

"*The dogs still trapped in their cages. We need to go back for them.*"

"*Ha!*" the Pitbull spat. "*No chance. I'm never going anywhere near that place again and if the animal services people come anywhere near me, I'm going to bite someone's leg off.*" He moved to go around Rex who blocked his path once again.

"*We are all going back, my friend. We have strength in numbers and surprise on our side. We can rescue everyone and if you want to bite someone, there are humans there who very much deserve it.*"

The Pitbull bared his teeth, a viscous growl emanating from deep within his chest.

"Challenging my decisions, eh? *Ready to fight me for the right to lead the pack, are you? I've been in eight fights over more moon cycles than I care to count, and I won them all. Think you can take me on?*"

Rex held his ground. "*Fighting between ourselves would be counterproductive and I have no desire to challenge your position as alpha. But we do need to return for those we left behind.*"

"*Maybe he's right, Brain Scar,*" said the Rottweiler. "*I don't like that they are still trapped back there.*"

The Pitbull shot around to growl in the Rottweiler's face until he backed down.

"*Learn your place, Battle Tank. I won't warn you again.*"

Rex had witnessed leadership in action, and this wasn't it. This was bullying. It was toxic. While the Rottweiler cowered, Rex spoke calmly.

"*If you really want to abandon your brothers back at the warehouse and leave them to their fate, no one will stop you.*"

"*Good.*"

"*But how will you feel tomorrow?*"

The Pitbull said nothing, but he looked around at the other dogs. None of them wanted to meet his gaze.

"*We have to go back,*" Rex repeated. "*Maybe the safest thing to do is run away, but if we are to hold our heads high and claim to be so much better than the humans, we have to face our fears and do that which would make our ancestors proud.*"

Rex lifted his head to look around at the dogs. "*We don't know each other, but we are linked by a unique experience that created a bond we can never escape. It unifies us with a glorious purpose ...*"

The Pitbull spat out a laugh.

"*My word you are laying it on thick. Come on, fellas, I'm off to find some place out of this wretched breeze. I'm freezing my undercarriage off.*" He walked around Rex without giving him another glance.

Rex could scarcely believe his eyes. How could they not want to help those still trapped back at the warehouse? They knew what it was like from first hand experience. Together they would be able to sneak in and get everyone else out.

The Rottweiler followed the Pitbull, the Doberman tagging on as one by one all the dogs followed the alpha. Ahead of them the bright lights of the city beckoned. There they would find food and shelter and maybe even figure out how to get back to their humans.

Rex watched them go, torn between his need to keep his promise to Kevin and the knowledge that he needed the pack's help.

Pausing when he drew level, the Afghan said, "*For what it's worth. I think you are right. I think we should rescue the others, but we're dogs. What can we do against humans?*"

Chapter 17

W edged into the bucket seat of Axel's Nissan GTR, a four-point harness holding him firmly in place, Albert tried to get comfortable. The car felt tight. That was the only word he could come up with to describe it. Where an everyday family car would bounce softly over a bump in the road, the Nissan's suspension was tuned for optimal performance. Apparently, that meant minimal comfort Albert noted as another jolt shot up his spine.

Low to the ground, with huge wheels and the smallest steering wheel he had ever seen, the car took corners as though stuck to the road and the slightest blip of the accelerator forced Albert back into his seat as though an elephant had chosen to sit on his chest.

"You say you spent a lot of money on this car?" Albert tried to make conversation.

Axel's eyes never left the road when he said, "More than many would pay for a house."

They were travelling through the centre of Amsterdam, two dozen brightly-coloured, heavily-modified cars in a long line that caught the eyes of young and old when they passed by. They kept to the speed limit, but every set of lights created a challenge to get from zero to the maximum speed allowed in the shortest space of time.

Albert felt the amount of money the street racers invested in their machines was ridiculous. Possibly even irresponsible, but it would be rude to offer his opinion, so he kept his thoughts private. They appeared to have the money to spend and if nothing else were supporting the industry underpinning the street racer culture and that meant keeping people in jobs. It was all cyclic and they were hurting no one despite the near certainty their races were always illegal.

They were en route to a garage where the racers fixed up their cars. Owned by Fishman – Albert wasn't bothering to ask for his real name – it was on the other side of town. There he hoped to get his investigation rolling.

There were several angles from which he could approach. To start with there were guilty persons at the animal services shelter. If they faked Rex's euthanasia so they could make him disappear, then they were directly linked to whoever now had him. He knew where they worked so could tail them but was angry enough to confront them directly if he thought he could force a confession or get a location for Rex.

Then there was the man Caprice claimed to know. If Ivan was employed by the people running the dog fight ring, he might be the only person Albert needed to speak with. For that reason alone Ivan would be the first priority.

However, Albert's focus on finding Rex had to be tempered with helping the car club to retrieve their cars. He felt a little bad about his pretence; they believed every word even though he made most of it up on the spot, yet they *were* still trying to steal cars tonight and he *did* know the identity of the two thieves he interrupted. Those things were true, and he held faith in his investigative abilities. If the missing cars were still in Amsterdam, or even in Holland, there was a real chance they could find them.

With a roar of the engine, Axel turned off the road and onto the forecourt of an autoshop. In Albert's head he imagined a dingy, greasy place with an old roller door or two and a faded sign on the front façade. In contrast the autoshop was brand new, sleek, and presented to the public with chrome and glass and a giant, blue neon sign. The sign shone the legend 'Bitchin' Modifications' for all to see.

The forecourt stretched across six large roller doors to a showroom on the right. Clad in twenty-foot-high glass, the dim lights inside illuminated several cars and displays of parts. Albert spotted chrome exhaust systems, racks of fat alloy wheels, engine blocks, and more. For those with money and the love for modifying cars, it was a paradise.

The roller doors started to rise as if by magic, the lights flickering on inside as Axel approached. They passed under the doors, but glancing left and right to spot the person operating things inside, Albert could see no one.

His brow furrowing, Albert said, "That's a neat trick. How did you do that?"

Axel twitched an eyebrow before he worked out what he was being asked.

"The lights and doors? That's Fishman," he replied. "It's his place. Started off working out of his dad's garage, tuning cars and fitting parts. Saved up to buy some equipment, made more money, rented a bigger place. Ten years later, he owns this. Anyway, he's got it rigged so he can open it and turn on the lights from a switch in his car. He's a bit like Batman except he doesn't have a cave."

Albert wasn't convinced the Batman analogy worked but wasn't about to argue.

The street racers were streaming in from the street. Some of them following Axel into the autoshop, others parking outside rather than crowd the building. There were two cars on ramps in various stages of build, the parts and tools abandoned until the morning when the mechanics returned.

Axel parked, but applying the parking brake, he turned to look at Albert, his face set with a determined gaze.

"You really think you can get the cars back, old man?"

"Was Caprice lying about her former boyfriend?" Axel was still acting wary, but doubt wasn't something that bothered Albert. He responded to the challenge with one of his own. Axel would come around in time.

Breaking the gaze, Albert reached for the door handle and let himself out. Most of the street racers were out of their cars and making their way inside. They were not heading in his direction though, rather their feet were aimed at a door on the far side of the workshop. It was already open and light shone from within.

Albert followed everyone else to discover the door led to a recreation area that his generation might have called a clubhouse. It was somewhere for the racers to hang out. A tall fridge in one corner held both cans of soft drinks and bottles of beer. There was a pool table, a couple of upright video game machines, and an assortment of comfy chairs arranged around a couple of coffee tables next to a giant screen TV.

Someone hit a button and the screen swam into life, a football game showing with the volume down low.

Most of the racers were paying Albert no attention, helping themselves to drinks and talking among themselves. Two of the guys grabbed pool cues while one of the women racked the balls.

Rotating on the balls of his feet, Albert looked about for Fishman. He was in an office to one side, his face lit up by a computer screen. As though feeling Albert's eyes, he looked up and waved him over.

Axel followed, as did three or four others – those whose cars had gone missing and were most invested in the old man's claim to be able to get them back.

"I want to meet Ivan," Albert repeated his earlier demand. "The fight could be tonight for all you know."

Axel jumped in with, "On a Thursday? Highly doubtful. Besides, that's not the deal. We agreed to help you find your dog and we will. Once you help us to locate the missing cars."

Albert's jaw clenched. Sick with worry for his friend, he was desperate to learn something. If he could just prove he was alive it would be enough for now. The street racers were not about to budge though and fighting them would just eat up time.

Regardless, he said, "Your cars don't have a dwindling lifespan."

"Yes, they do," Axel argued, his tone still aggressive. "If we don't get them before they leave the country, they will be gone forever. For all we know they are being shipped right now and that makes them a higher priority than your dog."

A muscle in Albert's jaw twitched. The street racers in the room said nothing, their eyes on Albert with a mix of emotions displayed. Some were impatient like Axel, others showed a modicum of sympathy for Albert's plight, but none were going to jump in to argue on his side. He could refuse to help, but striking out to find Rex by himself would be a foolish choice. If he helped the street racers, they would help him, that was the bargain they struck.

He just had to hope they would keep to it.

Chapter 18

F ishman had his computer on and his fingers poised over the keyboard.

"What were those names again?" he asked.

Albert needed a second to recall them. "Song Bin and Park Ji Hoon. They are Korean," he added, "So we will need a translator."

"What for?" questioned Shaggy.

"For when they choose to pretend they don't speak English or Flemish or any other European language." Albert's mind was operating at full speed, his need to rescue Rex acting as fuel to push it harder than normal. The sooner he disrupted the car theft ring, the sooner he could turn his attention to finding his dog.

"I've got one of them," said Fishman, leaning back from the desk so others could see the screen.

He was on a social media site that even Albert recognised. He also recognised the man in the profile picture.

"That's Park Ji Hoon," he stated, though he then noticed the name was emblazoned across the screen in bold letters next to the picture. "He's one of the men who tried to steal your car earlier."

Fishman rolled his finger over the little wheel on the mouse, scrolling down the page where his 'feed' as Albert had learned it was called, showed Park Ji Hoon in various poses and with other people, almost all of which shared his racial heritage.

"And that's his friend Song Bin," Albert aimed an index finger at a photograph before Fishman could scroll past it. The two men were with two white women. All four appeared to be similar in age. They were pictured at night, posing in front of a car with the lights of the city behind them. In the background and all around were other cars and people.

Axel bent at the waist and put a hand on the back of Fishman's chair to steady himself as he scrutinised the face of a scumbag car thief.

"He's a racer," he murmured at a volume that was little more than a whisper yet still loud enough for those present to hear. Gripping Fishman's shoulder, he said, "Check out the Skyline he's running."

"Man, that thing is slammed," said Shaggy.

"And shaved," remarked Fishman. "I bet those are Lambo doors. I love those on a Skyline."

To Albert it was a foreign language the chaps were now speaking, but the comments had caused those around him to press closer. They all wanted a look at the shaved and slammed car. Whatever the heck that meant.

Teagan, a mixed-race woman with blue highlights in her jet black hair was one of the racers whose car had been stolen. She suggested, "See if anyone is tagged."

Albert didn't know what that meant either but found out when Fishman used the mouse to hover over the individuals in the photographs. Song Bin's name popped up, hovering over his head when the mouse pointer went near him. Neither of the women had been 'tagged' but there were other photographs and they soon found someone they knew.

"That's Janice!" said Axel's girlfriend, who Albert now knew as Kerstin, clearly surprised to see someone she knew. "What's she doing there?"

What had become obvious in the last five minutes of trawling through Park Ji Hoon's life was that he was part of the same street racing culture Axel, Shaggy and their friends enjoyed.

Axel straightened himself back to upright and looked out through the windows to the recreation area beyond.

"I don't know," he replied. "But I'm sure she can tell us."

Albert's right eyebrow twitched in question. Kerstin was already on her way to the door, heading back to where the rest of the racers were playing pool and relaxing.

Axel made it sound like she was here. Watching through the glass, Albert spotted the woman in the photograph lift her head when Kerstin called her name.

There was music playing in the recreation area loud enough to drown out what was being said, but Janice was on her feet and coming to the office. As developments go it held promise, but Albert did not expect the revelation Janice brought with her.

"Say that again," he requested.

"They have a meet tonight," Janice repeated her previous statement. "It's over in Osdorp, I think." She claimed to not really know the Korean guys, but knew them through a mutual acquaintance.

"Can you confirm it?" Albert pressed.

Despite looking a little confused, Janice took out her phone.

Albert turned away to face Axel and those pressed in around him.

"This is a chance for us to track them and find where they have the cars. Your cars all have trackers on them, right?"

"Yes," said Shaggy, "but as we pointed out earlier, they are not showing up when we search for them. Most likely that is because they have the cars inside somewhere that is shielded or made from thick concrete, or they remove them as soon as they can. Either way the trackers are of no use to us."

Albert grinned. "But what if they took another car. A car that we know they want and watch the tracker until it goes dead? Wouldn't that show us where they had taken the car?"

Fishman nodded his head, a smile showing that he was impressed. "That would absolutely work." He fell silent, his features thoughtful for a moment. "But how do we know what car they want?"

Albert tilted his head and looked right at Axel, the question he needed to ask going unspoken while he waited for the street racer to catch on.

It took a second.

"Uh-uh. No way, man. I'm not risking my wheels!"

Explaining to the bewildered faces in the room, Albert said, "Park Ji Hoon and Song Bin tried to steal Axel's car. I believe they are trying to fulfil an order of stolen cars that will be exported and never seen again. Chances are they remove the trackers from the cars they take within hours, if not minutes, of getting them into their secure facility. They likely doctor the engine, chassis, and VIN numbers too so they can never be traced back to the rightful owners."

"And you want to tempt them with my Nissan GTR!" growled Axel, doing his best to ignore the faces around him. However, surrounded by those who had already lost their cars and could now see a glimmer of hope in the plan to get them back, he was fighting a losing battle and knew it.

"I have an address for the meet tonight," announced Janice, who had been texting feverishly and was largely oblivious to the latest development.

Albert shrugged in an exaggerated manner. "If we get this right we can get the police involved, get back all your cars, and break up the ring of thieves stealing them in one fell swoop."

"If we get it right," Axel highlighted.

Albert shrugged again. "No plan is without risks."

Chapter 19

S ylvia van Lidth gazed down at the two men on their knees.

"You really expect me to believe the dogs found a way to escape from their cages and that they then staged a mass breakout neither one of you could prevent?"

Hans knew they were in big trouble. There really hadn't been any other option than to report the breakout and be honest about what happened, yet the bitch, as everyone called her when she wasn't around, didn't believe them. What were they supposed to do about that?

"Well, it's the truth, I swear," Hans mumbled, his eyes aimed at the cold concrete rather than look up and see the lack of compassion in her gaze. "We were watching the football. There was no one else here to let the dogs out ..."

"Yeah, and we saw one of them flip his cage onto its side so the latch fell open," interjected Levi unhelpfully. "They were conspiring all this time and none of us realised it."

Hans cringed and tried to move away from the man they were now labelling as his accomplice.

"Dogs are a lot smarter than people think," Levi droned on.

They argued about the best way to present their defence before Sylvia arrived. Levi believed they should show it wasn't their fault and refused to see that claiming the dogs were organised was the worst strategy possible. He wanted to blame the newest arrival, the big German Shepherd, because everything had been fine until he showed up.

Hans suspected such a claim would be seen as an insult to Sylvia's intelligence and get them both killed.

"And they opened the emergency exit all by themselves, did they?" Sylvia growled.

Levi nodded his head vigorously. "That's right, they did! It was the craziest thing. The German Shepherd that came in a few hours ago, he was behind it all. He's the one to blame."

Hans shook his head and silently prayed the ground would open and swallow him.

Five minutes later, Sylvia smoked a cigarette outside in the cold. Her staff knew well enough not to disturb her when she was thinking. Or angry. And right now, she was both. Not all of the dogs who escaped were set to participate in the event which was now less then twenty-four hours away, but some were and it was too late now to replace them. Ivan reported the German Shepherd as a great find. An unexpected find to match up against a champion dog being brought in from Russia. There were tougher breeds out there, but Sylvia van Lidth didn't need the shepherd to win. She wasn't betting, she was hosting the event and that meant she took a fat share of the money wagered because the bookkeepers all worked for her.

The Russian champion, worryingly nicknamed 'The Death' because his fighting name 'Eviscerator' wasn't scary enough, had only come up against one opponent who gave him any trouble: a German Shepherd. He won the fight, but only barely and the crowd were looking forward to seeing him tested once more.

Sylvia set the whole thing up months in advance, paying The Eviscerator's owner a sizeable advance to ensure he turned up and that his dog was in top shape. Now, less than twenty-four hours from the biggest fight night yet, she had no contender to offer.

Well, it just wouldn't do.

Chelsea approached, Sylvia's assistant waiting patiently a few feet away until her boss was ready to speak to her.

Dropping her cigarette butt, she ground it under one stilettoed foot and blew the smoke into the air where the breeze tore it away into the night.

"I need them found," she stated flatly. "Especially, the shepherd and Brain Scar. The Pitbull is everyone's favourite because he's so vicious. He's scheduled to open the event."

"I have already sent people to search for them," Chelsea reported.

"Send twice as many. No ... send everyone. I need those dogs. And get everyone else to scour the city for another German Shepherd. I don't care if they have to rob people in broad daylight or break into their homes. I want a large German Shepherd before the sun sets tomorrow."

"Yes, Mrs van Lidth. I will get *everyone* on it." Chelsea knew well enough not to point out that 'everyone' appeared to now be doing at least two tasks alongside setting up the event, meeting and greeting the highest of the high rollers flying in to bet their money, and moving the dogs to the venue, a task Sylvia had just moved up by twelve hours due to the escape.

Sucking a little air through her teeth, Chelsea dared to wait when she knew Sylvia expected her to zip away to oversee her instructions.

Noticing that her assistant was yet to move, Sylvia fixed her with a curious expression. The Harvard graduate had already lasted longer than her previous ten assistants, all of which had been men. Sylvia believed that was probably the crux of the problem and her error in the first place. Men were just so darned unreliable and so easily distracted.

"There is something else?" she enquired, certain Chelsea would not loiter without good reason.

"Hans and Levi? Are they to be disposed of?" Chelsea felt certain she knew the answer but believed it prudent to check. It wasn't like the deed could be undone if she had misinterpreted her boss's intent.

Sylvia opened her mouth to answer only to close it again. She had been about to say, "Yes," but a better idea presented itself before she could form the words.

"No, Chelsea. I have something else in store for them. Have them involved in moving the dogs to the new location. Then ..."

Chelsea listened to Sylvia's idea and took notes, all the while doing her best to keep the horrified grimace from her face.

Chapter 20

R ex couldn't figure out what to do. The other dogs were not going to challenge Brain Scar's ruling and it didn't seem to matter what he said, the Pitbull had no interest in returning to rescue those they left behind.

It was new territory for him. He was used to having all the great ideas and other dogs following his lead. He was a leader and while he wasn't trying to usurp Brain Scar, it was looking more and more like that was his only option. Of course, starting a fight with a Pitbull was anything but a clever idea. But what did that leave him? He couldn't talk them into helping him and he couldn't force them either.

Worse yet, in choosing to follow them in the hope he might be able to talk them around, he was moving farther and farther away from Kevin and the other captives.

The pack of fighting dogs found an alcove under one arch of a railway bridge. A dilapidated sign above a hole that used to house a door read 'Wageningen Tyres'. Long abandoned by the owners, it still bore a faint trace of rubber inside.

The dogs were cold and tired, but they were not hungry for the humans keeping them captive ensured they were well fed. It was the only kindness any received though they knew it was not one born out of generosity or empathy.

Rex watched the dogs form a huddle. They were closer together than normal in deference to the temperature, but out of the wind they could expect their shared body heat to keep the worst of the winter at bay.

No one paid him much attention, and the few glances he got were no more than cursory. They wanted to sleep until the morning when the temperature would rise. Then they would set out to find their homes, even though some appeared to be a long way from where they needed to be.

When gentle snoring began to fill the air, Rex turned away. He could backtrack to the warehouse with ease, but convinced he would not be able to affect a rescue by himself, he chose to stay put.

He was tired too, but doubted he would sleep. Not right away at least. Instead, he kept watch, his eyes closed but his nose and ears alert. Perhaps in the morning when they were rested he would be able to talk some sense into everyone. He was going back for Kevin and the others no matter what.

Chapter 21

Albert had never been to a street racers' meet. In fact, Albert had never even heard of such a thing. When Fishman attempted to explain it to him as they drove back across Amsterdam, he did so with references to a franchise of films called *Fast and Furious*. Albert could claim to have heard of them but had never been inclined to check them out. Thus the comparison was lost to him, but he saw it with his own eyes soon enough.

What shocked him most was the abundance of female flesh on display. The ladies, as though oblivious to the near-zero temperature, were out in short skirts and low tops. Most had coats over their shoulders, but none thought it necessary to zip them up.

The gentlemen were more appropriately dressed, though few thought to wear hats or gloves and most still had their coats open at the top to show off the layers beneath. Observing the behaviour for a few moments, Albert came to realise it was a show of plumage as one might get with birds. Both genders were showing off for the other. Making themselves as noticeable as possible so they might stand out.

The cars were an extension of the same and while most of the cars were driven and thus presumably owned by men, twenty percent of the vehicles appeared to have a lady at the helm.

As Albert understood it, the street racer scene in Amsterdam was subdivided into two main factions. The Korean racers, of which Song Bin and Park Ji Hoon were a part, ran with other Asian gangs. There was some overlapping, and the separation wasn't due to a long-running feud or anything that might cause a fight the moment Axel and his friends arrived. It was simply that the messages to meet were sent out in code among the members of each group, so without being on the inside, which Axel's gang were not, there was no way to know a meeting of the Asian faction was going to occur.

Until tonight because Janice went to college with Song Bin's little sister.

Heads turned when they pulled into the street where the meet was already taking place. When he asked what exactly a 'meet' entailed, Albert learned that it was little more than an informal gathering of likeminded individuals. They would compare cars, show off their latest modifications, drink and dance to the music blasting from music systems fitted to the vehicles, and quite often race.

The races were quite illegal, not least because of the danger they posed to anyone else on the road. It was why they tended to meet in remote locations at the edge of the city where they stood a better chance of getting away with driving in excess of twice the national legal speed limit.

Just as they approached the cars parked in haphazard rows on either side of the street, a foursome of racers were waved into a line and set off by a woman wearing a skimpy dress and the highest heels Albert had ever seen on a person. Defying both logic and gravity, she spun around when the cars swept past her to watch as they accelerated into the distance at a speed close to that of a space shuttle on take-off.

Fishman drove a Toyota GT86 which he explained was fitted with a rebored V6 engine that ran more than five hundred brake horsepower. It had a Veilside bodykit and twenty-inch alloy wheels. The interior was filled with neon lights that glowed a deep green from under the seats and behind the dashboard. There were more neon lights fitted beneath the car. It guaranteed the car would be seen wherever it went, and the rest of their convoy were little different.

Certainly the lights and engine sounds made it certain their arrival would be noticed, so by the time Axel, Fishman, Shaggy, and the rest were getting out of their cars, the attention of everyone already present was on them.

Albert had to twist around, fight to get his feet out, and then use the handle above his head to extricate himself from the Sparco bucket seat. A younger person might perform the task with ease, but Albert slugged his way over the doorsill and onto his knees on the tarmac before he could rearrange his limbs to be able to stand up.

By the time he was straight and had his flat cap back on his head to keep out the cold, Axel was talking with a trio of Asian men. Fishman came around his car to stand at Albert's side.

"You know Axel is risking a lot here. There's no guarantee they will take his car to where the others are. How sure are you that they won't have shifted them yet?"

Not even slightly sure, the reply rang out in Albert's head. He was risking Axel's pride and joy on a hunch. A series of hunches maybe. Under other circumstances he would not act in such a carefree manner. However, with Rex missing and the street racers refusing to help him until he helped them, he was willing to flip a coin and hope for the best.

They were going to bet ownership of the Nissan GTR and then make sure to lose, but only if they could get a race against the right people – the people who they knew wanted it.

Ahead of Albert, one of the Korean's aimed an arm back toward the gaggle of racers and shouted to get someone's attention.

A man turned his head, acknowledging the call and an exchange in rapid-fire Korean took place. Albert only understood one word. It was a name: Song.

They were looking for Song Bin, one of the thieves from earlier. Axel and his friends had questioned whether he would run when confronted by the owner of a car he was almost caught trying to steal just a few hours earlier, but Albert promised them he wouldn't.

Yes, he would know that they knew, but there would be no cops present, so he would have no reason to run. Moreover, he would feel he was on home ground, and surrounded by people who would have his back, would stand his ground. Throw in Albert's conviction that he was stealing the cars to order and therefore needed a high-end, modified Nissan GTR, the chance to race and win it would be too tempting to turn down.

The familiar face of the car thief emerged from the crowd just as four more cars were lining up to race each other. Just behind Song was the other man, Park Ji Hoon.

"That's them?" asked Fishman. He was draped over the passenger door, so it did the job of supporting his body. According to him, racing for ownership was rare.

More usually, those willing to test their cars did so for money and bragging rights, the latter being the more important element.

Albert nodded, exhaling a cloud of warm air from his nose as he watched and waited for the two Koreans to register the Nissan GTR and spot him. Unlike Fishman, Albert was fully in view and was getting noticed by everyone.

There was no mystery behind the attention coming his way, the nudges and unheard remarks. He was forty years older than the next oldest person at the meet and sixty years older than some of them. It made him stand out. As did his wardrobe choices which would look right at home on the streets of his village or in the local pub. However, among the street racers his clothes set him apart like a polar bear in a penguins only club.

"Yes, that's them," Albert confirmed, lifting his right hand to wave for their attention.

Song and Park were almost at Axel where he stood talking to half a dozen other men from the Asian side of things. When Albert caught their collective eye, the response was nothing short of comical. Song saw him first, a quick glance to check the waving arm caused a double take of epic proportions. His feet simply stopped moving and the colour drained from his face. His left arm shot out to stop Park who had also glanced but not registered who the old man was.

Albert waved again, this time with a friendly smile on his face. Both men were stationary, urgent whispers passing back and forth between them. They looked about ready to bolt despite Albert's prediction, so he started toward them, hands up in a show of surrender he hoped might put them at ease.

Song Bin turned accusing eyes at Axel.

"What is this?" he growled. "Who's that old man?"

"The old man is of no concern," Axel replied, cool as anything. "I believe you have interest in my car." The statement was a threat and a warning combined. It told the Korean car thieves they were busted, but the lack of cops present conflicted with Axel's words. If he was looking for Song Bin because he knew he was guilty of tonight's attempt to steal it, why wasn't he doing anything about it?

Song Bin didn't seem to know what answer to give, and despite Axel's claim that the old man was of no significance, his attention remained split between them.

"Because if you do," Axel continued, "I am ready to race for it."

The engine noise and music blaring in the street made it hard to hear conversation, but a glut of the people present were interested enough in the unexpected situation to be listening. The offer of a high-stakes race rippled through them like a breeze shifting a field of corn.

Song Bin's gaze came to rest firmly on Axel.

"You want to race me for your car?" It was almost too good to be true. He could call back to the boss and let him know they were back on track, and it would all be legal. They wouldn't even need to rush to get to the lockup in Westpoort.

A confident grin spread across Axel's face. "Nah, I want to race you for your car. I've never owned a Supra and by the look of yours, I will enjoy fixing it up to make it run right."

Laughs and gasps arose in equal measure; Axel's insult was a surprising goad.

"Think you're going to show me your taillights?" Song Bin sneered.

"From what I hear about your driving. I won't even need the nitrous."

The second insult drew a bigger gasp from the crowd. Smack talk wasn't unusual, but this wasn't Axel's turf or his people.

Song Bin raised his right arm, aiming at Axel like a lance to pin him to the spot. The press of people fell silent to hear what he had to say.

"Okay. You've got yourself a race." The crowd cheered. "But if your car is so good …" silence fell, keen ears hanging off his every word. Song Bin kept his eyes locked firmly on Axel but swung his arm through an arc to point at someone else. "Then let him drive it."

All eyes turned toward Albert.

Pinned to the spot by Song Bin's arm and everyone else's faces, he had to fight not to gulp. He wanted to argue. He wanted to claim he was too old to have a licence, but that would be a lie. Axel wasn't going to let him get behind the wheel though, so it was all moot, surely.

"Sure," said Axel, shocking Albert right down to his boots.

Chapter 22

"O kay?" asked Fishman. "Think you can remember everything?"

Albert dropped his eyes to the dashboard, across to the centre console where an extra panel showed nitrous oxide pressure and a whole host of other information he'd been told to ignore. The instructions were simple enough: Drive the accelerator pedal into the floor and try not to crash into anything.

The aim of the race was to place Axel's car into the hands of the Korean gang of car thieves. They wanted them to drive away in it so they could see where it went. By tracking its location, they hoped to be able to find where the rest of the cars were stashed. It was a gamble, but one the street racers were willing to take.

Axel had agreed to the proposed plan, but now that Albert was behind the wheel of his car and about to lose it, he looked positively sick. The Dutch racers argued with Song Bin, but Axel's smack talk worked against them, charging the Korean crowd to get behind their man. They wanted to see him win.

Arriving as the challenger worked exactly the way the street racers said it would, but they failed to anticipate the clever demand to put the old man behind the wheel. It was that or withdraw. It didn't matter that Albert wouldn't be able to beat Song Bin, that was the aim. The concern was whether Albert could pilot the darned thing to the finish line without crashing it.

Albert looked back up, gripping the tiny sports steering wheel with both hands. He was surprised to find they were not shaking, but questioned if that was because he'd gone through terrified to arrive somewhere beyond where the certainty of imminent fiery death allowed him to operate.

"Albert," Fishman clicked his fingers to get his attention.

Albert snapped his head around and up to look out the open driver's window.

"Yes. Yes, sorry." He swallowed hard and ran through the instructions to show he was able to recall what they said. "Watch the girl with the flag. The moment she starts to lower her arm, I go. Keep it in first until the crank shaft speed hits six thousand five hundred RPM then upshift fast. To maximise thrust and speed I should continue to upshift each time the engine speed reaches six thousand and never let it reach seven thousand."

"Why not?" Prompted Shaggy, hanging through the passenger's open window.

Albert racked his brain. "Um, because I will pass peak torque and thus negatively impact the car's ability to continue accelerating."

"That's right, my man," agreed Fishman. "Now that's going to take about six seconds. What do you do after that?"

Albert's right hand moved instinctively down to the button next to the hand-brake.

"I hit the nitrous."

"Aaaaaand?" drawled Shaggy.

"I hold on to my butt because it will feel like I am going to leave the surface of the planet."

Fishman and Shaggy both laughed. The way the old man said it … possibly just that it was an old man saying it in the first place, was funny to them. He looked so out of place in the car it was like seeing a baby in a business suit or a skinny guy stepping into a wrestling ring.

"Hey? Are we ready yet?" shouted a Japanese man with spiked hair. He was acting as race organiser, setting the cars up and making sure they were all obeying the rules.

The crowd was impatient, not used to being made to wait while a driver gets a quick tutorial on how to operate his car. All other meet activity had pretty much ceased so they could all watch the event of the evening.

Mutters were passing around to question the identity of the aging man strapped tightly into the driver's seat of the Nissan GTR. Was he some faded British race hero from Formula One? Was he someone from the world of drag racing brought in as a clever ringer?

Two more cars were running with Albert and Song Bin, just to make it more interesting. They were in no danger of losing their cars, they were just taking part for bragging rights, but to Albert's mind it upped the stakes significantly. It wasn't just one car he had to race now, it was three, and they were all squeezed into a narrow street between industrial units on either side.

It looked too skinny for them all to fit. Thankful that all he had to do was lose, he couldn't deny the competitive edge blooming in his chest.

A horn beeped, the sound loud enough to break through the fog of Albert's concentration. He looked through the windscreen to find a sea of faces waiting for him to get on with it. Three cars were arranged against a spray-painted line on the tarmac, their noses hovering over the top of it, but not a millimetre beyond.

"Hey, good luck, man," called Shaggy, a sentiment echoed by Fishman who showed a thumbs up.

Albert powered up the windows; another thing he remembered they told him to do. Leaving them open created drag and racing a quarter mile was a sport of fractional margins. The slightest thing could win or lose the race.

Peering over the long bonnet, Albert edged his way up to the line and overshot it much to the amusement of the crowd. In his head, driving was a simple thing he mastered more than six decades ago, but diminishing eyesight and dwindling reaction speed convinced him to give up driving more than three years earlier. At the time, his wife was still in good health and happy to drive them wherever they needed to go. It had not occurred to either one of them what would happen if he survived her.

So, in theory driving a car was easy, but as he crunched and ground the gearbox into reverse to get back to the starting line, he acknowledged that many of the skills it required were ones a person's muscles forgot over time.

The onlookers were having the time of their life. The men and women found Albert's antics most entertaining and they lined the street on both sides from one end of the quarter mile to the other. It thinned in the middle with the glut of the crowd either at the start or the finish line.

When the spikey-haired Japanese man was finally happy Albert had the car in the right place, he backed away a few metres and took a moment to confirm each of the drivers was looking at him and ready to go.

Song Bin was two cars along, occupying the number two spot, if you will. Albert was fourth in line on the left hand edge. The finish line looked to be no distance away at all and he knew from Fishman and Shaggy that the race would be over in ten seconds or less.

He spared a glance to his right, looking down the line of drivers to find Song Bin's narrowed eyes staring his way. The Korean car thief gripped his steering wheel tight and turned to face the way they needed to go.

He recognised Albert from their earlier interaction, but couldn't figure out what the old man's play might be. That he stopped the theft could be put down to simple bad luck. The right guy in the wrong place at the right time. Turning up at the meet, though, that changed things and Song Bin did not like some of the thoughts swirling around in his head.

Heart thumping in his chest, Albert watched the Japanese man hand over to a woman, a different one to the inappropriately clad lady he saw setting a race off when they arrived. This one wore a one-piece tartan playsuit that covered her skin from the top of her thighs to the swell of her breasts and very little else.

Thinking that she had to be freezing, Albert almost missed when she dropped her arm and was last off the line. He was only a fraction of a second behind the others, but that equated to half a car length.

Music blared, audible inside the car even over the insanely loud engine. Albert flicked his eyes to the dials visible between the spokes of the steering wheel. The RPM needle hit six thousand five hundred RPM and he pumped the clutch, snatching the gear lever back into second.

His right foot barely left the floor and the car continued to accelerate. It felt like he was flying and for a brief moment he understood the allure of racing. The adrenaline high was not to be underestimated, but his heart felt like it might explode if it attempted to beat any harder.

Snapping the gear lever forward into third, he drew level with the car to his right. It was a VW Golf, not a car he associated with racing of any kind, yet it was able to hold its own. It was driven by another Japanese man, this one wearing his hair bleached and buzzed into a crew cut. He had piercings in his eyebrows which were also bleached, and his lips were pulled back in a grimace of concentration to show his gritted teeth.

With a gasp of horror, Albert's eyes relayed a terrifying message: the road narrowed ahead. Either it wasn't visible from the start line or he was just too scared to see it before now, but in less than a second he was going to run out of room. There just wasn't space for four cars ahead, but should he let off and slip in behind the Golf? Or floor it to get ahead?

Flooring it wasn't an option, his foot was already making a dent in the steel panel beneath the accelerator pedal, but his thinking time delayed taking action for too long and the second he once had evaporated.

Opening his mouth to scream, Albert yelled, "Arrrrrrgggghhhh!" and moved the speeding Nissan closer to the Golf. They shot into the narrower portion of the road to defy his belief that they would fit. His nose was ahead now and when he slammed the accelerator back into fourth, he left the Golf in his wake. The differences in acceleration were marginal, but the GTR was faster than the other three cars. The half a car length he gave them with his slow start was gone and suddenly there was only three of them in the race.

On the far side, a Subaru clung to the tarmac like it was using glue, its fat tyres holding the road as the people and buildings either side of them vanished into nothing but a blur.

Albert felt like he had tunnel vision. The finish line was coming up and he was pulling ahead of the Subaru. Only Song Bin in his Toyota Supra had a marginal lead.

The finish line was ahead. It was easy to see because it was where the crowd ended. How long did he have? Two seconds? Three? He was perfectly positioned to finish the race in second place, but now was the time to hit the nitrous oxide button, and according to Fishman and Shaggy the mix of odourless gas would shunt him back into his seat like having a giant standing on his ribcage. The car would leap forward as it achieved new heights of acceleration.

Albert needed to lose, but it was imperative that he looked as though he was trying to win. Song Bin had to believe his victory was fair and square. If Albert gave him any reason to suspect he was handed the race, the chances were that the thieves would become wary and choose to protect themselves. They were not the bosses, and in such a cutthroat criminal operation, exposing the organisation to risk would be met with swift reprimands. So if he wanted them to take the bait and lead them to the cache of stolen cars, his loss had to look real.

Nevertheless, when the Supra sprang forward with a blast of blue flame from its exhaust, Albert jabbed his nitrous button in response. For a fleeting moment nothing happened. It was long enough for Albert to glance down at the button. Had he pressed it hard enough? Was there something else he was supposed to do first?

His right hand wavered, just off the steering wheel so that when the nitrous blend hit the engine, exploding with a violent surge of torque, he was neither looking the right way nor holding on. The force of sudden acceleration made the loose skin on his face gather by his ears. The back of his skull pressed into the thinly padded head rest and his body appeared to be trying to merge with the seat material.

To say the Nissan shot forward would be a gross understatement. It crossed the remaining two hundred metres at what Albert assumed was roughly the same speed a fighter jet achieves when in a full dive. He wanted to check to his right to make sure the Supra was still ahead but by the time the thought had occurred to him he was across the line and the wild cheers from the crowd were falling into silence.

The boost from the nitrous oxide tanks fell off, reducing the car's speed down to a level called 'merely suicidal'. Albert heaved in a lungful of air thinking it might be the first since the lady who forgot to dress for the weather dropped her arm.

He let the car slow, applying the brakes and checking his mirrors to find the other racers. They were all behind him and heading back to the finish line having already turned around.

By the time Albert got the Nissan pointed back the way he had come, his competitors were parked, but there was something distinctly wrong with the picture.

Song Bin looked ready to kill. He was arguing with Park Ji Hoon, and the crowd of Koreans, who Albert expected to be cheering and congratulating him, were quiet instead. In direct contrast, Axel, Fishman, Shaggy, and the rest of the street racers Albert arrived with were running toward him. They were excited and animated and there could only be one reason for it.

He'd won.

Pursing his lips, Albert spat, "Nuts!"

Chapter 23

“That was some of the best driving I have ever seen!” exclaimed Axel.

“Yeah, man, it was totally dope,” agreed Shaggy.

Albert received similar praise from almost every member of the street racer crew and found two of the young women looping their arms through his when he got out of the car.

“I was supposed to lose,” he pointed out. “We were using your car as bait, remember.”

Axel’s smile was too broad to be dented by Albert’s concerns. To his mind they had just won a great victory the Koreans couldn’t hope to argue against. They tried to get the better of them by insisting the old man drove and his car still crossed the line first. As a reward, he now had a Toyota Supra to take home and it was a heck of a car despite the insults he threw Song Bin’s way earlier.

“Don’t worry, Albert. All is well. Can’t tell you more here, there are too many people listening, but we have a solution to the problem that should work.”

Given a cryptic answer, Albert wasn’t sure what to think, but had no choice other than to go with it.

“So what now? Do we need to get out of here before they get uppity about losing a car?”

Fishman clapped both his hands on Albert’s shoulders.

“Nah, man. You won. Now you get to revel in glory and enjoy the victory. Racing for ownership is rare, man. They’ll be talking about you for years.”

"And the rest of the community would never let Song Bin get away with anything other than handing over the keys," added Shaggy. "He bet his car and he lost. That's just how it is."

To confirm their claims, Song Bin was heading their way now. Outnumbered at least ten to one, if not closer to twenty, Albert expected some backlash from the Asian street racers but there was a respect thing going on that he genuinely admired.

"Fair and square," said Song Bin offering his keys to Axel. The conflict was clear in his face. His mouth failed to match the words coming from it, and his eyes looked tortured. Albert didn't think it was possible for a nose or ears to look disappointed and angry, but Song Bin's were giving it a good go.

Park Li Hoon was a few feet behind him, the other car thief undoubtedly now charged with driving his partner home.

Axel kept his arms at his side, jinking his head toward Albert when he said, "Give them to him. He's the one who beat you."

Had he not known the man holding out the keys was a criminal, Albert might actually have felt sorry for him.

He raised his right hand, holding it below Song Bin's until the Korean opened his fingers and the keys dropped.

"Thank you," Albert said. Lines made a hasty queue in his head as he fought to decide whether he ought to dispense some advice on the subject of criminal behaviour and where it leads, or to warn them that he wasn't done yet and would be bringing down their whole operation in the coming hours or days. Would that send them running back to their bosses? Would it help to panic them into making a costly mistake?

Ultimately, the moment passed, and Albert found himself hoisted aloft, lifted to the shoulders of Shaggy and Fishman who then paraded him all the way to Song Bin's car.

Albert had no idea what he was supposed to do with the car, other than hand the keys to Axel since it was his car they staked and Albert had no use for it even if they did think it was now his.

However, halfway to it, a cry of alarm warned of incoming police patrol units. The crowd scattered like ants, everyone running for their cars. Axel raced to his Nissan. Fishman legged it back down the quarter mile to get to his car, but Shaggy went with Albert.

"Come on, Albs! It's time to get out of here. The fuzz don't like us one little bit."

Albert slapped the Supra keys into Shaggy's hand, insisting he drive. He'd had enough for one night.

Chapter 24

DCI Garfield had watched the illegal street race with interest. He knew very little about Albert Smith beyond what he'd read and seen online and on the television, yet he was clearly a remarkable man.

When Daniella asked him if he had any time he could give her to help look into her missing dog, he made it sound as though it was a terrible imposition and that she was wrong to even ask, yet he did so to mask how he almost said yes before she finished asking.

Truthfully, he didn't have time for it, but he knew how much she loved her dog and he wanted her to feel obliged to give their relationship a second chance. Or a third chance, if he was being more accurate. It wasn't the right way to woo a woman and he knew it, but she had resisted romantic gestures, even the bigger ones and he risked looking like a fool if he continued to pursue her that way.

Saving her dog would ingratiate her to him and if he had to manipulate her into admitting she still felt the same way then so be it.

He was dressed to blend in with the street racers and though he was a little on the old side compared with everyone except Albert Smith, he believed he looked the part. The Asian contingent assumed he was just another one of the Dutch racers there to interrupt their evening with the big race throwdown, and he kept his distance from the Caucasians lest they question who he was.

His car was parked a block away, the unmodified Ford too stock standard to be brought to the meet.

Garfield's plan was to tail the old Englishman and see where he went, yet his behaviour thus far was inexplicable. Danielle expected Albert Smith to be looking into his dog's supposed euthanasia, yet he was participating in a street race with a bunch of punks a quarter his age.

According to Danielle's officers, who Garfield relieved more than an hour ago, he got into a fight with a pair of muggers, who he then chased off and had been with the gang of street racers ever since.

When the alert came to tell the racers the police were inbound, Garfield thought about ditching his quest. Danielle had overplayed her hand and the old man genuinely believed his dog was dead. That her guess they would make the German Shepherd disappear in the first place came out on the money was coincidence enough. That she would get any further with it was too much to hope for.

Regardless, when he reached his car, out of breath and left behind by everyone else, he decided to give the case another hour. If he went home he had nothing but an empty apartment waiting for him. He would drink a few shots of whisky he didn't need and watch rubbish on the television.

It wasn't with any great conviction that he pointed his car toward Bitchin' Modifications but so he could be honest when he told Danielle he gave it his best shot.

Chapter 25

The jubilation continued back at Bitchin' Modifications where the majority of the racer crew were breaking out the beer and hard liquor.

Albert made a beeline for Axel who was intertwined with Kerstin in a manner that suggested they ought to be somewhere more private.

"My dog," Albert started, too consumed by his need for the racers to uphold their end of the bargain to consider any further patience. "You promised to help me find him. I need you to take me to Ivan."

Allowing a sliver of air to creep between their bodies, Axel levered himself away from his girlfriend.

"Yes, Albert, but the agreement was for you to help us get the stolen cars back." He made a show of looking around the workshop. "I don't currently see them."

Albert's fists closed into balls. He'd already thrown a few punches tonight and was boiling with the need to chuck a couple more.

"My dog cannot wait," he growled. "Look ..."

Axel pried himself away from the woman whose arms were still hooked around his neck.

"Don't fret so, Albert. You did me a solid tonight. We will have great fun with the Supra. I'm inclined to sell it to make some cash to get new parts for the GTR. I've been wanting to upgrade the suspension with some new coilovers for a while now." He put two fingers in his mouth and whistled, the abrupt noise making heads rise around the room. "Hey, Shaggy," he called. "Anything on the tracker?"

Shaggy was inside the office again, bent over the terminal with Fishman and half a dozen other men and women. He looked up and waved, pointing down at the computer screen before giving a thumbs up.

"We put a tracker on Park Ji Hoon's car," Axel revealed, crossing the room with Albert in his wake.

"That's what you didn't want to tell me with so many people around us at the race," Albert guessed correctly.

"Trackers have been getting cheaper and more readily available for years," Axel explained. This one is designed to be attached to anything you think you might lose. I use them for my luggage when I fly anywhere." He pushed open the glass door to access the office, leading Albert into a room filled with excited conversation.

"They just stopped," said, Teagan, once again in the thick of things. "But it's nowhere near the docks or anywhere where they could have the cars stashed. It's probably where one of them lives."

Axel walked around until he was facing the screen, the people there parting so he could see. Albert joined him. The computer showed a street map of Amsterdam that appeared to not only be coming from a satellite but looked to be live. A red dot with pulsing circles like ripples on a pond blipped away in the middle.

Fishman was doing something on a second screen to the right of the first one.

"I have the address," he announced. "They are in Clarissenhof over in Duivendrecht. Looks like they might have parked."

Albert seized his chance. "Until they leave there and go somewhere more promising, there's nothing we can do. But they are part of the gang of car thieves, and they will lead us to the stolen cars if we are patient. In the meantime, I need to see Ivan. I have to look for my dog and if you won't help me now, you can forget having my help to catch these guys."

Axel held his hands up, the alpha male of the street racer crew grinning as he surrendered.

"Okay, Albert. You win. Let's go find Ivan."

Chapter 26

Rex awoke from his upright doze when the sound of tyres crunching on gravel reached his ears. The tyres had stopped, that was what woke him. He opened his eyes, lifted his nose, and sniffed the air. It was cold, but not unbearably so. Unlike the Pitbull and the Doberman, to name just two, Rex had a thick coat of fur to keep the cold at bay. He could only imagine what prolonged exposure might be like for those with short coats.

He heard doors closing. One set and then the rumbling sound of a sliding door to indicate they were travelling in a van. He could smell the men too, but he didn't recognise any of them. Humans in their immediate vicinity ought not to be a reason for concern, yet it was getting late and Rex was on high alert following their breakout.

He came up from sitting to standing. Lurking in the doorway where he positioned himself more than two hours ago, Rex questioned whether he ought to wake the dogs snoring fitfully behind him. They would not be grateful for the disturbance, yet if the approaching men turned out to be the dognappers searching for escaped fighting dogs, the advanced warning might be the difference between getting caught and putting more distance between them.

Counter to that argument was the very real possibility that the men were nothing to do with the dog fighting ring. If that proved to be the case, he would wake the Pitbull and the others for no good reason. They were already against the concept of helping him and upsetting them wouldn't aid his cause.

He waited, feeling his hackles rise as tension crept through his body.

The humans were talking, but in their own local language. Rex often struggled with English simply because humans talk so fast and habitually mumble. He stood no chance with a foreign language. Regardless of what they were saying, they were coming closer and soon he was going to have to make a decision. The choice of location dictated it. The dogs were asleep in an abandoned business arch beneath a railway bridge. It kept them out of the cold, but the singular entrance made it a trap if the humans found them.

Rex took a deep breath in through his nose, holding it for long enough to sift through the odour profiles to find that which he feared might be there – the smell of the warehouse where the fighting dogs were being kept. It was tenuous, a partial smell that could be from a different warehouse, but it was also too much coincidence to risk.

"*Get up,*" Rex nudged the Afghan Hound, the one dog who voiced his support even if he subsequently chose not to give it. "*The humans are here. It's time to move on,*" Rex hissed as loudly as he dared.

Shadow Fang lifted his head. "*Hmmm, wassup?*"

Brain Scar awoke too. "*What now, Rex? We are sleeping,*" he grumbled.

"*There are humans here. They smell of the warehouse where you were all kept. We need to move.*"

The other dogs began to wake, some voicing their concerns, but Brain Scar the Pitbull wasn't of a mind to go anywhere.

"*He's just trying to get us to go back with him again,*" he argued sleepily around a yawn.

The ridgeback wasn't so ready to dismiss the possibility that Rex was telling the truth. He went to the door where he stuck his head outside. It proved to be poor timing on his part for he did so just when Sylvia's men came into sight. They were just one search party out of almost a dozen sent on what they all believed to be a wild goose chase. The dogs were either long gone or spread out in a dozen different directions. No one expected to find them, but when the boss lady gave an order, no one dared to question it.

"There!" yelled the first of the men to spot the ridgeback's head and shoulders poking from the open doorway.

Eyes wide in panic, Ball Biter ducked back inside knowing it was already too late to hide.

The chance to employ whispered conversation squandered, he barked, "*Rex is right! Scarper!*"

Warning given, he burst from the building beneath the railway arch. One look was all he needed to know the dogs would not all escape. They had been too complacent. Too willing to listen to Brain Scar's opinion that they were away and clear and had nothing to worry about.

The humans were closing in fast and they had nets at the ready. The expressions each man carried told a story of determination. They had a shot at rounding up the missing dogs which would place them all firmly in Sylvia's good books. She was well known for her polar opposites. Please her and she would reward and do so generously. Disappoint her as Levi and Hans had just a few hours ago and her retribution might be the last thing you ever experience.

They saw the Rhodesian Ridgeback slip through their fingers and chose to let it go. It was just one dog and by the sounds coming from the darkness under the railway arch, there were plenty more there to catch.

What they could not see was Rex rounding them up. The only calm one in the building, he had to stand his ground to keep the dogs from fleeing blindly into the night.

"*We have to rush them,*" Rex insisted. "*But not until they are inside.*"

"*What?*" the Pitbull scoffed. "*You are even crazier than I thought. If they get inside, we won't be able to get out.*"

"*That's where you are wrong. Humans are next to hopeless in the dark. They will be relying on little devices that cast a beam of light. They will wait outside with their nets at the ready, expecting that we will try to escape. They will be thinking in terms of individual dogs, not organised pack behaviour.*"

"*I've heard enough. We are leaving. Every dog for himself!*" The pack alpha turned toward the door, his body lowering into a slight crouch ready to launch himself forward. He would have raced for the door, but had expected that the others would also make a run for it and was hoping to let one or two to go out ahead of him so they would get caught and he could escape in the confusion.

Coming out of his poised crouch, he snarled, "*Well, what are you all waiting for? I said let's go!*"

Bite Knight the Doberman, pinned to the spot by the Pitbull's glare said, "*I don't know, Brain Scar. Rex was right about how to get out of the cages, and he got us out of the warehouse when we had no clue how to open the doors.*"

"*Yeah, and he said the humans would come after us, Brain Scar,*" said Battle Tank the Rottweiler, adding weight to the argument.

"*Maybe we should trust him, Brain Scar,*" suggested Shadow Fang in his usual laconic tone.

"*I'm the alpha,*" Brain Scar reminded the assembled dogs with a threatening snarl. "*You obey my lead. Not his.*"

"*But what if he is right?*" replied Battle Tank, his voice meek and quiet.

The Pitbull's lips curled back to snarl something new, but instead he backed toward the door. "*To hell with all of you. Follow the German Shepherd for all I care. I'm getting out of here right now!*" He spun off his back paws, lowered his head, and charged out into the night.

The dogs inside heard the humans' excited cries and the sound of their rushing feet. They heard Brain Scar's snarls of threat and his panicked attempts to evade the men and their nets. It sounded like he fought hard to overcome them, scrapping and trying to bite, but his snarls turned to pitiful whines and there was nothing Rex and the rest of the dogs could do except learn from the Pitbull's mistakes.

"*They'll be coming soon.*" Rex murmured in the quiet of their hiding place. "*Spread out. Wait until I give the word. Then do exactly as we planned.*"

Chapter 27

Albert looked up at a tall apartment block. It was a nice enough place. The front façade was devoid of graffiti, the grass and shrubs around the entrance had been pruned and mowed, and the cars parked along the street were newish models.

Albert didn't know one suburb of Amsterdam from another, but he knew low rent when he saw it, and this was a long way from it.

Caprice stepped up to the intercom firm in her conviction that Ivan would open the door the moment she spoke. A few text messages had already confirmed he would be home, but before she pressed the buzzer, she said, "Ivan can be a little ... touchy at times. He's a former body builder, but he still takes the steroids to maintain his size and they can have an effect on his mood. He was always gentle with me, but if he thought someone was looking at him in a way he didn't like ..."

Albert knew the sort. Surly from the moment their eyes open, all they needed was the slightest push to make them violent. Men like that use their size to solve problems, getting their own way often enough that it shocks them when they don't. As a police officer it had been his great pleasure to see hard men reduced to tears when they finally came to realise there really was no way to escape the law.

Warning delivered, Caprice pressed the buzzer, announced her arrival and grabbed the door when it buzzed open. Heading into the building, Albert wondered if they would find Ivan in a receptive mood.

They did not.

"What is this, babe?" He had kind eyes for Caprice, but eyed Albert, Axel and everyone else as if they were keeping him from being with her.

Caprice tried to be apologetic. "Ivan, we're just looking for a little information."

Upon Albert's insistence, they were not to reveal that his dog was missing. Doing so would ensure Ivan took a defensive posture and they would learn nothing. Instead, they presented Albert as Axel's rich uncle. He had money to gamble and liked blood sports.

"What makes you think I am involved in a dog fighting ring?" Ivan demanded. He stood six feet and six inches tall with a head like a piece of polished granite and a neck that simply tiered from the base of his skull into his overdeveloped trapezium muscles. Everything about him was twice the size of anyone else in the room. His forearms were the size of Albert's thighs. The tattoo on the side of his head did nothing to soften his features.

There was no hope they could force the information from him, not unless they employed a bulldozer and a wrecking ball, so their only hope was to convince him to give the information up willingly.

Thus far he seemed disinclined.

Caprice shrugged one shoulder. "You told me about it, sweetie. Don't you re-member? You came to see me when you got out of the hospital. It was when you got bitten. You showed up with a fat roll of Euros and when I asked how you were so flush you told me you have a new gig working for some hardass lady boss and it paid really well."

"We just want to know about the dog fights, man," added Fishman, thinking he was being helpful.

Moving fast for a big guy, Ivan surged across the room to get into Fishman's face. The street racers all tensed, sensing violence was about to ensue, but the giant stopped when his face was an inch from Fishman who was leaning back to keep some distance between them.

"I don't know you. And I don't think I like you. Keep your mouth shut while I am talking to the lady. Understand?"

"Yeah, okay, sure thing, man." Fishman wasn't about to argue.

Albert cleared his throat and spoke for the first time. "All we desire is a location for the event, sir. If you can assist us with that, I can assure you your employers will be pleased to receive me."

Ivan twisted around to glare at Albert, his giant skull blocking out the light hanging from the ceiling to give his face a worrying halo effect when he sneered down with an evil smile.

"It's invite only."

Albert made his face look innocent when he asked, "What is?"

"Huh?"

"What is invite only?" With Ivan's face displaying confusion, Albert said, "Since we arrived, you have denied any association with or knowledge of the dog fighting ring in which I am interested. However, you just revealed that the event is by invitation only." Albert made a big show of reaching into his coat for his wallet. "I can make the information worth your while."

Annoyed with himself, Ivan stepped back from the old man. He didn't look like much. He certainly didn't look like he was swimming in money. Not that it mattered, Sylvia van Lidth controlled the client list and secrecy was one of her biggest rules. Even if he thought he could get a little extra cash by giving the old man the address, it would cost him far more in the long run when she found out.

"No deal. I'm not telling you lot anything. If you were connected enough, you would already know where to go." Ivan looked around the room, making eye contact with as many of the street racers as possible before saying, "Now get out. All of you."

There was no question resistance would cause Ivan to use force to eject them. If Albert read his expression correctly, it was what the giant hoped for.

He gritted his teeth and pressed his brain to devise a new strategy. One that would get him the information he needed. Rex was out there somewhere in the city and heading for a fight that was sure to leave him injured or worse. Ivan was his only lead. He could not ... he would not leave without learning something that would get him closer to finding his dog.

His right foot twitched. He was going to place himself right in Ivan's path and if he had to beg, then so be it. Dignity, money ... nothing mattered. Only finding Rex held any importance.

A hand caught his elbow when he started to move. Surprised, Albert jerked his head around to find Kerstin holding him back. She flared her eyes and dropped them to her other hand.

When Albert looked, she leaned in close to whisper, "I swiped his car keys. His satnav will show us where he's been recently."

Albert felt his eyebrows rise. He wanted to ask, "You can do that?" but acknowledged his understanding of modern technology was severely limited. Rather than sound dumb, he patted her hand where it held his arm and whispered, "Good idea. Well done."

The racers were going back out the door of Ivan's flashy apartment, but when Caprice turned to go, a hand the size of a chair base caught her left shoulder to hold her in place.

"Angel, I thought you wanted to see me. Why do you keep breaking my heart like this?"

Caprice looked at his hand until he removed it. Then turned to face him.

"Babe, I'm happy to be your friend. That's what I was trying to be tonight, but I asked for your help, and you wouldn't give it."

Ivan looked sorry when he said, "You don't know the people I work for, Caprice. If you did, you wouldn't want anything to do with them."

Ivan watched his ex-girlfriend leave and stood back so Albert and Kerstin, the last two, could slip out without having to squeeze past him.

Once the door shut behind them Albert found himself tugged along behind Kerstin when she took his hand and tried to run.

"Come on, Albie!" she hissed, excited yet trying to keep quiet. "He's going to notice his keys are missing and I don't want to be anywhere near when he does."

"Surely he will know that one of us took them."

Kerstin shrugged and Albert accepted that he didn't actually care. Finding Rex was the priority and he was ready to break whatever rules it took to get him back.

Outside in the street Kerstin released Albert's hand and darted forward, aiming the plipper device on Ivan's keys at the cars lining the street. They knew from Caprice that he drove a Mercedes, but the vehicle flashing its indicators was distinctly more car than Kerstin expected.

An expletive slipped from her lips. "That's an SLS!" she gasped.

Caprice had commented on Ivan's sweet ride, but Albert was surprised to find that meant it had gullwing doors and looked like something James Bond should be driving.

Pausing to admire it for a moment, Kerstin growled, "I would shred the hell out of this thing."

"What's going on?" asked Fishman, his eyebrows performing a little dance.

Axel said, "I told Kerstin to get his keys. We can check the Satnav log. It will show where he has been."

"No," Fishman clutched the sides of his face. "No, no, no. This is bad. Did you not see that guy? He's going to know it was us."

With a big shrug, Axel said, "We're not going to steal it. I'll take the keys back and drop them on his doorstep when we are done. He'll think he must have dropped them or something."

Kerstin opened the car door and swung inside. "This won't take a moment. He'll never know we even had them."

A banshee scream of rage echoed through the night. It came from high above them causing heads to turn and look up. Ivan was hanging over his balcony, his face visibly red with rage.

"You're all dead meat!" he promised just before running back into his apartment.

"Or maybe he will notice," quipped Kerstin from inside the car. The lights of the dashboard illuminated her face, but the system was taking its time to boot up.

Fishman and Shaggy ran to their cars, Jerome and Caprice piling in next to them. Axel reversed course and went to his, shouting for Kerstin to make it quick.

Albert, suddenly alone on the pavement, attempted to calculate how long it would take the enraged bull of a man to reach the ground floor. Not long was the most accurate prediction.

"Dead meat!" echoed out from inside the building, reinforcing the need to be elsewhere.

Albert glanced back along the road. It was forty metres to the waiting street racers and their cars, but only two metres to Ivan's Mercedes. Ultimately, biology made the decision. He was too old to run fast enough to get to a different car.

Arriving at the Mercedes at the same instant as Ivan burst through the doors, knocking one clean off its top hinge so it came to hang at a drunken angle, Albert wrenched the passenger door up into the sky and fell in.

"Drive!" he barked, jolting Kerstin who was still trying to interrogate the satnav history.

A squealing of tyres brought their heads up to find Axel alongside them.

He yelled, "Get in!" But there were already two fully grown men in the GTR and while it had space for backseats, they had been removed to make way for oversized speakers and more neon lights.

Kerstin might be able to bundle in on top of the passenger by diving through Axel's open window, but it wasn't an option for Albert. Not without popping a hip.

Kerstin glanced through the Mercedes' windscreen, saw Ivan charging and came to the same conclusion. She swore again, but her street racer instincts kicked in and they were moving.

Throwing the car into reverse, she angled the wheels to get away from the kerb, narrowly missing the car parked behind when she rocketed into the road.

She was almost fast enough.

Almost.

Ivan landed on the bonnet with a thunk that shook the suspension and made the front end dip like it was unexpectedly carrying a walrus. His wingspan was so vast that he was able to grip under each wheel arch and that allowed him to hold on when Kerstin sent a plume of smoke into the air from the rubber burning off his tyres.

The backward inertia sent Albert into the passenger's footwell from which he had to clamber to get back into the seat. The car had a standard seatbelt – hardly sufficient for the impending manoeuvres Albert knew would be coming, but as he heard the clasp click home, he pulled it tight and hoped for the best.

In a heartbeat they were doing thirty in reverse, the engine and gearbox screaming in protest.

Following them, Axel and the others kept a small amount of distance, but all they could do was watch as the man mountain clawed his way up to the car's windscreen.

Albert could only guess what Ivan had planned once he was close enough to the glass. There was no question he possessed the power to break it, but Albert thought it equally likely he would just bite the top off the car, chew it twice and spit out a ragged ball of twisted metal. His eyes were wild, showing the madness inside.

If Kerstin didn't lose him soon they were in deep trouble. They were in trouble anyway for that matter. They had just stolen a car for goodness sake.

With a grunt of effort, Kerstin cranked the wheel, dropped the clutch and powered the car through one hundred and eighty degrees.

Albert's whole body squashed into the passenger door with enough force that he worried it might buckle and pop open.

Straightening up, Kerstin floored the accelerator once more with a yell of, "Hold on!"

Albert's head and torso snapped back the other way before coming to settle in the middle of his seat.

Ivan was still clinging to the bonnet. The manoeuvre made him slip a little so he was no longer right on the windscreen, but it wasn't going to take him long to get back to where he had been and now he had the wind pushing him toward them, not away.

With a gasp of breath, Albert said, "I have a tip for you. A request if you will." Kerstin risked an incredulous look his way. "Next time, tell me to hold on before you send the car into a power slide or try to jump a bridge."

Kerstin grinned. "Gotcha. Hold on."

Albert's brain had just enough time to register what she had said before she stomped on the brakes.

Ivan was on one knee, gripping the edges of the car with both hands and about to drive his skull through the windscreen when suddenly the car stopped moving and he wasn't able to.

He shot off the bonnet, his eyes meeting Albert's for a nanosecond to show his utter disbelief and horror before he hit the tarmac. Still doing close to forty miles per hour, he tumbled and rolled, his limbs flailing.

Kerstin was not of a mind to wait for his momentum to exhaust itself and certainly wasn't hanging around to check he was okay. The moment he was off the bonnet, she floored it again, burning yet more rubber and praising Ivan for buying a manual car instead of the more common automatic box fitted to most high-end German models.

Albert twisted to check the road behind, watching with relief when the half man half rhinoceros not only got up but began to give chase. The rest of the cars were already past him, leaving Ivan in their dust cloud.

They shot through an intersection with Ivan falling farther and farther behind, but Albert was still looking his way when the cars coming crosswise were forced to swerve. They missed him, but not each other, the crunching of metal as cars collided an echoing epitaph to their crime.

Slumping back into his seat, Albert took a deep breath and gave himself a two count to get his heart rate under control. Closing his eyes, he prayed no one was hurt.

"Now," said Kerstin, prodding the car's centre touchscreen with a delicate index finger. "How about that satnav history?"

Chapter 28

The men filtered through the hole where a door used to be, holding their nets ready, but finding it difficult to do that and aim their torches into the inky blackness. It was dark outside, especially in the shadow of the railway bridge, but inside the old tyre fitter's place so little light penetrated they might as well have all been blind.

Two stayed at the door, ready for any dogs who tried to make a break for it. They expected resistance – they were fighting dogs after all - and had a plan to take them one at a time. They believed the dogs would cower and that would make them easier to pick off. Throw a net, catch a dog, wrestle it outside and go back for the next one.

Rex watched and waited. His eyesight, like the rest of the dogs, was many times greater than the humans when it came to seeing in the dark. He rarely relied on his eyesight, using his nose to find things and to know where he was and where he needed to go, but the current situation called for eyeballs.

With Brain Scar and Ball Biter gone; one caught for sure and one they hoped had escaped, it left ten dogs. In Rex's opinion that was more than enough for what he proposed.

The humans filled the doorway, blocking their exit. It caused a few fearful whines that brought the torch beams to bear on their location.

"There you are," said one of the men in a friendly sing song manner. "Don't worry, little fellas. We're not going to hurt you. Not with a fight tomorrow. We just need to get you back where you belong."

They split at that point, the two inside the room stepping away from their colleagues at the entrance.

Rex bunched his leg muscles, dropped his head and barked, "*Now!*"

Thrusting with his back legs, he felt as much as heard the other dogs move with him. A unified attack was key to their success, and it worked better than he could ever have hoped. Neither of the men advancing toward the dogs saw it coming. They had their nets at the ready, but juggling their torches to spot the dogs, they had too little control of either thing to be effective. When that was combined with the dogs' unpredicted behaviour, they were nothing more than sitting ducks.

Rex ran through the shin bones of the man on the right, catflapping him into the air. He heard a grunt from his left; confirmation Battle Tank the Rottweiler had just done the same to the second man.

The impact jarred Rex's neck, but with so much adrenaline pumping through his body it barely registered.

The two men blocking the doorway didn't have their torches at the ready. They were waiting to be handed dogs the first two trapped with their nets. They had nets of their own but planned to hand them to their partners as they took the dogs to the van.

They heard cries of surprise when their colleagues went airborne but the time between registering what they heard and calling out to check everything was okay turned out to be half a second longer than the time it took Rex to close the distance between them.

Repeating the catflap tactic, because he knew it worked well and allowed them to keep their forward momentum, Rex exploded out of the darkness with a second human flying through the air above his head.

The dogs shot from the old tyre fitting place like an out-of-control freight train and they were just as unstoppable.

Except they did stop.

Twenty metres beyond the doorway, Rex hung on the brakes. Not because he felt safe, or because he had just heard Ball Biter calling to them. The ridgeback was a hundred metres away and tucked in a shadow in the hope someone else would make it out. No, Rex stopped because he heard Brain Scar's pathetic whimpers.

He was inside the van, back in one of the cages.

"*Help me, Rex,*" he pleaded, barking through the bars of his cage. "*Work your magic. Get me out of this thing.*"

The rest of the dogs continued when Rex stopped. They were twenty metres farther away from the building and though they paused to see where Rex was going, they were not about to come back.

Rex ran to the van. The cage was bolted into place, removing any chance that he could roll it as he had back at the warehouse. Doing so wouldn't have achieved anything though because the cage was secured with a padlock instead of a peg, humans demonstrating their ability to learn for once.

He met the Pitbull's eyes. "*I'm sorry.*"

To drive home Brain Scar's predicament, the men were getting up. Rex had seconds if he was to escape and that went for the rest of the dogs as the humans would be able to give chase once they were back in their vehicles.

Brain Scar cried, "*No! you have to help me. I should have listened to you. I should have let you be in charge. Don't leave me here! Don't send me back to the fights!*"

Rex backed away a pace and was about to apologise again when a shot got close enough to part the hair on the top of his head. One of the men was angry enough to open fire in spite of Sylvia's demand to bring them back unharmed.

Rex bolted, running with all his might, but over his shoulder he barked, "*We're coming back for you!*" and this time he suspected it would prove to be true.

Chapter 29

R ex didn't stop running for ten minutes though his pace inevitably slowed from the breakneck pace he started at. He got to the pack as they reached Ball Biter and the lot of them kept running until they felt safe. Rex knew distance was their friend along with alleyways and paths where humans would struggle to follow. The pack snuck though gaps in fences, cut through abandoned buildings, and crossed more then one narrow bridge in their bid to make sure the humans would not be able to follow.

When Rex stopped, he was out of breath and panting again, but content it was okay to slow down.

For now.

"Everyone okay?" he enquired. They were all with him, but it felt like the right thing to ask. He got a round of confirmations and a few comments about how scary their situation had been, but Rex chose to wait for someone to echo Brain Scar's comment.

"We should have listened to you," said Battle Tank the Rottweiler.

Rex said nothing, choosing silence so the Rottweiler's words could sink into everyone's heads. Lifting his muzzle to sniff at the sky, he made them wait. He was the alpha now, there could be no questioning it. No one else would want to lead, and that made what needed to happen next all the easier.

Bringing his nose back down to level, he met the eyes of his new pack. They were all looking his way.

"Do you know where we are now?"

The dogs looked at each other or lifted their noses to sniff the air as Rex had. Before they could start guessing, he supplied the answer.

"We are back at the warehouse. Back where our fellow dogs are still being held." A few whines of fear escaped the pack. Rex had led them on a circuitous route, right back to almost where they started. *"Back where they will take Brain Scar."* He let the final sentence linger on the wind, reminding them all what was at stake. *"We are going back in and we are getting everyone else out. Then we will go in search of humans we can trust. The police probably. I don't know how, but we are going to find a way to reunite everyone with their humans. Everyone."* He stared right at the pack, daring any of them to argue.

When they did not, he turned around, sniffed the air once more and set off. The warehouse wasn't far.

Chapter 30

K erstin pulled the car into the forecourt of a petrol station. She wanted to confer with her friends and ditch Ivan's car, which she said was intoxicating to drive, but needed better suspension than they fitted as standard, the ECU remapping to provide greater torque in the mid-range, and a bunch of other technical stuff Albert heard but didn't understand.

The satnav listed a host of recent destinations, three of which she felt were possible locations for the impending dog fight. They could investigate them all, but Kerstin hoped someone else might know more and be able to narrow the search.

From the convenience store attached to the petrol station, Albert bought a road map of Amsterdam, the kind of thing designed for tourists. Using that and the information taken from Ivan's satnav, they pinpointed the likely locations.

Circling one with a pen, Kerstin said, "He's visited this one four times this week including today. And this one he's been to twice." She made another mark.

"Where's the third location again," Albert enquired, peering at the first two.

Kerstin drew a third circle.

Albert studied the map, his lips pursed in concentration. The location he frequented most often was out of town in what appeared to be an industrial district.

"I think we can rule that one out."

"Why's that?" asked Shaggy.

"Because we believe the dog fights are catering to rich people. They will want somewhere plush, not an abandoned unit somewhere miles from the city centre."

He jabbed a finger at the map, right in the middle. "I think that is where they will hold the fights. Can anyone tell me what is there, please?"

In an instant, phones were in hands, fingers flashing across screens as the street racers fought to be the first to find the answer.

"Beat, ya," declared Kerstin, holding up her phone for Albert to see.

They were competitive at everything, Albert noted.

"That's not fair," teased Axel. "You already knew the location. You didn't have to copy it from the map."

Kerstin pretended to scratch her forehead, sending banter Axel's way by making an 'L' for loser.

The city centre location was a hotel and casino, the website for which boasted private party areas and a sports arena below ground. It was the perfect place to host an illegal dog fighting event. But no sooner did Albert decide it was the first place they needed to look than a new thought occurred to him.

While the casino's private spaces might be ideal for the event, they wouldn't want to keep the dogs there the whole time. They would move them in at the last moment, hours before the fights. If they went there now they might find the people behind it all, but Albert just wanted Rex. Taking down the guilty ones could happen afterward.

"So, we're going there next?" Shaggy managed around a yawn. It was close to midnight and he was ready to call it a night.

Albert shook his head. "No. I think the dogs are here." He pointed to the map once more, prodding the point furthest from the city centre. "It's out of the way and it looks like warehouses in an industrial park. If Ivan went there four times this week including tonight, that's where the dogs are."

Chapter 31

DCI Garfield called an ambulance and waited with Ivan van der Pol. He placed him under arrest for jaywalking which was all he could come up with at the time. Ivan screamed blue murder, claiming his car had been stolen and that his efforts to prevent the theft resulted in him running down the street in traffic.

Had he not caused an accident when cars swerved to avoid him, Garfield probably would have driven straight by and continued after the street racers. However, worried that he'd been tailing them for hours and was going to get spotted sooner or later, combined with the blocked road and potential casualties someone had to deal with, plus the presence of a known criminal with a rap sheet longer than an elephant's trunk gave him good reason (and no choice) but to alter his plan.

He called in backup, waiting several nervous minutes until uniforms arrived to help him with van der Pol. It wasn't so much that he couldn't handle Ivan by himself, which he couldn't, but that cuffs wouldn't go around his wrists. If he put him in the back of his car for the ride to the station, the chance that van der Pol would get out halfway was significant.

That he didn't need medical treatment stood as testament to the man's powerful physique. Being thrown from the bonnet of a speeding car would be enough to put a normal person down, but van der Pol brushed it off like it was nothing.

With uniforms on scene, paramedics treating those with minor injuries, and van der Pol on his way to the nick in the back of a squad car, Garfield called Danielle.

"He did what?" she needed Garfield to repeat it all.

"Albert Smith is with a group of street racers. Punks with souped up cars. I'm not sure what that's all about, but I think one of them is the guy whose car was being stolen when Albert Smith got involved."

"Okay, but what's he still doing with them?"

"Well, that I don't know, but he identified two Koreans as the thieves, did he not?"

"Yes. Song Bin and Park Ji Hoon. They're nobodies. Punks like your street racers. They've been busted stealing cars a dozen times each. I suspect they work for Lee Yoo though I have no evidence to support it. What's that got to do with his dog?"

Garfield pulled a face Danielle couldn't see, rolling his eyes at himself and questioning if maybe he should have gone home to drink the whisky and watch a bad movie after all.

"Nothing so far. But listen, there was a car accident. They caused it … kind of, but if we bust them for it, we effectively stop Albert Smith and whatever he is up to. You don't want me to do that, right?"

"No. No, I don't think I do. I just hope I am right about that crazy old English man."

"Ok, well I need to finish things up here and deal with van der Pol. You get some sleep and I'll call you with an update in the morning."

"Get some sleep?" she laughed. "I'll see you when you get here. I'm still at work."

"Still at work?" Garfield rolled his eyes again. Her dedication to career was one of the reasons they broke up the first time. He wanted to spend time with her, and she believed she had to work harder than all her male rivals if she wanted to overcome the gender prejudice he claimed no longer existed.

"Let's not get into that again. What are you doing now? You lost Albert Smith, right?"

Garfield scratched at an itch on his chin. "Yeah. I don't know where he is right now. He went to see van der Pol and when they left his place, they stole his car. I'm betting van der Pol is up to his neck in the dog fighting thing. It's just the kind of criminal activity he would be caught up in. If I want to find out more, I'm going to have to lean on him."

Chapter 32

Rex led the pack to the warehouse, his nose guiding them in the right general direction until they crossed the path they took in their flight from captivity. It felt like days ago, yet Rex knew it was no more than a few hours.

The dogs were all getting hungry, but there was no food to be had and this was not the time to eat. They could deal with their base needs once they had Kevin and everyone else safe.

Approaching the building cautiously, the dogs kept to the shadows. It was just as quiet as before, but the soft glow of light Rex expected to see emanating from inside was absent and there was something wrong with the background scent.

Those were concerns to be tackled once they got inside and it was that task that presented their first challenge. Getting out required nothing more than his police dog training. Emergency exits were precisely that and were never locked. However, they were designed to be opened from the inside and might as well have been part of the wall for all the hope he had of gaining access from the outside.

They circled the building, going slow out of wariness for human activity but the warehouse was quiet. Quieter than Rex thought it ought to be.

The pack were coming back to their start point having completed almost a complete loop of the building's outer perimeter when Shadow Fang the Afghan hound called them to stop.

"*Up there.*" He looked where he wanted everyone else to train their eyes.

There was no way in unless they waited for someone inside to open a door and try to rush them, but above their heads was an open window. They could tell from the odour drifting out that the room was a toilet. The dogs all held their own thoughts about humanity's disgusting need to do their business in their homes, but none of that mattered because the window presented an opportunity.

If they could reach it.

It was ten feet off the ground. Rex inspected the wall. It was brick which provided decent purchase. His police dog training had him perform stunts such as wall-running to get into high windows, but it had been a long while since he'd attempted such a feat.

"*Me,*" said Bite Knight. When everyone turned to look at him, he sighed. "*I used to do doggy agility,*" he admitted, his voice loaded with embarrassment.

Amid sniggers from the other dogs, he added, "*I can run up that wall and get in through the window without needing to pant afterwards. If anyone else wants to have a go first, they can be my guest.*"

There were no challengers, just as the Doberman expected, and the pack backed away to give him space. Rex felt relief that he wasn't going to have to try it because he recalled how much it hurt when you fail and fall back to the ground. Even when you land right it hurts your paws. He didn't want to think about the times he hadn't landed right.

With a deep inhale, Bite Knight set off, running directly for the wall as though he planned to go through it, only to convert his horizontal motion into vertical at the last moment. Reaching out with his front paws, he took one big bound, dug in with his back paws and thrust upward again.

In full view of the pack, he sailed through the open window, nudging it wider with his body to land on the other side. A crashing noise and several canine swearwords came back to the ears of those above. Then silence.

"*Bite Knight?*" Shadow Fang ventured.

"*I'm okay,*" his voice drifted down. "*Stupid humans had clutterments on the windowsill. I skidded right through them. One of them was a bowl of smelly wood shavings. They are stuck to my coat.*"

"*Potpourri,*" Shadow Fang supplied. "*It's called potpourri.*"

"*Well, whatever it is it stinks.*"

Interrupting the conversation, Rex said, "*You need to go to the ground floor and look for an emergency exit.*"

"*Then what? How do I open it?*"

"*Just like I did. Get on your back legs and throw your front paws at the bar in the middle with your bodyweight behind it.*"

Bite Knight's final comment that he wouldn't be long turned out to be accurate, the Doberman's happy face grinning at the pack when he opened a door a few metres down the wall. He held it open with his body until everyone was inside, but no sooner had it banged shut behind them than they knew there was something wrong.

The warehouse still smelled of dogs, but the scent was old now, not fresh. The dogs were no longer here.

Chapter 33

O n the other side of the warehouse, four modified cars were creeping slowly toward the building.

"There's no sign of life," remarked Fishman, scanning the area around the warehouse. "And unless they are parked on the other side, there are no cars here."

"They could be parked inside," Albert pointed out.

"Good point."

They continued to approach with caution, keen to see if this was indeed where the dogs were being kept, but staying rightfully wary. If Rex was here, Albert was going to find a way to get him, but attracting unnecessary danger to the street racers was not on his agenda. The people behind the dog fights would be hardened criminals, of that he felt certain, but whether the police would react with an appropriate response he could not say.

They skirted the entire building at a distance of roughly a hundred metres, confirming there really were no cars parked outside. There were also no lights to indicate there might be people inside and that incongruity made Albert question if this was indeed the right place.

Ahead of them, Axel stopped his car and got out. Fishman powered down his window and pulled up next to him.

Axel crouched to bring his head down to their level.

"What do you think?" he aimed the question at Albert.

Albert puffed out his cheeks, debating how to answer. "It looks deserted, but we know Ivan came here. I'm going to need to check inside at the very least."

They chose to all get closer to the building but kept their engines running with someone at the wheel for a swift getaway should it prove necessary. How to get into the building would have proven to be problematic on any other occasion, but with Albert's mind attuned to solving challenges with a straight-line approach, he took a tyre iron from Fishman's car.

"Wait," said Kerstin, caution in her voice. "Will it be alarmed?"

Albert shrugged. "Let's find out." The steel of the iron was cold to the touch, chilling his fingers, but his first jab wedged it between door and frame, popping the door open easily enough when Axel lent his weight.

Chapter 34

"*W*hat was that?*"* Battle Tank voiced the question everyone was thinking. They all heard the same noise. It had echoed through the building accompanied by a slight shift in the air.

A door to the outside had been opened.

That meant humans were back and it was time to leave again.

But Rex wasn't ready to go. The pack were in the space where the lines of cages once stood. They were gone now with nothing to show they were ever there other than a few lines in the dust and the lingering scent of the dogs they left behind.

In the few hours since their escape, the humans packed their operation and moved it. They had done so in a hurry, taking only that which was necessary. They were not done with the warehouse, vacating it a day early was nothing more than a precautionary move in reaction to the dogs' breakout. After the fight, the surviving dogs would return to wait there until the next event.

"*Rex, we need to get out of here,*" whined Shadow Fang. The humans were being quiet, but the dogs could hear their muffled footsteps in the corridors at the front of the building.

Rex sniffed the floor. He promised Kevin he would come back for him, and nothing was going to stop him from making it true.

Lifting his head, he said, "*Split up and get sniffing! The humans have taken the dogs somewhere and we need to figure out where it is.*"

The pack obeyed, each dog dropping their sensitive nose to the floor where they snuffled up the scents left behind.

Rex watched, his brain working fast.

"*Battle Tank, you were forced to fight before, weren't you? What did the place smell like? Would you recognise it again even from the outside?*"

The Rottweiler lifted his head. "*Yeah, maybe. Don't ask me where it was though. Other than in the middle of the city, I can't tell you anything.*"

"*But you just told us it's in the middle of the city. That's known as helpful information.*"

"*Hey, I found something,*" announced Shadow Fang.

The pack looked his way in time to see him haul a pizza box out of a bin.

Rex shook his head. "*I'm sure that smells great, but we don't have time for leftover pizza crust.*"

The rest of the dogs were not ready to agree with that statement. They felt there was always time for leftover pizza crust, especially given how hungry they were all beginning to feel.

However, the Afghan Hound had more to say.

"*No, I'm not talking about the leftovers. This pizza comes from a place near where I live. I'd recognise the smell anywhere. It's a privately owned place, not one of the big franchises, so they must have got it from there.*"

Rex blinked. "*So what's your point?*"

Shadow Fang brought the box across to Rex, dropping it at his feet. "*My point is that the pizza place is right in the middle of the city and that's where Battle Tank said they took him for the fight. The humans who were here eating pizza had to have been there, so either it's a coincidence, or the pizza place is close to where we need to go.*"

Rex's heart beat just a little bit faster. "*And you can take us there?*"

"*Once I get my bearings and get back to a part of town that I know it should be easy.*"

The sound of the approaching humans was drawing ever closer. Rex wanted to explore some more; there could be more clues if they only looked, but the chance of getting caught again increased with every passing second and his pack were already looking scared.

"Okay, it'll have to do. Everyone get to the door!"

They ran for the emergency exit, the same one they escaped through earlier. This time Ball Biter got there first, showing off his new skill for the rest of the pack to see. Bounding out into the night, Rex kept his head down and his legs pumping which was a shame. If he had only aimed a glance back inside before the door swung shut, he might have seen his human coming into the warehouse from the other end.

Chapter 35

A lbert was too busy checking the vast open warehouse for bad guys to notice the emergency exit door softly shutting more than fifty metres away. Creeping through the corridors from the front of the building where they entered, he fully expected to find someone working in an office as they passed.

That the building appeared to be devoid of life dented his hope. If Ivan hadn't been coming here for something to do with the dogs, then why all the visits? Albert needed answers either way, so they pressed on, entering the warehouse proper with the same amount of caution.

However, the need to be sneaky dissipated the moment they stepped into the cavernous space. There was no one here; that was immediately obvious, but they could also see they were in the right place.

To their left, a pallet of dog food in twenty-five-kilogram sacks left little doubt the space had recently been catering to a large quantity of dogs. They found a relaxation area with couches and a television, plus a fridge filled with human food, a bin overflowing with discarded food waste, and a short way beyond that an area with a few empty cages.

Albert crouched to get a better look at the floor.

"They were moved this evening," Albert announced, groaning slightly and using his hands to push against his knees as he came back to upright.

Kerstin asked, "How can you tell?"

He pointed to a spot on the floor. "There are paw prints in the dust and here," he moved to another spot, "the water they spilled when they moved the cages hasn't yet had time to evaporate. We missed them," he remarked, disappointment dripping from every word.

Kerstin and Axel looked about.

"We should get out of here," Axel warned. He didn't want to hang around any longer than absolutely necessary. Ignoring the part where they broke into a building, they knew it to belong to a criminal organisation. Getting caught would not be in their best interests.

Albert set off in the direction of the door they used to enter the warehouse, but he wasn't leaving, he was heading for the bin.

"We need to figure out where they have gone. The dogs must have been moved to the fight location and we are still not sure where that is. Any information we can turn up will help us." To demonstrate his point, he upended the bin, spilling the contents onto the floor.

He needed to get on the concrete to sift through it but turned to face his companions first.

"Well don't just stand there. Kerstin, go check the computer. Axel, make yourself useful and have a look at the desk. Names, addresses, times, locations ... anything that might tell us something more about the dog fight and the people behind it."

Leaving them to it, Albert placed his right hand on the cold concrete and lowered himself down to his knees thinking that he should have emptied the trash onto the sofa instead.

The rubbish was half food waste and half paper. He found a napkin from a pizza place that gave the address and placed it to one side. He could ask where it was later and see if that proved useful. The pieces of paper were coated in stains of pizza sauce and grease, plus coffee marks from discarded paper cups and other marks he didn't wish to consider.

Carefully holding each piece up and unravelling them where necessary, Albert inspected them for clues.

Five minutes passed fruitlessly until Kerstin said, "Hey, I found something!" The excitement with which she said it was enough to convince Albert to give up on the rubbish.

It took him a few seconds to get off the ground, the task requiring more than one manoeuvre so his limbs were in the right place. Once on his feet he could see Axel and Kerstin bent over something on the desk.

"It was in the drawer," she explained when he joined them. "There were a whole bunch of them."

On the desk was an embossed invitation. Inlaid with what looked to be real silver around the edges, it invited the holder to attend 'A grand spectacle'. It provided the address, the time the event started, and the dress code: cocktail.

Kerstin whipped out her phone to check the address. "Hey, this is one of the places Ivan has been visiting. It's that fancy hotel with the casino."

"Oh, my," Albert felt his pulse speed up. "This is it. Ivan said the event was invite only, but I didn't realise that meant there would be actual physical invitations."

"You think we can use that?" Axel voiced his doubt.

Albert picked it up carefully as though it was a delicate antique.

"I think this is our ticket to bring the whole thing down."

Chapter 36

L ee Yoo placed his face close to the rear wheel arch on the Ferrari F40 and looked down the length of the car. It was flawless. The engine made metallic pinging noises as it cooled, heat radiating off the bonnet where it had only just been switched off.

The Ferrari ticked off another car from his list which was now nearing completion. It wasn't complete though and that presented a problem. The earlier conversation with Uncle Kim had him on edge. Uncle Kim has always been a supportive force in Lee Yoo's life, but with the possibility of failure hanging over his head, Lee's uncle showed his true self.

If Lee failed to get the final cars there would be repercussions. Uncle Kim chose not to elaborate on what those might be, and Lee Yoo wisely didn't ask. His girlfriend said it was probably nothing more than added incentive – his uncle wouldn't really do anything if the order wasn't complete. Surely, the missing cars could be added to the next delivery or follow in a week's time. Wasn't that better than getting caught going after rare models that were too well protected?

Lee agreed, but the gruff tone of his uncle's threat still reverberated in his ears and made his stomach squirm. His uncle made it sound as though there were something bigger riding on the order. They had to have all the cars and there was no option to fail.

Four cars, that was all he had to find. It didn't sound like much, and he knew where to find each of them, yet the security around them dictated he had to get the timing of each theft just right. The Nissan GTR spent its life locked inside a secure facility with a guard on the gate. For that reason alone they had waited until it was parked outside the house of the owner's girlfriend. However, Lee Yoo's patience was defeated by an old man with a dog according to Song and Park. It sounded ridiculous, but he knew them well enough to trust they were telling the truth.

Arguing from the front of the lock up created a knot of worry in Lee's gut. There should be no need for raised voices but coming out of his crouch to look over the top of the Ferrari, he saw the origin of the uproar: his uncle.

Flanked by two men carrying machetes, Uncle Kim prowled through the lock-up holding Lee's most trusted lieutenant with his arm twisted behind his back.

It had been months since he'd last seen his uncle, but he looked no different. His hair was thinning on top but retained its natural black colour. He was five feet and eight inches tall with thick glasses and a terrible scar that ran from the left side of his mouth all the way to his ear. He'd asked once how it had happened and was told to never ask again.

"Ah, there you are, nephew," Uncle Kim declared as though he was pleased to be reunited.

The ball of worry changed to full-blown panic. What was his uncle doing in Amsterdam? Lee had thought he was in Korea when they talked not more than five hours ago, yet that clearly wasn't the case.

"Uncle," Lee stammered. "I have the Ferrari," he aimed his arms at the F40.

"Yes, I can see." He gave Lee's right hand man a rough shove that pitched him sideways to sprawl on the floor. "But do you have the rest of the cars?"

"I have men out working on that right now. The final models carry significantly greater risk."

"That was a 'no', nephew. You do not have them. I thought if I gave you the opportunity to rise above the position life granted you that you would grasp onto it with both hands, yet I find you hiding behind excuses."

Lee couldn't believe what he was hearing.

"Uncle I have tried my hardest ..."

Uncle Kim cut him off with a shout. "Your hardest!"

Lee flinched.

"If you had tried your hardest, we would not be having this conversation."

"But uncle it is just four cars. I can have them in a week and will pay to ship them myself."

Uncle Kim observed his nephew in silence, Lee feeling more and more like he was supposed to say something more as the seconds stretched out.

Turning away, Uncle Kim paced to Lee's right, his hands behind his back and his eyes looking at nothing much in particular when he started to explain.

"The problem you face here, nephew, is that you dare to think. I do not give you the full picture because I do not need you to have it. I need you to obey and in this case that meant finding the list of cars. The cars will be shipped to Korea where they will each find their way to a valued customer. Failing a customer is not a good way to demonstrate that we value them. However, the cars are only a small part of the bigger picture. I have partners here in Amsterdam who provide me with 'product'."

"Product?" Lee repeated the word. His uncle said it in a way that loaded it with meaning.

"Yes, nephew. Don't be dense now. This 'product' has far greater value than the cars which serve the purpose of acting as shipping containers. Each of the cars in your lock up have already been loaded with the 'product'. The men guarding them work for me, not you. The product will be unloaded at the destination prior to delivery." He stopped pacing to face his nephew. "Did you really think we were interested in making money from selling stolen cars?"

Lee had thought precisely that. To him the value of the cars was enormous. Yet now that he gave it consideration, they were only talking about a few million Euros. Twenty-five at the most even with the rare nature of some of the models.

"The business model is slick and operates well. Should I fail to supply the expected cars and the required amount of 'product' there would be questions and I cannot allow that."

"I will redouble my efforts," Lee blurted, desperate to appease his uncle. The man was famous for his wrath and though Lee had never seen it in person, except as a child when his father pushed Uncle Kim too far, he had no desire to have it aimed his way.

"I rather think that you will," agreed Uncle Kim with an encouraging smile.

Lee returned it, relieved that he appeared to be off the hook and keen to get on with the task.

"Because if you don't ..." Uncle Kim held out his phone and fiddled with the screen to bring up a picture. "Well, let's just say this young lady will be accompanying me back to Korea when I leave."

Lee's eyes felt like they were popping from his sockets. The picture on his uncle's phone was of his girlfriend, Sookie. Tears tracked marks through her makeup to the gag in her mouth. She was bound to a chair in a dimly lit room in the same dress she was wearing when he took her out for dinner only a few hours earlier.

"You have until midnight tomorrow, Nephew. I advise that you do not let me down."

"It will be done, Uncle."

"Let me know when it is. But do not bother me tomorrow evening, if you please. I have an event to attend while I am in town and won't be taking any calls. I wouldn't want to miss the grand spectacle." With that Uncle Kim left, the two machete wielding thugs flanking him just as before.

Lee Yoo watched him depart, unable to make his mouth or feet work. He wanted to shout at his uncle, he wanted to rage that there was no need to threaten Sookie or anyone else. He would get the final cars. But he knew there was nothing to be gained begging for forgiveness or leniency.

His body shook with fear and adrenaline, rendering him unable to operate for more than five minutes. When it finally began to subside, he found his phone and started to call numbers. He needed everyone.

Chapter 37

Albert was tired. He'd been on the go for far more hours than he'd intended and was struggling to keep himself from yawning. His companions were all younger, and imbued with what he'd come to think of as a European attitude toward going out, were talking about where to go next. Bars and clubs would be just getting busy at midnight, the hip and trendy types leaving their homes for a little nightlife.

They were high on the events of the evening thus far, the street race victory and the breaking and entering they had just got away with sufficient to make them want to stay out.

Not that Albert wanted to go to bed. His sole focus remained the pursuit of Rex, and they had clues to follow up, but he didn't have to worry about what to do next because the decision was made for him.

In Fishman's car, he saw when Axel pulled over to the side of the road, his arm held high out of the driver's window to make everyone else stop too.

Fishman swung in behind the GTR with the typical breakneck method of driving that demanded maximum acceleration and braking at every opportunity. Thrust forward and only held in check by the four-point harness, Albert sighed with relief when the car stopped, and he was able to take back control of his limbs.

He wanted to get out and stretch, possibly even to massage some life into his backside, but Fishman was much faster. He jumped out, talked to Axel, and got back in all before Albert could extricate his shoulders from the stupid harness.

"They're on the move," Fishman reported, firing the engine to life and snatching at the gearstick. He was animated and awash with fresh enthusiasm, but his news lacked the detail Albert needed to be able to understand what he was trying to convey.

"Those two Korean car thief dudes. Song Bin and Park Ji Hoon. Their tracker has been stationary for hours. I guess they didn't feel much like partying after Song lost his car the way he did, and they went home. Anyway, they are moving again, and Axel says they are heading in the direction of the docks."

This was news. Okay, so it got him no closer to finding Rex, but Albert still felt invested in the mystery of the missing cars, nevertheless.

"Carter and Pixie are tailing them," Fishman added. "Did you meet them earlier? They're two of our guys, I guess you could say. Pixie lost his Mitsubishi Eclipse a week ago and man is he keen to get it back. When Axel said what we were doing, he was first to volunteer. They've been sitting outside Song Bin's place since the race."

Albert took it all in. They were hot on the trail of the car thieves and if they were lucky, they would soon find the location of the missing cars. The possibility raised a new question. That of what to do if they did.

The obvious solution would be to call the police. The detective he met, DCI Hoeks, came across as a capable sort, but the street racers were anything but fans of law enforcement because their cars came loaded with illegal modifications they wouldn't want the police looking too closely at.

Albert thought that was a minor concern compared to the danger of trying to rescue the cars themselves, yet suspected that was precisely what Axel and his friends would attempt to do. Not least because if the police were involved, the cars would be seized, and it could be months before the rightful owners were reunited with them.

He would dispense some advice if and when they found the right location and the cars. Until then it was all moot, so Albert stayed quiet and tried hard not to think about Rex.

Chapter 38

DCI Garfield slammed a fist into the table, jolting Ivan van der Pol.

"I'm not giving you a choice, Ivan. I know there is an illegal, big money dog fighting ring operating in this city and I know that you are involved." Garfield wafted his right hand at the array of materials they had taken from his apartment. It included print outs taken from Ivan's personal computer which proved shockingly easy to hack.

Ivan had a headache from landing on his skull. They'd given him painkillers and had a doctor confirm he was medically fit to be questioned, but the thumping in his brain continued unabated all the same.

They had him on a bunch of charges following the raid on his apartment. Foolishly he had more than a kilo of marijuana stashed in his sideboard for a friend; enough to be considered too much for personal use which placed him into the bracket of distributor. That would get him five years and it wasn't the only charge.

Garfield was offering him a way out and he was going to take it, but he couldn't do so without putting up a fight. If he caved too quickly, the detective would suspect he had ulterior motives and for his plan to work, Ivan needed to play it just right.

For the last thirty minutes he'd denied any knowledge of a dog fighting ring. It was clear the police had no clue who was involved, how big it was, or where it would take place. It was why Garfield was leaning on him to reveal the truth, but the truth can be a subjective thing.

Additionally, Ivan knew how cops thought and how they operate. They are always after that next big bust that will get them recognition and DCI Garfield was no different. Ivan was willing to bet he would want to infiltrate the dog fight himself. Inside he would be able to coordinate the police raid and take it all down in a way that would ensure he claimed all the glory.

Police were so easy to predict.

Ivan rubbed his head and stared at the evidence laid out on the desk. He was going to capitulate, but not just yet. He had to wait for Garfield to come up with the idea himself. Only once the idiot suggested Ivan could get him into the event would he begin to sway.

He would express that it could be done, but that he would need to be there to make it happen. That would get him out of custody and back into the folds of the organisation who would make DCI Garfield disappear as though he had never been.

Ivan would need to leave the city, or just take his medicine and spend the next couple of years in prison, but that was okay. For him it was little more than an occupational hazard and it was in jail that he made the contacts that got him his current gig. There were always so many interesting people to meet behind bars.

Garfield slammed his fist into the tabletop again and Ivan did his best not to smirk.

Chapter 39

Rex and the dogs didn't need to do much navigating on their way to the city centre; they could see the bright lights from where they were. They could also see that it was miles away, a distance they could cover in an hour if they chose to run the whole way, but they were tired and hungry, and Rex knew it was time to properly rest.

Unlike before when Brain Scar led them into the first sheltered spot they came across, Rex kept the pack going until the warehouse was more than a mile to their rear and the search radius included enough ground that the humans would never find them.

In another sheltered spot where they could hide from the wind and cold, the pack snuggled in close to greet sleep like a welcome friend.

They had a distance to go, but Rex knew there was nothing to gain by arriving exhausted. They would sleep for a while, rising before the sun to continue their journey in the dark. Along the way they would find food – a dog can always locate something to eat even if it has to be stolen, but they would not delay, for even though they had many hours before the fights were due to start, they could not be sure of their destination.

It was enough to make Rex's slumber fitful. They were heading for the vicinity of the pizza place in the hope that Battle Tank would then recognise the smells and sounds of the place they took him for the last fight. Or maybe they would detect the scent of the other dogs – that many in the same place would give off an unmistakable odour, but it was guesswork because that was all they had.

His eyes fluttered open, a sound he couldn't place interrupting his sleep. He listened for a while until he felt content there was nothing to fear and when he closed his eyes again, he thought of Albert.

The old man was out there somewhere, exposed and unprotected without Rex to stand guard at his side. His human was more capable than most, but that knowledge did nothing to stop Rex worrying. Albert had a habit of getting into trouble, but drifting back to sleep, Rex told himself the old man was probably tucked up in bed and completely safe, the only concern troubling his aging brow that of his missing dog.

Well, that was a worry Rex planned to resolve just as soon as he rescued Kevin and the other dogs.

Chapter 40

"Is that ..." Kerstin questioned.

"Yes," Axel replied, "I'm fairly sure it is."

They were looking down at Song Bin and Park Ji Hoon from the top of a shipping container. The steel shell was freezing cold to the touch, the chill penetrating Albert's layers to make him wish he was back in Fishman's uncomfortable car.

They had tracked Park's car to Westpoort, one of the many areas in Amsterdam where ships dock. The racers told him the Dutch capital acted as a central conduit for export, firms sending their goods by road or rail to one of the ports that lined the city's waterways.

Prudently, their cars were parked a few hundred metres back so they wouldn't be heard. It meant approaching on foot but allowed them to be stealthy.

"You know him?" Albert questioned.

The person they were talking about was not one of the two car thieves Albert identified, but another Korean street racer they knew by reputation more than anything. He had money and was known to be connected. They just hadn't realised he was connected to Song and Park.

They were too far away to make out what he was saying, but he was saying it loud and gesticulating wildly to make his point. Song and Park were just two of many listening to what Lee Yoo had to say.

"Yeah," Axel responded to Albert's question. "That's Lee Yoo. He's a bad dude by all accounts. I heard he cut a guy up for insulting his girlfriend. He's clearly in charge down there and that building looks big enough to house a bunch of stolen cars. We need to get a closer look to confirm it, but I would guess this is the place and that we've just found the guy behind the car thefts."

It was after one o'clock, a time when criminals found themselves busy in Albert's experience. They were car thieves and he'd already surmised they were stealing high end cars to order. The remote port location confirmed it or came close enough so far as Albert was concerned.

Lee Yoo issued a final command and the people gathered around him split, running back to their cars as though instilled with a time-sensitive purpose.

"They'll be after more cars," Albert guessed. "Trying to get whatever it is they haven't yet been able to obtain."

"Like my GTR," murmured Axel.

"Precisely."

Lee lifted a hand to bang on a roller door, the sound from it echoing across the dock and bouncing off the still water flowing by just a hundred metres from his building. Nothing happened for a couple of seconds, then the roller slowly started to move. Made from metal, not the modern plastic a new door might employ, it made a grinding, wheezing noise as it lifted slowly into the roof.

On top of the cold shipping container, no one dared to breathe.

Two men ducked under the rising door, coming out to join Lee. He spoke and they listened, his words once again too quiet to carry to the ears of the racers, however they all saw when both men produced handguns from behind their backs, checked they were loaded and put them away.

One moved into position near the door, ducking back into the shadows to become invisible and, most likely, to hide from the cool breeze. His partner set off around the building's perimeter.

"Guards," murmured Axel.

"No," Albert countered. "Armed guards." He knew it made a significant difference.

Lee Yoo ducked inside but the roller door was halfway up now and in the next second got high enough to reveal what was inside.

"That's Teagan's Evo," hissed Axel. It was right next to a Ferrari, a car that even Albert was able to identify. They had the right place. Now they needed a strategy.

Kerstin shuffled back from the edge of the shipping container, just as keen as everyone else to get off the cold metal.

"So what now?" she asked. "I mean, I'm all for stealing back our cars, but as Albert already pointed out, that won't solve the longer-term problem."

Albert had spoken at length on the subject of repercussions and root causes. If they took back their cars they would absolutely solve the immediate problem, but how long would it be until the Koreans came after them again and the moment they figured out they were back in the street racers' hands, the gang of car thieves would know who broke into their storage facility. No one needed a target on their back and now that they knew Lee Yoo was behind it all, the threat of retribution was all the higher.

"Do we accept this is too big for us and call the police?" asked Shaggy, helping Kerstin, then Albert back to the ground.

"Not a chance," said Axel. "Do that and the cops will know exactly what mods we have been making. They'll be crawling all over Bitchin' Modifications in a heartbeat. Not to mention the distinct likelihood that the Koreans will figure out who sent the police their way. It's not like they will get locked up for good. I'd be willing to bet their lawyers would have them out the next day, and even if it goes to plan and they do go down, there will still be members of their gang on the outside. If they want to make us pay, they will be able to."

"I'm not just letting my car go, man," argued Pixie. "That building they came out of; I'm going in there and I'm getting my wheels back."

Axel held up his hands to beg for calm. The argument was heating up and everyone was both right and wrong at the same time.

Albert cleared his throat to make everyone look his way.

"I believe I have an alternate solution."

Chapter 41

"Well, Albert," Axel shook his head, "I've got to hand it to you. That is the craziest plan I have ever heard in my life. You really think we can pull that off?"

"Yup." Albert ran the whole thing through his head again, checking for flaws. Obviously, to pull it off and win there were certain elements that had to go their way, but in principle it was pure genius. The street racers didn't trust the police, the Koreans were essentially an organised crime family, and the people behind the dog fights had to be seriously dangerous given the clientele they catered to. Viewed separately and up close they were each an insurmountable problem Albert could not hope to overcome, but with a few steps back to see it all as one giant ecosystem, a holistic approach came into sight.

They were going to steal back the cars, but they were not quite ready for that yet. There were other tasks to which they had to attend first. It pained Albert to put rescuing Rex on hold, but he believed his best shot would be at the fights when he could be sure of his dog's location.

He knew where the event would take place, but if he went there now and the dogs were still being held at a different spot, he ran the danger of tipping his hand. He could get caught and even if he feigned dementia or confusion they would remember his face when he returned with his invitation for the event itself.

He needed sleep and so did everyone else. Especially if they were going to be ready for the following evening and all the adventure it promised.

The racers drove away from the port leaving the stolen cars where they were. They would be back in a few hours.

Dropped back at his little hotel, sleep found Albert far more swiftly than he expected.

Chapter 42

Rex woke to a twitching paw tickling his left ear. Used to his own space, spending the night sandwiched and overlapped by other dogs had been less restful than he might have hoped. The only good thing to come from it was the warmth so many bodies created. It kept the winter cold at bay.

The paw twitched again. Rex leaned back and shifted his weight to see who it belonged to.

"*Sausages,*" muttered Battle Tank dreamily, his other paws twitching too as he chased something unseen in his sleep.

Rex rolled to get his legs under his body and stood up. He stretched in place and looked out from their sheltered spot at the dark sky above. It was night still, but the moon had shifted across from one side of the horizon to the other, denoting the passage of time accurately enough for Rex to know morning and daylight were on their way.

They had slept and it was time to get moving.

Accentuating an altogether different need, his stomach grumbled. Unlike the rest of the fighting dogs, he did not get fed at the warehouse. Arriving after their dinner was handed out, his last meal was a couple of hours earlier and that felt like a long time ago now. If they were to find Kevin and the remainder of the fighting dogs and then stage a rescue, they would need to have food in their bellies.

He padded around the jumble of dog limbs to find Shadow Fang. The Afghan Hound's long, silky coat hid his face so completely that looking at his confused form Rex wasn't sure which bit was the head end and got it wrong on his first attempt.

Shadow Fang lifted his head. "*Why are you talking to my butt?*"

Dismissing the question, Rex lowered his backend to the ground and looked out at the lights of the city twinkling in the distance.

"We need to get moving and we need to find food. You're our guide for this leg of the journey. Is there anything you recognise yet?"

Shadow Fang tilted his head back to raise his nose and sniffed deeply. He could smell the river but that was like saying he could see the sky, the scent of the tidal waterway running through Amsterdam was everywhere. He ignored it, focusing on the subtler odours, those lurking in the background.

As though lifted from the ground by his nose, Shadow Fang followed it upward, rising to his paws to step outside where a light breeze made his long fur shimmy. With his eyes closed, he tested the wind looking for anything familiar.

Rex stayed silent, waiting.

Shadow Fang lowered his muzzle and opened his eyes. *"Sorry, there's nothing that I recognise. We'll have to get closer."*

It was disappointing, but not unexpected. If the one local dog had been able to lead them on the trail of a scent he knew it could have short cut their journey, but they had visual markers to guide them into the city, the taller buildings high enough that they could be seen from almost anywhere in Amsterdam.

Rex roused the other dogs, led them to a puddle where they were able to slake their collective thirst, and with breakfast thoughts dominating their minds, they headed for the city.

Chapter 43

Sylvia van Lidth dabbed at her lips with a napkin. Clad in a silk dressing gown, hair pulled into a ponytail for sleeping, and bereft of makeup, she looked nothing like her usual self. The version she presented to the world was impeccably dressed at all times, her face and hair flawless as though she were a Hollywood actress about to step in front of the cameras.

Appearance was everything in her opinion. If a person looked vulnerable, those around them who might vie to usurp would see them as such. She showed no such weaknesses.

However, alone in her penthouse apartment high above the city streets below, she permitted her fatigue and age the opportunity to surface. At sixty-three she did not consider herself old, but there were days when she felt it. Twenty years ago, she would have shrugged off a bad night's sleep with indifference. Now it plagued her. She felt as though there had been no sleep at all.

It was too late to call off or postpone the event set for tonight. Months of planning went into each of her 'parties' and they made so much money it was hard to conceive that she rose to control her empire from a job as a cleaning lady. No one knew her humble beginnings. No one in her employ at least, and they never would.

Ruthlessness, cunning, and a blind determination to win ensured each of the victories she scored and the loyalty her staff displayed. They won when she won, that had always been a rule, but what lesson might they learn tonight?

She was missing several of the dogs due to take part in the fights, and though they could be replaced by grabbing someone's domestic animal off the street, getting them to put on a good show wasn't so simple as people might believe.

The average pooch would back into a corner when faced with an opponent they could not hope to defeat. Or simply roll onto their back. If that happened even once she would be a laughingstock, the bets would all have to be returned – further embarrassment – and it would be talked about which would damage the popularity of future events.

It had taken too long and she had worked too hard to see it all go to waste now. Trying to fix it had kept her up into the small hours and worrying about it troubled her sleep when she finally slipped between the sheets.

There were still people out looking for the missing dogs, but Sylvia held little hope they would be found. It was small consolation that the American Pitbull had been caught and returned. He was one of the star attractions and about to be pitched against a vastly bigger opponent. That was the opening bout and a spectacle sure to get the crowd talking. They wouldn't know how to bet and her bookies were all set to take advantage of the indecisiveness that came from the unknowable.

She downed her coffee, a double espresso, and glared through her window to the grey sky outside. It was going to be a trying day.

Chapter 44

C laude and Rutger worked the night shift at Amsterdam's Animal Services and had done so for years. It paid better than the day shift and the lack of other people about let them goof off and generally skive far more than they could otherwise.

One of their first jobs the previous evening had been to collect a German Shepherd. When they saw how massive he was, they made a couple of hurried calls and netted themselves a nice bonus. That should have been the end of it, but the stupid dog escaped a few hours later along with nearly a dozen others and they were offered another fee to find them all. The task had them scouring the city all night while pretending to look for strays.

Not that they saw that as a problem. The reward on offer was five times what they usually got paid for delivering a worthwhile specimen, so when their shift ended and they were forced to return the van and their equipment, they stole what they needed, raced home, and went straight back out to continue the search.

The dogs could be anywhere in the city, that was the advice given, but Claude and Rutger knew that wasn't true. For a start the building they escaped from had the river in one direction. That meant they had to head away from it which drove them toward the centre of Amsterdam. That still left a lot of territory to cover, but they knew the dogs had been found under a railway arch when Sylvia's men attempted to recapture the dogs themselves. They ought to have called in the professionals.

If they were near the railway they were most likely heading toward the city itself. There they would find food and it sounded plausible that some of them might be trying to find their way home. Claude and Rutger argued about the concept, Rutger adamant no dog was bright enough to navigate in the manner he described while Claude recited stories he'd read or heard about faithful hounds doing precisely that.

"Haven't you seen *The Incredible Journey*?" he asked at one point.

Rutger shot his colleague a look of disbelief. "The Disney film? Dude, that's fiction."

"Yes, but based on a book that was based on a true story."

"No, it wasn't," replied Rutger. His partner had a habit for believing everything he heard. "It was a load of guff made up to keep kids quiet for ninety minutes."

Claude was about to snap his response when he caught sight of something from the corner of his eye. They were passing a side street near Geuzenveld-Slotermeer on their way back to the Zeeburg area and he had to yell for Rutger to stop and back up.

"What?" Rutger demanded impatiently as he coasted to a halt. "You think they made it this far already."

"It's only a few kilometres from where they started. A dog could easily travel that far in a night."

"Yes, but why would they? They don't know where they are going, and don't give me any more of that claptrap about *The Incredible Journey*, they are not trying to find their way home. They will be trying to find food and there's a fish market not far from where they set off. That's where they'll be."

"I just saw them!"

Rutger sighed. He wasn't going to get his way until he showed Claude how foolish he was being. He probably had seen a dog or even some dogs, but they would be scruffy, flea-bitten strays scavenging for food, not the hardy fighting dogs they were looking for.

Drawing level with the side street, he cut his eyes to the left where Claude's gaze was already trained.

The pack of dogs froze in place. Spread out across the empty road with Rex at the front next to Shadow Fang, the dogs felt they were making good progress. They still had a long way to go, but the city loomed closer and having detected a food scent drifting on the wind a few minutes ago, they were zeroing in on the smell's source.

However, the van now blocking their path exuded a sense of menace they could all detect.

Rex narrowed his eyes and sniffed the air. However, he learned nothing about the van or the people inside it until Claude opened his window.

"Hey, doggies," he cooed. "Who wants a nice treat?" he dangled a large gravy bone in his right hand, a succulent morsel he carried at all times. It was standard practice for anyone working in animal services. Of course, most of his colleagues packed straight up gravy bones whereas the ones he carried today were laced with a drug that would knock a dog out in under a minute.

Shadow Fang's jaw dropped open, a dribble of drool spilling from his mouth.

"*Friendly humans!*" he exclaimed excitedly, wagging his tail and staring forward.

"*And they have food!*" cried Bite Knight, breaking into a run.

Rex barked, "*No!*" and had to throw himself into Bite Knight's path to stop him. "*These are the men who brought me here last night. They're dog catchers!*"

"*But they have food!*" whined Battle Tank, equally desperate to sample the flavoursome gravy bone.

Claude, an old hand at luring dogs into his clutches, dropped the gravy bone to the ground and produced several more.

"I've got enough for all of you," he cooed in friendly, soothing tones.

"*He's got so many!*" whimpered Ball Biter, ready to believe Rex's claim, but hungry enough to risk trying to get the treat anyway.

Rex barked the other dogs down, stamping his authority as the alpha before turning back to face Claude and the van.

"*The treats are probably drugged. They'll taste fine, but ten minutes later you wake in a cage in the back of their van.*"

The thought made the dogs whimper.

"You think they are friendly? Watch this."

He walked toward the van, watching Claude to see when he would move.

Claude twisted in his seat to grin at Rutger. "Easiest money ever. They're going to come to us. We won't even need the poles." He was still looking his way when Rutger's expression changed from upbeat to horrified and Claude realised he could feel warm breath on his neck.

Gulping, Claude leaned away from the open window and slowly turned to look at the dog. Rex had his front paws up and his face in the van, his teeth on show.

"Oh, dear, chaps. Oh, deary, deary me. We do appear to have something of a situation here, now don't we. You see, I recall my last journey in your van, and I hold the pair of you responsible for everything that has happened since. The only question I have, if you wish, is which one of you I am going to bite first."

Seeing Rex run toward the van and stick his head into it startled the pack who, to a dog, assumed Rex was going to do what alpha's do and claim all the treats for himself. Instead, he was taking the fight to the humans, something no dog would ever do, and they wanted to get a closer look.

Stunned by the German Shepherd's behaviour which went against everything they had ever experienced working in animal services, Claude and Rutger were momentarily unable to make their limbs respond. The dog's head was in the van, forcing Claude to one side just to stay out of snapping reach of his teeth.

However, when Rutger spotted the other dogs moving in to surround them, terror overcame shock to unfreeze his body.

With a scream to get himself moving, he lunged for the control pole hanging on the hooks behind his head. Rex saw it coming and ducked back through the window, but rather than dropping back to the ground and making off, he bit hold of the passenger side door mirror, clenched hard with his jaw muscles and ripped it off.

The hoop end of the control pole shot out through the window above Rex's head.

"He was right!" barked Battle Tank. *"Rex was right! These guys are dog catchers! Scrag the van!"*

The instruction, easy to understand and simple to follow, generated an instant response from the pack of fighting dogs.

Rex thought the statement about him being right was perhaps the most redundant sentence any dog had ever used, but he kept the opinion to himself and joined the fun as the dogs descended on the van en masse.

With the control pole shoved through the passenger window and being operated right in front of Claude's face, it was only a matter of time before Rutger accidentally caught his colleague with it. Smacked on the nose with the plastic pole, Claude slapped Rutger's arm away and he fumbled his grip, losing the pole which tumbled through the window.

It reappeared a second later in Rex's mouth when he raised his head to glare at the humans. Saliva dripped from his jaws before he demonstrated his strength and bit the pole in half.

Battle Tank rammed the side door of the van with his head, rocking the suspension and leaving a sizeable dent while Bite Knight, Ball Biter, and some of the others ripped the front bumper from its mount.

"My van!" squealed Rutger.

Bracing himself against the roof and the dashboard Claude spat, "Nevermind your van! Get us out of here!"

The van rocked again from yet another Rottweiler head strike just as Rutger slammed the stick into first and stamped on the accelerator. The van shot forward in a cloud of smoke, narrowly missing the dogs as they leapt to get out of the way.

Rex watched the humans go, a satisfied grin on his face as he watched the pack celebrate their victory.

Shadow Fang sidled up next to him, crunching something between his teeth.

"Hey, I reckon you were wrong about the gravy bones, by the way. This one tastes fine."

Rex started to snigger, only realising what the Afghan Hound had said a moment later. Spinning around to face him, he wanted to ask if he was joking, but Shadow Fang's left eye was already three times more dilated than the left.

His tongue lolled from his mouth and he tried to scratch at his head with a back paw only to miss and stumble into Rex.

"*Hey, what's with him?*" asked, Bite Knight.

Shadow Fang wriggled his tongue around in his mouth. "*I feel kinda funny,*" he announced, looking squarely at Rex with his eyeballs pointing in different directions. "*You might have been right about that gravy bone after all.*"

With that he promptly fell over onto his side, his tongue spread along the street like a spill of strawberry yoghurt. His eyes closed and their guide to the city passed out.

Rex sat his butt on the ground and looked up at the sky.

"*Well, that's just great.*"

Chapter 45

Albert allowed himself a lie in, not because he was in any way relaxed about Rex's predicament, but due to the simple fact that he had time to kill. The event was due to take place that night, giving him almost twelve hours to get through before he could hope to be reunited with his dog.

They needed to infiltrate the venue without getting caught – a task that was going to require steel nerves and some luck, then they had to find the dogs which almost certainly meant sneaking into the back area behind the scenes where they were being held. To do that they would have to find a way around the security employed specifically to stop it from happening, security that was undoubtedly made up of people like Ivan van der Pol who might well kill them on sight if they had the misfortune to run into him.

If they managed to get into the back areas they still had to find Rex and get him out, assuming the dogs were kept in cages of some kind, and then escape the building once again without encountering security who would seek to stop them.

Laid out like that the odds were stacked so high against them only a complete idiot would ever attempt to pull it off. Mercifully, Albert was not an idiot, and his plan to disrupt the dog fight organiser's slick operation would eliminate more than half their challenges provided it worked.

Provided it worked.

Albert allowed himself a wry grin. The possibility for abject failure was huge, but he could see no way around the task and he would do it alone if he had to. He would need the police, but it wasn't time for them yet and he didn't have enough information to bring be certain they would respond. Well, he believed he knew the location of a building in which several dozen stolen cars were currently hidden, and the police would take that information as actionable, but that wouldn't get him any closer to Rex and he needed the cars as part of his plan.

So it would be without local law enforcement that he went up against two of Amsterdam's criminal organisations, a big day for anyone, let alone a man nearing his eighties in the country by himself.

Swinging his legs out of bed, Albert stretched and scratched and set off for the bathroom. There was much to be done, but first he needed some breakfast.

Chapter 46

DCI Garfield fought to stifle his yawn. In the captain's office to explain what he'd learned and what he now planned to do, his sum total of sleep for the night amounted to just less than three hours which he'd grabbed on a couch in the far corner of the cafeteria.

"Not keeping you up, are we?" questioned the captain in a tone that was half joke half serious.

Garfield didn't reply. He saw Captain Verbeek as a brown noser who got his promotions through saying the right thing at the right time rather than by having any talent for police work or even a modicum of leadership ability. There were plenty like him about. Not just in the police, but everywhere in life.

When the yawn finally subsided, Garfield said, "Where's Dani?"

"DCI Hoeks is otherwise engaged, Garfield. You asked that she be here, but she is working elsewhere in the city, as you ought to be. Did I not assign you to an international taskforce investigating cross-border drug trafficking? I'm fairly sure I did because I was there when I gave you the assignment and can recall the event quite distinctly."

Ignoring the captain's stupid attitude, Garfield said, "The cross-border drug case is progressing. I took a moment to look into something else on my own time and I have good reason to believe there will be a big money dog fighting event in town tonight."

"Dog fighting? Well, that is big news. I'll call SWAT and get them geared up."

Garfield lost his cool, opting to raise his voice when he demanded, "What is your problem? We pursue criminals. I'm handing you a bunch of criminals. Arrests will be easy since everyone at the event will be engaged in criminal activity purely by being there."

"Is that a fact?" Captain Verbeek replied cooly. "So this is nothing to do with DCI Hoeks' missing dog and your infatuation with her?"

Garfield felt his fists clench. "What if it is? That changes nothing."

Verbeek raised an eyebrow in challenge. "Drugs take priority over dogs every day of the week, Garfield. Carry on this way and you'll make yourself redundant."

Garfield toyed with the idea of punching Verbeek in his annoying face.

"I have a man in custody with a rap sheet longer than a cat's list of things it finds curious, and he is going to get me into the event. We don't need a warrant, there's minimal investigation to conduct prior to the arrests … I'm handing you a dream ticket and you are questioning my motives."

Captain Verbeek hadn't thought about the upside. He hadn't given it much thought at all to tell the truth. He didn't like Garfield because he knew Hoeks was still hung up on him and even though Verbeek was married, his union was not a happy one. He would drop his wife in a heartbeat if Danielle Hoeks looked his way, but she never would because of Garfield's stupidly perfect face and physique.

Putting all that to one side, a big score, if that was what it turned out to be, was just what he needed to boost his visibility. The commissioner was just a few years from retirement and Verbeek rather fancied the city's top law enforcement job. More than one commissioner had gone on to be the mayor and from there anything was possible.

"You don't need anything now? No extra funding, no overtime bill?"

Garfield felt the tension seep away; he had him.

"No, sir. I'm going home to get a little rest and will be back later to coordinate with SWAT. The man in custody, Ivan van der Pol, will be released to me this afternoon. Once I am inside and can confirm the event is what I believe it to be, I will call in backup and liaise with them to secure the exits and make arrests. I believe we will need as many officers as you can muster."

And a man to lead the charge, Verbeek thought to himself.

"What about the drug trafficking case?"

Garfield reached for the door handle, he needed to get some sleep. Paused in the doorway, he admitted the truth, "No one can figure out how they are shipping it out. We know where it is being manufactured, but the boss of the taskforce wants it all. Otherwise, the distributors will just move to a different supplier and we achieve very little."

There being nothing more to say, Captain Verbeek let Garfield go. He needed to speak to Hoeks. If there was a bust going down that might reveal what happened to her dog, he wanted to be sure she knew he was driving it.

Chapter 47

Lee Yoo felt better than he had a few hours ago. Caffeine from far too many cups of coffee was making him jittery, or perhaps it was the perilous situation he found himself in that had his nerves all strung out. But the guys had come through, finding three of the last four cars during the night. Though the term 'finding them' was misleading. They had known where they were all along, and left them to last because they were going to be the hardest to obtain or were the riskiest.

Yet it was done, and no one got caught in the process. Maybe his uncle had been right to push as hard as he did. Lee was trying hard to view the experience as a lesson he could learn from, but he was yet to hear from Sookie and he didn't dare call Uncle Kim.

Not until he had the final car.

Nissan GTR's are rare but not so rare that there was only one in the city. There were eleven that he knew of, but the demand was not for a stock GTR, the customer wanted one fit for street racing and that reduced the list from eleven cars down to one.

At this point, Lee wished he'd looked farther afield than Amsterdam. He would have found other options if he'd looked for them, but he knew Axel Janssen by reputation and wanted his car. That was before he learned the leader of the city's rival street racing outfit had thrown down a challenge and won Song Bin's prized Supra. That he had the gall to bring in a ringer of an old man to pull it off was insult to injury.

He had no choice but to supply the one race ready GTR available to him, but it was not a job he was prepared to give to anyone else. He was going to handle this himself. He would prove to Uncle Kim his doubts were unfounded. That he was a man who could be trusted to deliver.

Just one more car, that was all he needed.

He downed the last of his coffee, his umpteenth for the night, and grabbed his jacket. It was time to go hunting.

Chapter 48

Rex was feeling frustrated. They could push on into the city, but they would have to do so without their guide. The Afghan Hound's local knowledge would get them to the pizza place and from there the hope was that Battle Tank's nose would take them the rest of the way.

The plan was tenuous to begin with, but losing Shadow Fang meant they would only find the right area by chance. Not that Rex was going to chance it. To move onward while the Afghan was out cold was to abandon him to fend for himself. There would be crows pecking at his unconscious form within seconds. Splitting up wasn't an option either because they would have no way to get a message back to those they left behind to guard Shadow Fang and it was too far to go into the city, maybe find where the other dogs were being held, and make it back to collect the others.

All they could do was wait.

Except waiting was boring and did nothing to silence their increasingly loud bellies.

"*I'm starving,*" moped Bite Knight, an emotion echoed by everyone present. Most had voiced much the same in the hour since Shadow Fang collapsed.

Rex got back to his feet. "*I'm going to look for food. I need a couple of volunteers to help me. Ball Biter and Battle Tank, you're it.*"

"*Huh? Why not the rest of us?*" asked Snow Beast, an Alaskan Malamute almost half as big again as Rex.

"*Because I don't want everyone wandering off. We will scout the area and come back. If we find food we will bring it back here. Is that understood?*" He fixed the ridgeback and the Rottweiler in place with a glare.

"Yup, gotcha. Don't eat what we find," agreed Battle Tank, lying through his teeth.

Rex knew they would scoff the first thing they found; it was in their nature, but hoped they would show the good sense to bring something back with them.

Unlike in the city, where there were places to find food on every street, trapped between the industrial area and the suburbs ahead there was nothing. Vague food smells carried on the wind found the dogs' noses periodically, but none had been strong enough to make the pack think they were worth pursuing.

That was still the case, but the collective hunger, made worse by lack of activity, was becoming a distraction. Rex prayed they could find something worthwhile without having to search too far.

Battle Tank set off in one direction, Ball Biter in another. Rex aimed his paws to the west and ran at a steady pace for a while, his nose searching for likely food sources the whole time. What he wanted was a human food outlet, something selling burgers or sausages. It didn't even need to be open. In fact, it might be better it if wasn't. Humans were careless and wasteful with food, so the bins around the place would have rich pickings inside. If he could find a place and it was closed for business, he could knock a bin over and eat his fill, drag out the liner inside and heft it all the way back to the pack.

He ran on, looking for high ground so he could get above and have a better view. Perhaps his eyes would spot what his nose could not find, but when his legs began to tire, he slowed. There was no high ground. It was as though Amsterdam had no gradient. Rex wondered if it really was as flat as it seemed.

Accepting defeat, Rex turned around to retrace his steps and hoped Ball Biter or Battle Tank fared better.

Ball Biter had not. He was already back with the pack, whining about his ever-thinning waistline and how he was going to fade away if he didn't eat soon. Goodness knows he was lean enough to start with.

However, the slower-moving Battle Tank trotted into view a few minutes later with something dangling from his mouth. He was simultaneously spotted by more than half the dogs in the pack. Most of them were moving before the Rottweiler could take another step.

They surrounded him, each trying to see what he had. Rex stayed with Shadow Fang and gave his head a nudge to check if he might be coming out of his drug induced state.

As Battle Tank came closer, Rex could see that what he held in his mouth was a large cardboard box. It measured four hundred millimetres square and was a hundred and fifty deep. Not that Rex thought of the size in those terms, to him it was roughly the same size as the Rottweiler's head if not the same shape.

The pack continued to fuss around him, but no one was going to try to take the prize from his mouth. They were impatient, but no one wanted to start a fight.

Arriving next to Rex, he dropped the box and placed a paw on top of it. The smell from inside was unfamiliar yet enticing. It possessed a sweet, confectionary tang that also hinted of vegetation. Lurking behind it was a piney, skunky odour he recalled smelling in the street the previous evening. There was something very familiar about it that he knew he would be able to place if he gave it enough thought.

"*What did you find?*" Rex asked, adding, "*Well, done, by the way. Ball Biter and I struck out.*"

Battle Tank pulled an uncertain expression.

"*It's food. I'm sure of that. I found a place making these so we can go back for more. They were boxing them up, so I waited until no one was looking and took one. I would have brought more, but I've only got one mouth.*"

Bite Knight whined, "*I'm starved. Let's just eat them!*"

Rex agreed so the box was opened and the smell from inside wafted out at twenty times the strength.

"*Ooh, what are they?*" asked Ball Biter. "*I've never smelt anything like that before, but the scent alone is making me feel happy?*"

"*Really?*" questioned Shadow Fang, startling everyone. He was back on his feet and staring into the box like everyone else. "*The smell is making me feel anxious. That's weird, right?*"

Too hungry to discuss it any longer, Rex used one front paw to flip the box, spilling the contents onto the ground. The things inside looked like brownies, but not like any brownie he had ever eaten. They weren't chocolate, that was for sure, but with the rest of the pack diving onto them like the ravenous hounds they were, he wasted no time questioning what secret ingredient they might contain.

When they were done, he thought as he munched and munched, they would set off again. Shadow Fang was back on his feet after close to two hours on his back, so they could finally get moving. Food first though.

It felt good to be putting something in his belly, but converse to his expectations, he was feeling more hungry, not less. He vacuumed up the last few crumbs and sat back to question what he had just ingested.

Something about him was very definitely not the same. He couldn't claim that it was 'not right', it was just different. His heart was beating faster than it had been, his head didn't feel connected with the rest of his body, and he could see colours.

HE COULD SEE COLOURS!

Battle Tank ambled over to him. "*Hey, Rex, have I ever told you that you are da bomb?*" Swaying a little, the Rottweiler rotated to face the pack. "*Hey, everyone, isn't Rex just da bomb?*"

Rex was aware of Battle Tank speaking, but was transfixed by his own right front paw. If he held it in front of his face and moved it, it left a streak in the air where it had just been.

Shadow Fang bumped into him, giggling uncontrollably.

"*Hey, Rex. I don't know what was in those brownies, but they were the best brownies I have ever ... I have ever.*" His eyes unfocused and he moved his lips around like he had lost his place and couldn't now find it. "*What was I saying?*"

Abruptly, Battle Tank started howling with sadness, and Rex's last lucid thought was that it might take them a little while longer to walk to the city than he'd previously calculated.

Chapter 49

With breakfast behind him, Albert went shopping. He wasn't short of money, but he was far from rich, and with no income beyond his police pension, he had to give some consideration before he threw money around.

Not so very long ago, he'd won a fair amount betting on a horse, but as fate would have it, he gave it all away to a group of people whose need was far greater than his would ever be.

So, pushing open the door to what was reputed to be the best tailor in the city, Albert had to hold his metaphoric breath. Axel, Shaggy, Fishman, and Pixie were with him, those four selected as his personal bodyguards because their body shapes fit the bill more closely than any of their friends.

They needed suits, the kind of black two-piece affair that fades into the background where a bodyguard should be. That wouldn't do for Albert though. To play the part of a rich Englishman, he wanted a look that was somewhere between King Charles and Hugh Heffner.

The owner of De Oost Bespoke Tailoring accepted Albert's credit card with the same care one might afford a used tissue, placing it behind the till for later. At five feet and eight inches tall, Yorick van Rijker was the shortest man in the room, but he also commanded the space. This was his domain and though happy to receive anyone who wished to pay for a rush service, he wasn't about to let them rush his process.

Whipping the tape measure from around his neck, he called the first man forward.

An hour later, with a deposit for the eye watering bill paid, Albert and his fake bodyguards left the tailors to find Kerstin and Caprice waiting for them at the kerb. They were the next part of the plan.

It involved more shopping, but their outfits for the event were every bit as necessary as those for the guys. Albert elected not to go into the shop with them; he felt lecherous enough without getting involved in the process of picking outfits that said 'gold digger' loud enough for it to be easily understood. The ladies would be in figure hugging dresses that were somehow both elegant and revealing at the same time.

Albert had no experience to lend, so waited in a coffeeshop across the street with a latte and a stroopwafel. The shop was yet another high-end affair where the garments were one-off originals and came with no price tag attached. If you needed to ask what it cost, you were in the wrong place.

For the sake of his heart, when the two girls and four guys exited the shop more than an hour later with more bags than two dresses ought to warrant, he chose not to ask what he'd spent.

He did ask why there were so many bags though.

Kerstin snorted. "You can't just buy a dress, Albert."

"You can't?" He wasn't sure why that was the case. Was it some kind of store policy?

"No," agreed Caprice. "What would we pair it with? A pair of fifty Euro heels we happen to have in our closet at home?"

"We needed heels and clutches, new underwear that fit with the dress ..." Kerstin continued.

"Speak for yourself, honey," Caprice laughed. "There's no room inside my dress for underwear. I'll be going commando."

Albert wasn't sure what to do with his face. Young ladies discussing their underwear as an optional garment was not something he was used to nor wanted any part of. Unfortunately, while he could be sure to study the pavement or the sky with great interest, there was no way to make his ears stop listening.

The good news was that they had their outfits. The guys would have to return for theirs, before close of business – the tailor assured them even with his staff working flat out it would not be ready before late afternoon, but that part of the preparation was complete, and it was time to move onto the next element.

Fortunately, the next outfits on the shopping list would be cheaper.

Chapter 50

"How do I look?" Shaggy asked.

Caprice straightened his tie. "Like a custom's official."

Shaggy beamed.

"Who slept rough last night," she completed her assessment, wiping his smile away with a single cruel blow.

"She's not wrong," agreed Albert. They had all the props they needed, but the guys needed to tidy themselves up a bit if they were to pull off the car heist he proposed. "You all need to shave, and Shaggy ..."

"Yeah?"

"You need a haircut."

Shaggy backed away like he was being threatened.

"No way man. No one is touching my luscious locks man." He swished his head from side to side, showing off how long and thick it was. "I haven't had a haircut in ten years."

"And it shows," remarked Caprice. "Albert is right. You can't pull this off looking like that. Especially not tonight's gig. You need to look like a bodyguard which means looking like you are ex-forces or something, and you don't see soldiers with hair down to the middle of their backs."

"And we are going to have to use your real names. Fishman, Shaggy, and Pixie are out." Facing Fishman, Albert asked, "What is your real name."

Colour bloomed in Fishman's cheeks. "I'm not telling you."

Caprice raised an eyebrow and the guys all looked his way with curious expressions.

"Really? It's that bad?" asked Kerstin.

"You'll never know," Fishman shot back.

"Oh, come on, Gerald," said Axel. "Tell them your real name."

Shaggy sniggered until Albert aimed a glare his way.

"And I'm betting your mother didn't call you Shaggy."

"No," said Axel. "His real name is Carel."

Albert nodded. "Carel. Good. Now you." They all looked at Pixie.

"Todd," he admitted quietly. Clearly the name was not something he wished those around him to know, but Albert couldn't figure out how a grown man would prefer to be called Pixie.

Regardless, shaves and a haircut were in order, or they would fool no one. Thus, another half an hour ticked by with Albert twiddling his thumbs and it was after two when they were finally ready to go.

Packed into two cars, Axel's mum's Citroen C3 and a Ford Ka Fishman, sorry, Gerald borrowed from one of the girls at his showroom, they drove back to the port. Behind them, Kerstin and Caprice drove a van, also taken from the showroom. It wasn't designed for passengers but that was what it held, the entire street racing crew packed inside like sardines.

Gaining access to the port itself was easy enough, there were public entrances and vehicles going back and forth. Once inside, they aimed for the squat building where the stolen cars were stored.

Leaving the van behind so as not to spook the guards outside the lockup, Axel with Pixie and Albert in the C3 pulled up next to the lockup. They were followed by the Ka with Fishman and the almost unrecognisable Shaggy who now required a new nickname.

The customs officials' outfits were far from exact replicas. Anyone who actually looked at them would know they were off the peg pieces, but they didn't need the subterfuge to last for long. Just long enough for them to get close.

With Albert leading the way, convinced his age would do more to fool the guard of his authenticity than the uniform, they approached the door. The two men blocking it while trying to act casual were not the same two they saw last night, but in Albert's book all henchmen were equal. They would be bored, tired, achy from standing around, and undoubtedly armed.

He held up a clipboard, another item borrowed from the showroom, and frowned disapprovingly as he came within earshot.

"Am I not expected?" he barked, his tone catching the guards by surprise. "This is a routine, planned inspection. I expect to be met by the head of your organisation, which I can tell just by looking, is neither one of you."

The guards looked inward at each other, both silently hoping their partner had some clue as to what was happening. Albert expected they would do something like that and had coached Axel and the others to be ready for it.

They were armed but couldn't afford to have their weapons on display. Most likely they were tucked into the back of their jeans, so it was with confidence that Fishman and Shaggy ducked around Albert's right shoulder and Axel with Pixie went around to the left, all four arriving on top of the guards before they had any chance to react.

Albert expected the street racers to have stun guns or tasers, or just some plain old actual guns at their disposal, but firearms, even moderately safe ones, were not their thing so they weighed in with fists alone.

It proved sufficient for the task.

Axel waved to make sure the girls had seen their success and were coming with the van.

Albert checked around to make sure no one saw or was watching when the guys dragged the guards into the building. They needed to fish around in their pockets to find the keys and open the door, but once inside the street racers dropped the unconscious forms and stared with open mouths at the treasure trove of automobiles arranged in neat rows from one end of the building to the other.

"Sweet Mary mother of Jesus," murmured Axel in the same tone one might employ for a prayer. The others muttered variations of the same, all with their eyes agog and their jaws hanging open.

"Yes, yes," grumbled Albert, hustling past them and down the first row. "It's a building full of very nice cars. We appear to be alone, so how about we tie these nice gentlemen up, relieve them of their phones, and get on with the next part of the plan?"

He left them to deal with the guards. They were not badly hurt, not that Albert felt the slightest soupçon of remorse. It was the henchman's job to take the hits, but they needed to be restrained until someone found them. Walking away he heard the riiiiip of duct tape being torn from a roll.

Albert checked over his shoulder once, looking back at the door as the mass of street racers came through it. They reacted in a predictable manner, but were quick to descend on the cars. Light streamed in from the opening roller door, illuminating the interior though the sun was already heading for the horizon.

He continued down the line, looking for something particular. He was going to an exclusive event in just a few hours and could not arrive in a modified street racer's car. He needed something from a different end of the car market. He found what he was looking for three rows across.

"Oh, yes," he nodded to himself. "This will do nicely."

Chapter 51

T he stream of cars leaving the lockup was a sight to behold. They were not able to take everything; they failed to anticipate just how many cars there might be and needed to have brought more people along, but they got more than half and that was enough.

Led by Kerstin, who was disappointed to be driving the van still, a procession of luxury vehicles made their way from the port. Italian sports cars, rare models or classics, and all the modified cars drove through the gates in a long line that ended with Albert in the backseat of a Rolls Royce. It was brand new and even with Fishman at the wheel, who claimed he'd always wanted to have a go at modifying the world's premier luxury marque, the ride was as smooth as silk.

It was the perfect car in which to arrive at the event that evening. It was just a few hours away and they still had plenty to do.

Leaving the port behind, Fishman questioned if now was not the time to place an anonymous call to the police. The lockup was left open and half the stolen cars were still in it. The police would find the guards bound and locked inside one of the offices and that would lead them to Lee Yoo and his gang where they could make the appropriate arrests.

Not pointing the police in their direction now granted the Koreans time to discover the break in and free the guards who would immediately point a finger at Axel and his merry band of street racers. Retribution would follow. Fishman believed this was a bad thing.

He made good points, but Albert wanted the Koreans to know. His plan relied upon it. If he involved the police too early, it would ruin everything and diminish his chance to recover Rex.

Just outside the port, the cars split up. It would be fun to parade the freshly unstolen cars through the city, but massed together they would draw too much attention. Yet again they ran the risk of alerting the police. They were going to hand the cars over, their owners deserved to get them back, but not for a few hours yet.

Taking separate routes through the city, many of them involving back roads to reduce visibility, the street racers took the cars home or to the house of a friend with a garage. Others went to Bitchin' Modifications' showroom and workshop where they were parked out of sight in the workshop.

Stage one of the plan had gone better than anyone could have expected. It left the street racers buzzing with adrenalin from the stolen car heist. Albert called for calm. It was, after all, just stage one.

Next they had to return to the tailor to fetch their clothes and the ladies needed to go home to start their preparations. Albert knew from his many years of marriage that a lady getting ready for a night out was a distinctly different proposition to that of a man. Albert would comb his hair, apply some aftershave and think the time spent was indulgent.

Petunia would start getting ready at least a day before him.

Anything but a fan of waiting, Albert settled into a chair with a book and tried to tune out the worries circling his brain.

Chapter 52

The dogs reached an intersection and stopped. The marijuana they ingested was slowly wearing off, but they were all still feeling the high. Not that any of them understood what had happened. They ate food all the time, plenty of it stolen when their humans were not looking or snaffled from the gutter because it got dropped and humans then weirdly considered it inedible.

Never had any of them encountered a meal that made walking feel like they were swimming through the air. Shadow Fang had been giggling for two hours straight. Battle Tank kept trying to see if he could knock down lampposts by running into them with his head, and Ball Biter jumped at every shadow, convinced they must be hiding some unspeakable monster that was after his ears.

Of them all, only Rex was semi-lucid. Taking the opposite stance to that of every other alpha he'd ever met, when the brownies hit the ground, he refused to grab the biggest share. He let the others dig in first and consequently had less cannabis in his body than anyone else.

He blamed himself for their predicament. As a trained police dog he should have questioned why he recognised the smell, but he hadn't. His head too filled with thoughts of rescuing Kevin and the other fighting dogs, of finding his human and what he might be up to, made worse by the all-consuming emptiness in his belly, he'd pushed the nagging concern to one side and plunged in like the other dogs.

The pack voted to stay where they were and sleep for the rest of the day. Except Battle Tank who wanted to return for more of the delicious snack. They got to do neither. Stoned from the tip of his tail to the damp of his nose, Rex nevertheless retained enough purpose of being to get the pack moving. Waiting for Shadow Fang to sleep off the effects of the drugged gravy bone ate up time they could ill afford. Waiting any longer simply wasn't a choice Rex would entertain.

He checked for traffic, waited for a van to pass, and chivvied his pack of stoned-out dogs across the road. They were reaching the outskirts of the city centre with the high-rise office blocks stretching into the sky ahead. Another hour was all it would take to cover the remaining distance, but to track their path to the dog fight he needed both Shadow Fang and Battle Tank alert and at their best.

They were a long way from that.

Food would help. At least Rex doubted it would hurt and he was just as hungry as he had been since the day started. Thankfully, there were plenty of places to find food in a city, but they would have to steal it, and more than half the pack still couldn't walk in a straight line.

Of additional concern was the looks they were already attracting. A pack of large dogs would go unnoticed in a park or recreational area, but sauntering along city streets, every driver gave them a glance.

How long would it be before someone called animal services? When that call was placed, who would receive it? Rex knew the animal services people were dirty. They took him to the warehouse and started his nightmare.

To make them a little less conspicuous, Rex slowed his pace until a couple walking arm in arm got ahead of them, then edged the pack forward until they were trailing in the humans' shadows. It wouldn't fool anyone who bothered to look, but the curious looks from passing motorists reduced.

With the sun setting and the cold air returning, the pack meandered onward, onward to a showdown for which they were anything but prepared.

Chapter 53

"This is him?" Sylvia van Lidth asked.

Garfield hung limply between two thugs, making himself look more beaten than he was. His gut hurt from the punches they gave just to soften him up a bit, but he could stand and fight if he needed to. There was no point right now. Surrounded, trapped inside the criminal empire's stronghold, and finally meeting the person behind it all, his best play was to look like he was ready to give up.

"Yes, ma'am," replied Ivan. He played along with DCI Garfield until they got inside the building. Once the door shut, he swung a sucker punch with enough power to lift the smaller man off the floor. It felt good to land that punch.

The police had him on a bunch of charges, so he was going to vanish for a while once the night was done. If he got caught when he returned to his home city or in the time he was away, he would find himself incarcerated, but that was better than betraying Sylvia van Lidth or letting her down.

Either thing would result in ... well, he didn't want to think too hard about what might happen, but it would not be pleasant. At a basic level he was far more scared of her than he was of the police and what they could do to him.

Garfield listened to the clicking of high heels as the elegantly dressed woman paced to his left.

"What does he know?" she asked.

Ivan sucked in a deep breath. He was going to have to speak with great care. There was no point lying about it, he revealed information about her business and the event itself but claimed to be a low-level lackey with no knowledge of who ran the operation or where the money came from. Under interrogation, he gave up the least he could, but to lure Garfield in, there was no choice but to give him something.

"He knows this is a dog fighting ring. Beyond that he doesn't know much at all." He continued to explain what he had revealed to the police in great detail.

Sylvia's right hand woman, Chelsea, eyed Ivan with great scrutiny. She didn't like him. He was a basic thug, a blunt tool to be used when the situation called for it, but he displayed ambition beyond his ability and was foolish enough to make advances on her when they first met. Being found attractive wasn't offensive, but he touched her without permission, and that crossed a line from which he would never return.

"You told them where to find us though, didn't you?" she accused.

With the eyes of the room boring into him, Ivan took a second to make sure his voice would come out calm and in control when he said, "No. I provided a false address for the event. If they come looking for him, they will be a block away from our current location at The Grand Hotel. I fooled this one," he poked Garfield with the toe of his right shoe, "into thinking we had to park and walk because there would not be enough parking here. If they come looking for him, they will be in the wrong place."

"And he wasn't followed? He has no tracker on him?" Chelsea wasn't about to let Ivan off the hook.

"He was followed, but I made sure to lose them on the way here and he was searched on the way in, as was I. The security at the door," he didn't need to mention that Chelsea was responsible for event security, "found nothing on him to indicate anyone might know where he is."

Garfield sagged a little. It was all true. He was in trouble.

Sylvia pursed her lips, thinking.

"Okay, dispose of him, but don't do it here. Put him somewhere safe for now and deal with him after the event."

The blow to the back of Garfield's skull stole his consciousness before he had a chance to consider whether helping Dani out had been the best idea.

Chapter 54

C ruising through the streets of Amsterdam, heading for the port, not away from it, Lee Yoo felt euphoric. The Nissan GTR was a joy to drive, but it was the thrill of victory that filled the wind beneath his wings.

He'd done it. He had all the cars and could call his uncle. He would have done so already but staying up all night with too many things going around in his head he'd completely forgotten to charge his phone and the stupid thing was dead.

It mattered little. He was on the home stretch and about to turn into the port. It felt like a victory lap, not least because he'd found the GTR so easy to steal.

For once it wasn't secured in Axel's garage inside the gated street in which he lived. The fool left it unattended along the street from Bitchin' Modifications just begging to be taken.

He'd never driven a GTR before, but now that he was, he had to admit it was something he could get used to. Maybe he would treat himself to one with the money he got from the order of cars. It would be a fitting gift and an insult in the face of a street racing rival who would suspect Lee was behind the theft of his prized possession yet unable to do anything about it.

He drove through the port wishing it was still daylight so he would be able to admire the Nissan properly, but the sun had all but set and now was not the time for preening. Now was the time to borrow a phone, let Uncle Kim know the order was complete, and get Sookie back.

Approaching the lockup, there was no reason to suspect that anything was wrong, and it wasn't until he angled in towards the front of the building that he spotted the thing that was amiss. The roller door was open for no good reason, but it was the lack of guards he noticed first.

That the guards were absent was going to get them a butt kicking, and he was still thinking evil thoughts in their direction when his brain finally caught up. The roller door was open, and that ought to have registered the moment he saw it, but it was the lack of cars parked in neat lines behind it that drove the shard of ice through his heart.

With a snatch of the brake pedal, he gawped through the windscreen in dumbfounded horror. The cars were gone. Not all of them, but even one would leave him short of Uncle Kim's order and Lee could see as many spaces as he could cars. The place had been raided.

Not by the police though, which was his first panicked thought. If the authorities were involved, they would still be here.

Numb and shaky, he rose from the car on unsteady legs. The gun in his jacket pocket was suddenly in his hand. He couldn't remember deciding to draw it, but holding it in both hands to keep it steady, he entered the lockup through the roller door.

It was worse than he could believe. Half the cars were gone, but whoever took them chose to cherry pick the best ones. The ones that would be nigh impossible to replace. The Maybach was gone. So too the Rolls Royce.

A muffled mumble came from his right and Lee almost put a bullet through the wall. The sound caught him by surprise at a time when he felt more stress than he ever had or believed he ever would. Wanting to hurt someone, he stalked toward the sound which still echoed out from the front office in an ever more insistent tone.

Halfway to it, Lee registered what he was hearing – the sound of someone yelling through a gag. Gun up and ready, he burst through the door hoping there would be someone beyond it he could shoot.

The guards he left behind stared up at him with frightened eyes. He almost shot them. They had let this happen, but he needed them to tell him who was behind it, so he tucked the gun into a back pocket and wrestled with the nearest man's gag.

He was going to get some answers, and then he was going to commit some murders.

Chapter 55

Rex looked up at the building. They had found it. It felt a little surreal given the challenges the day managed to throw at them. Yet there could be no doubt they were in the right place; he could detect the scent of the dogs from the warehouse and so could the rest of the pack.

The high they all suffered with all the associated side effects had diminished to a point where they were no longer aware of it. Finally lucid, Shadow Fang had been able to lead the pack to the pizza place and a thorough scout of the area led them to the back of the Grand Hotel where Battle Tank assured everyone he was brought to fight the previous time.

That didn't necessarily mean the next dog fight would be in the same place, so it was with great relief that Rex tracked the scent of the dogs still held captive to a door at the back of the venue.

There were two men guarding a ramp that led down to the subbasement. It was wide enough for vehicular traffic and high enough that large trucks could get in and out.

Rex led the pack to the edge of the fence where he made them wait for a van to turn in. That covered their entry, allowing them to slip in and around the humans. Pausing next to the ramp, the dogs peered into the subbasement.

"So what now?" asked Ball Biter. *"You want to rescue the ones we couldn't get out at the warehouse, but we are still just dogs, Rex."*

Rex drew a steadying breath through his nose and thought about slapping the Ridgeback on the nose.

"You see things from a very skewed perspective," he remarked. *"We are not 'still' just dogs. We are 'dogs' and therefore vastly superior to the humans even though they*

spend their lives trying to convince themselves the opposite is true. Their arrogance will be their undoing. Too dumb to think of us as threats, we will infiltrate their event and disrupt it, sabotaging where necessary to cover our escape. Our priority is to free the dogs they hold captive, never lose sight of that, but if you have a chance to repay them with a bite, do so only when exposing our presence will no longer thwart our mission."

The pack had no response to give. They gawped at Rex in much the same manner one might if he had just demonstrated how a dog could eat his own head.

"That was a lot of words," murmured Battle Tank, his tone full of reverential respect.

Ball Biter whispered in his ear, *"Yeah. What did any of it mean?"*

Rex jumped down to the ramp, leaving the pack scrambling to catch up.

Inside they could see and smell humans. Lots of them. The sight was enough to make the pack freeze at the open truck-sized entrance. There was another smell though or, more accurately, several of them.

They were unfamiliar to his nose, but Rex knew what they represented: wild animals. Carnivores for that matter. Recalling what Kevin told him about Hyenas at the last fight, Rex understood what the scent represented and why it was present. It was enough to make him want to go the other way, but he bit down on his fear and forced himself onward.

Rex walked a dozen paces before he sensed no one was following. Backtracking, he found his pack cowering among the recycling bins in the yard outside.

"What are we doing?" he enquired.

"Not going in there," whimpered Battle Tank. *"If they see us, they will catch us. All they have to do is shut the door and we will be trapped."*

"Until we let ourselves out through an emergency exit. All buildings have them."

"Yeah, but what if they cut us off?" questioned Shadow Fang. *"Those are the same people who snatched us from our humans. They locked us up and ..."*

"And treated you roughly?" Rex finished his sentence.

"*Very roughly,*" Shadow Fang agreed, wondering why Rex was trying to make his point.

"*And why did they do that?*" Rex asked the pack. When no one had an answer to offer he supplied one. "*So that you would learn to fight. They wanted to make you rough. To chip away the domesticated edge to reveal the animal instincts inside.*" His words were hitting home. "*Each of us is descended from wolves, the noblest beast ever to roam the planet. Now I don't give a stuff whether you lot come with me like the wolves that you are or cower out here like the frightened rabbits you appear to be, but I am going in there to free our captive brothers.*"

It was his second speech in as many minutes and there would not be a third.

Left outside when Rex headed back down the entrance ramp, the pack looked at each other, though they managed to do so without making eye contact with anyone else.

"*He laid that on a bit thick,*" complained Battle Tank.

Ball Biter stepped forward, his chest out and his head high. "*He was right though. It's time to be a wolf.*" He tipped back his head and was about to howl when Shadow Fang slapped a paw across his nose.

"*We get it. We're coming,*" he said, sotto voce. "*But let's not announce our arrival, eh?*"

They jogged after Rex, sticking to the edge of the slope and sneaking in using the columns, boxes, and parked catering vans as cover. Once inside, avoiding the humans required little more than some stealthy movement and patience, but they still had to find the dogs and get out.

Chapter 56

A lbert rubbed his palms on his trousers. They were clammy and his heart pounded with anticipation. They were moments away from the event and he knew he was about as far out of his depth as he ever got. Not on one single occasion in his long police career did he work undercover, yet here he was about to play the role of an ageing British billionaire playboy. The ageing part he figured would be easy enough, and the girls, Kerstin and Caprice, were dressed like they cost a million bucks a night to hire, so they supported the playboy concept, but he was just Albert Smith, a blue-collar man from a blue-collar background.

Infiltrating the dog fight event sounded like a good idea when it first occurred to him and it was far too late to back out now, but paranoia whispered in his ear and if the event security saw through him or suspected his invitation could be fake, then he and everyone he was with were in serious trouble.

Maybe he ought to have included the police in his plan. Maybe DCI Hoeks would have listened and agreed to support his play. It was too late now. Just a few minutes earlier they got a call to confirm Lee Yoo had arrived back at the lockup and their heist was known.

The caller, another of the street racers left behind with a buddy to watch and report, let Axel know Lee was driving his GTR.

Naturally, Axel had a few things to say about that, turning the air blue with his response. It changed nothing though; they were already committed to the plan. If it went the way they hoped, Axel would get his car back before the night was done.

"Ready?" asked Jerome as he stopped the car and two burly men in black suits stepped forward to get the door. He'd been able to recover his Nissan Skyline and was so over the moon about it he volunteered to be their driver for the night.

Was he ready? Albert knew that he wasn't, but to admit such a thing would put everyone else on edge, so he put on a smile and tried to channel his inner Hugh Hefner.

It seemed incongruous that they should be greeted at the hotel's main entrance like they were celebrities arriving for the Oscars. The Rolls Royce was in line behind a stretch limo which had another stretch limo in front of it. Behind them, a shiny Hummer with dazzling pink paintwork prowled toward the kerb, waiting to take their spot when the Rolls moved forward.

There was no paparazzi, no flashbulbs going off as people took pictures, but in all other ways it resembled the red-carpet events he'd seen on TV. It made him feel famous.

"Your invitation, sir?" requested one of the burly doormen. He was about as wide as two normal men, with hands like ham hocks and a face professionally devoid of expression. Faced with him, Albert observed how much like Ivan he looked. It made his pulse quicken again, a sense of dread weakening his confidence.

Was Ivan here tonight? Surely, he would be. There were lots of people around and he looked vastly different in appearance to the previous time they met, but if Caprice's ex-boyfriend spotted their party, the whole caper would fall apart in a heartbeat.

"Your invitation, sir?" the doorman repeated, this time with a little more force behind the words.

"Darling, what have you done with it?" demanded Kerstin, slipping her hand inside the paisley silk smoking jacket Albert wore. She found the slip of silver-embossed card, kissed Albert on his cheek with a look that would have made any man's toes curl, and handed it to the gorilla in the black suit.

It was filled out with a name 'Lord Henry Mountbatten' plus guests.

The doorman scrutinised it.

"Put your hand on my bottom," murmured Caprice.

"Hmm?" Albert wasn't sure he could have heard her right.

"Put your hand on my backside," she whispered with a little more urgency. "You're supposed to be a lecherous old playboy out with two gold diggers. Now play the role, grab my ass, and give it a squeeze!"

Feeling distinctly uncomfortable about it, Albert nevertheless did as he was told, angling his face down to nibble on Caprice's neck as he fondled her derriere. She giggled coquettishly, biting her lip as she stared at him with hungry eyes.

Not to be outdone, Kerstin acted jealous, pressing her ample cleavage into Albert as she tried to get his attention.

The display worked, distracting the doorman enough that his attention was off the fake invitation. One of their biggest concerns was what the real ones looked like when filled in. Were they all typed? Handwritten with a calligraphy pen? They had no way of knowing, so made it look fancy and hoped for the best. Distracting the doorman was nothing more than an additional strategy to aid their entry.

A horn beeped, the guests inside the Hummer becoming impatient.

Looking up, the doorman handed the invitation back to Albert and turned his attention to the next car in line.

"Have a great evening," he remarked in an automatic manner when they passed him trailed by his four security guards.

"Wow," hissed Caprice once they were inside and away from ears that might hear. "I thought we were busted for sure."

Albert nodded, aiming for a person holding a tray of champagne. It had been some years since either of his hands traced the soft curve of a lady's bottom, and perhaps five decades since his wife's felt as toned as Caprice's. He needed something else in his hand to shunt the memory sideways and a drink to calm his nerves.

They were in and that was the first hurdle negotiated, but now the real challenge began.

Guests were being funnelled away from the hotel lobby no sooner than they entered it. A carpet lined on either side with gold brocaded rope attached to waist high gold posts led them to a set of double doors. There was nothing special about the doors. No sign on the outside announcing what lay beyond. No floral displays on either side suggesting the portal would lead to somewhere interesting, but there were two more burly doormen waiting to check the invitations for a second time.

On the other side of the lobby in large gold letters, above a wide archway, the word 'Casino' announced what lay beyond. Albert had imagined that was where they would be heading, but that was clearly not the case. If anything, they appeared to be heading for a behind-the-scenes area.

The next two security guards were thankfully not Ivan either and they passed them with a nod and the most cursory of glances.

Albert aimed a glance back into the hotel lobby just before he left it. The staff behind the counter and at the concierge desk were paying no attention to the line of people passing through one end of the ornate reception area. It was as if they were oblivious. Did they even know what was happening beneath them?

The double doors led to an elevator operated by an attractive young woman in a sleek cocktail dress. She wore a radio on her right upper arm with a wire taped to her skin that led around her shoulder to her ear, and a badge pinned on her left breast to identify her as staff not guest.

Albert's party rode down, the quiet music in the car doing nothing to displace the nerves they each felt.

The doors swished open, spilling noise from outside as they walked out into the cavernous room beyond. Music and the hubbub of conversation competed for dominance with neither winning. Servers glided through the crowd with trays of drinks. Albert downed the one he had and took another as did Caprice and Kerstin. Albert smiled at the irony of taking Dutch courage in Holland.

They walked through the press of people. There were too many to count, but Albert estimated attendance to be several hundred. There had been cars still arriving when they moved inside the hotel, so the numbers would continue to swell.

It worked to their advantage – the more people there were, the easier it would be to slip away.

Moving farther into the room, they came across a fenced off area marked 'Pit One'. Roughly ten feet by ten feet, it had an open top and two doors set into opposite sides. Yet another burly guard in a black suit stood watch over it. The pit was clearly intended to house two combatants although thankfully it was empty still.

A pianist at a grand piano tinkled melodies next to a bar brought in for the occasion. It created the illusion of class and elegance at an event that turned Albert's stomach. Were all these people really here to witness animals fighting? How were they okay with that?

Next to the bar, a cluster of booths housed the bookkeepers behind Perspex screens. Alcohol, gambling, and rich people; how could the organisers possibly lose?

Albert pushed his dissection of human depravity from his mind. He was here to get Rex, that was all. Well, that and topple the people behind it all plus ruin the car thieves' night if he could get away with it.

He turned around intending to move deeper into the room, but hadn't looked where he was going. He bumped into a man, jogging his arm and spilling his drink.

"Goodness, I'm so sorry," he apologised.

The man looked annoyed, but forced a smile onto his face even as he shook the spilled champagne from his fingers. He peered at Albert through thick glasses.

"It's nothing," he replied from lips pulled out of shape by a large scar that ran from his mouth all the way to his left ear.

The next part of their plan was almost certainly the riskiest and the one most likely to get them caught. Since entering the room, Albert, the girls and the four guys dressed as security guards had all been focused on finding doors leading backstage. Wait staff were coming and going as they would at any event; bringing trays of glasses filled with champagne or loaded with canapes, and returning with the empties. There were others who were easy to identify as part of the organisation from their radios and handheld tablets. Likewise they used the doors set into the walls but each one Albert and his crew found had a security guard placed by it to ensure no one unauthorised could trespass.

To get past them they were going to have to create a distraction.

Chapter 57

Rex froze his body, the pack tucked in close behind his tail doing likewise. They were deep into the bowels of the subbasement, letting their noses lead them where they needed to go. They were closing in on the dogs, but the other scents, the worrying ones he couldn't identify with any accuracy, were in the same direction.

There were humans in every direction, but not so many that they couldn't find places to hide. Hunkered down behind some boxes, Rex watched two go by. They were talking and walking, too oblivious to notice the pack of dogs hiding just a few feet away. Rex usually despaired for the human inability to smell that which was right in front of them. Tonight it worked in his favour and he was glad of it.

When the coast was clear, he started forward again. The scent of the captive dogs was close; their fear and anxiety blending into one awful odour, but the other smells were closer.

He led the pack across the open floor of the subbasement, keeping to the outer edge since the centre was a wide-open space in which even the stupid humans would manage to spot them. Weaving around boxes of pallets stacked three or four deep, they reached a door and knew they had found where the animals were being kept.

Rex stopped again, this time turning around to face the rest of the pack. Forced to halt abruptly, the ones at the back didn't get the message fast enough so they walked into the rear end of the dogs ahead.

Gritting his teeth at the quiet sound of multiple apologies and 'excuse mes', Rex said, "*We've found them. They are just inside, but there are humans with them. Find hiding spots and stay out of sight until I call you. We might have to ramraid them to overwhelm the guards, but I'll know more once I've had a better look around. If we all go, they will see us for sure."*

Instructions delivered, Rex watched for just long enough to be sure the pack was complying. Then with a deep breath, he slipped through the door.

The dogs were not in the next room, but now he could see where the strange animal smell was coming from. Arranged in cages of various sizes, wild animals glared through their bars, paced, or just looked miserable. They were unhappy, as Rex acknowledged they ought to be, but there could be no question why they were here – they were part of the entertainment.

He'd never seen a bear before, but he knew what one was. It wasn't a large one; Rex doubted it was even fully grown, but it was five times his size and ten times heavier. He wouldn't want to fight it. Across from the bear, a large cat prowled.

"A cat?" Rex questioned.

When it spotted the German Shepherd looking its way, it stopped pacing, narrowed its eyes, and hissed a string of expletives.

"I'm not a cat! I'm a lynx, and if you're my opponent later, I'm going to take great glee demonstrating why cats rule and dogs drool. I'll tear you into confetti!"

That woke a black lump that unfolded to reveal a honey badger. Just along from it a wolverine looked up, and beyond that the next cage contained a Komodo dragon.

Inspired by the lynx, the other animals went berserk. The rising cacophony of noise drew the attention of the nearest humans.

"Here, what's got into them?" asked an unseen voice.

Rex ducked out of the way, darting into cover just before booted feet arrived to check the animals. He shouted and banged on the cages, demanding quiet which only served to make the animals louder. The lynx slashed at the human when his face came near the cage, but Rex didn't hang around to watch. The noise acted as cover for him to sneak through the next door where finally he found what he was looking for.

Now in the same room, he could filter out all the other smells and pick out the scents of the individual dogs. Many of them were curled into balls inside their cages, doing their best to block out the truth that was their immediate future. Others were sitting up, but none were making any noise until they saw Rex.

"*Hey! Hey, over here!*" cried a Doberman, desperate to get his attention.

"*Help us,*" barked another. "*Get us out!*"

"*Rex!*" barked Brain Scar.

There were more dogs than he expected; the humans had replaced the escapees with new animals presumably snatched in the last twenty-four hours. They looked utterly bewildered by their predicament.

Rex begged for quiet; their cries would draw people, but they were too desperate to listen or even hear him. Frustrated, he searched the line of cages, looking for one dog in particular. He was here to get them all out, but his personal promise, delivered dog to dog, had more meaning when it came to Kevin.

The giant Bullmastiff occupied the last cage in the row, filling it from top to bottom with his enormous frame as he pressed his head against the bars and wagged his tail like mad.

Rex bounded over to him.

"*I can't believe you are here,*" Kevin blurted. "*How did you do this? How did you find us?*"

Rex said, "*I had some help,*" but his attention was not so much on Kevin, but the padlock securing the latch on his cage where the peg used to be.

He couldn't open it. A step back to look down the line of cages confirmed his worse fear; they were all the same. He was determined and he was both strong and resourceful, but no dog on the planet could defeat a steel padlock.

"*What is it?*" Kevin asked, knowing it had to be bad from the look on Rex's face. "*Is it the locks? They fitted them after you escaped. You can't open the cages, can you?*"

Rex gritted his teeth, forcing his brain to work the problem.

"*It's okay,*" Kevin soothed. "*You did more than anyone else could have. That you found us is amazing. Now do what you should have done in the first place and save yourself.*"

Rex backed away. The longer he hung around, the more likely he was to get caught. And it wasn't just him. He'd brought the escapees here, right back into the last place on Earth they wanted to be. If he didn't get them out again soon ...

"Hey!"

The shout brought Rex's head around to see a man heading his way.

Kevin barked, "*Go!*" jolting Rex into motion.

He pushed off with his back paws, twisting his body around to get away. He would achieve nothing if he was caught, but the padlocks made it all but impossible to free the captives, and now that he'd been spotted, everything would get a good deal harder.

It pained him to admit it, but what he needed, what he could not hope to succeed without, was human help. Where the heck was Albert when he needed him?

Chapter 58

Albert skidded to a stop, his shoes sliding across the tiled floor. They were through the door but had to do it at a run.

Caprice and Kerstin volunteered to distract the guard, but getting his eyes pointing the wrong way wasn't going to be enough, so Caprice's offer to 'accidentally' spill out of her dress went on the backburner in favour of a plan that would shift him away from the door he blocked.

It involved a fight in which Kerstin shoved Caprice, hair got pulled, one got slammed into the guard and a drink went straight in his face. He was professional enough that he stayed at his post until a replacement could arrive, but the ten seconds where he was blinded and trapped between Caprice and Kerstin, who continued trying to scratch each other's eyes out, was all the men needed to shoot through the door and close it again.

Albert's pace being less than the younger men, they elected to drive him ahead of them with their hands hence the skidding shoes when they let him go.

They were in the rearward area, the biggest hurdle negotiated, but now the real test began for they had achieved nothing so far. The black suits Axel and the others wore came close enough in design that they would pass unseen until someone took a closer look at them. They had a simple enough mission and were splitting off to complete it.

Albert stood out like a sore thumb in his paisley smoking jacket and cravat, but his age worked for him. Anyone discovering him would find a bewildered old man unsure where he'd taken a wrong turn on his way to the restrooms. That was his plan at least.

He shook hands with the four men, wishing them luck for the task they had to complete, and struck out deeper into the subbasement to find his dog.

There was no path to follow, no direction that suggested success more than any other. Creeping about in the corridors, the muffled sound from the function room filtered through in the form of a bass beat and general background noise. It helped to hide his footfall but by the same token hid the approach of those he needed to hide from.

After five minutes that felt more like five hours, Albert froze when he heard barking. It made his heart soar to know he was in the right place, but the sound had bounced through the corridors before it reached his ears and he could not be sure if it came from in front or behind his current location.

Sucking some air between his teeth, he was about to make his choice when someone cleared their throat.

"Excuse me, sir. You appear to be lost."

Albert rearranged his face, making his features that of a confused old man with a spotty memory. Turning, he found one of the black-suited security guards blocking the path to his rear. It was time to engage his best acting mode, but as he sucked in a breath to deliver the line he'd practiced, his heart sunk.

The guard sported a wide grin. The guard was Ivan van der Pol.

Chapter 59

Rex lay flat on a stack of boxes high above the humans to watch them rush by beneath. Not one of them had the imagination to look up. Losing the man who first spotted him took no more than a few seconds, but the precarious situation he started with when he led the pack right back into enemy waters, was a good deal more dangerous now.

The humans knew there was a dog on the loose and were looking for him. Maybe he would continue to give the humans the slip, but what about Battle Tank, Ball Biter, and the others? He'd all but forced them into following his risky plan and would do anything to make sure they got out again. It was supposed to be with every captive dog in tow, but Rex failed to consider what action the humans might take in response to his escape. Of course they improved the cage security. He showed the fighting dogs how to get out and they would have continued to do so were there not now a padlock fitted to defeat their best efforts.

He cursed his luck and thought about how he could cut his losses. His mission had to change. Rex would get the pack back outside where they could put some distance between themselves and their captors. It would be the last he saw of them, casting them into the city to find their own way because he was coming back.

If it was the last thing he ever did, he was going to keep his promise to get Kevin out. They would take him from his cage when the time came for his fight and that would give Rex a chance to strike. They wouldn't expect it and with the element of surprise he would ...

Rex stopped thinking about Kevin and how to get him out. He stopped moving in the same way that a glacier can be considered quite good at staying still. His nose had just detected a smell and he needed to be sure it wasn't his imagination.

Rising to his feet on top of the boxes, even though it increased his visibility, he sniffed deeply. His tail twitched in excitement, freezing again a half heartbeat later when he forced himself to concentrate. Rex looked around, checking for smell, sight, or sound of humans before jumping down to the next pallet and then to the floor.

His human was here.

There could be no mistaking his scent; Rex was more familiar with it than any other on the face of the planet.

Albert was here and in the wag of a tail Rex had a solution to his problem. He couldn't open the padlocks, but the old man could. Feeling euphoric, he set off to find him.

Chapter 60

DCI Garfield was starting to think in terms of defeat. It seemed ridiculous that he would perish from the cold, but there was no way to fight the temperature in the freezer. Completely devoid of light, without his phone or watch, and doing all he could to stay warm, he had no clue how much time might have passed since they closed the door, but he felt sluggish and tired.

His brain was cold. It felt like there was ice running through his veins. Star jumps worked to get his heart pumping and blood flowing initially, but there was only so many he could do before the balance of fatigue worked against him.

That's where he found himself, teetering on the edge of accepting his fate and lying down to sleep when a blinding shaft of light lasered through his eyeballs. Someone was opening the door.

"Get in there," growled Ivan van der Pol, one meaty hand giving Albert a rough shove that sent him windmilling into the freezer. Catching sight of Garfield shielding his eyes, he chuckled, "What are you doing still alive? I thought the cold would have got you by now."

He knew Sylvia would want to know there was an intruder poking around looking for his dog, but now was not the time to disturb her. The first of the dogs were being taken to the main pit for the fight that would get the night underway. He would deal with the old man and let her know later. Perhaps much later. He knew what instructions she would give and believed he would be commended for his initiative.

Garfield knew this was his chance. Perhaps the only one he would get. His foggy brain identified Albert Smith as the old man coming to join him, and that he was dressed very differently to his usual attire. That didn't matter though. Only getting out mattered. He had to get his body to move.

With a determined shout to underpin his effort, he surged forward.

Except he didn't. The message to make his right foot move left his brain and arrived at its destination, but the cold numbing Garfield's muscles stopped them from operating. He stumbled and fell, crashing into the icy floor with his head up to watch the freezer door swinging shut again.

The light from outside was being cut off inch by inch until a blur of something ripped Ivan away and the remaining foot of light stayed where it was.

Confused, Garfield heard growling, snapping and cries of pain. He watched Albert Smith run back out through the still open freezer door with a frozen chicken in his hands. He raised it above his head, turned right, and vanished from sight.

Garfield had not one clue what sound a frozen chicken would make when smashed over someone's head until he heard it. Shivering uncontrollably, he watched a drumstick bounce back into sight a second before everything outside went quiet.

The quiet didn't last long.

Like an oak felled in the wilderness, Ivan van der Pol crashed backward to the floor doing nothing to protect himself from the impact. A small cloud of dust billowed out, washing over Garfield's face with the blissful warmth of the air beyond the freezer. All he had to do was get there. Focussing every fibre of his being, he started to crawl.

The dog came back into view, sniffing the inert form now blocking the freezer entrance. To Garfield's sluggish brain it looked as though the dog was checking Ivan was unconscious. Somewhere deep inside his head, he associated the German Shepherd with Albert Smith. It was his dog. The wily old detective had found and freed him before he got caught in the process of escaping.

Edging toward the door, Garfield was looking right at the dog when it turned around to face him and gleefully lifted a back leg to urinate on Ivan's head.

Albert reappeared. "Good work, Rex." He patted the dog's skull and looked down at the man in the freezer.

"Police," Garfield managed to wheeze and stutter through his frozen lips. "I'm police."

Albert was coming to help him up anyway. No one deserved to be locked in a freezer to die of the cold, but he would have guessed the man was police anyway. He looked like a cop and who else would the bad guys lock up?

Back on his feet and free of the freezer, Garfield leaned against the wall.

"I say," Albert held him upright. "I don't mean to hurry you, but I can't shift this lump by myself and I rather think he ought to cool off."

Garfield got Albert's meaning and agreed wholeheartedly. He still needed a minute to massage some life back into his limbs.

"Get his phone," Garfield stammered through chattering teeth. "Must call for backup."

Placing a knee on Ivan's chest, Albert patted him down, but he was looking for his own phone as much as he was Ivan's.

Ivan didn't appear to have one; he was wearing a radio instead which Albert hastily removed, however Albert's phone was inside Ivan's jacket. Extracting it from an inside pocket, he turned it over to find it was smashed and lifeless. Pointlessly he prodded the screen which remained resolutely black. They couldn't call for backup, but it didn't worry him. What the half-frozen police officer didn't know was that they were not alone.

Albert had brought some friends with him.

Chapter 61

A xel, Fishman, Pixie, and Shaggy had a simple task to complete.

The street racers were prowling the area around the hotel with the cars taken from Lee Yoo's lockup. To bring both the police and the Korean car thieves to the same location, they had to make sure their friends could get in. That meant accessing the street entrance to the subbasement and making sure it was open.

Albert believed the Koreans would crash the party prepared to do anything to regain that which they had already stolen once. Until now the street racers had kept the police at arm's length; they were not considered to be allies. However, when Albert said they could employ law enforcement as a tool to cover their escape while simultaneously placing the car thieves in the stolen cars and disrupting an illegal dog fighting event, it became a no brainer.

They could get their cars back and know the Koreans wouldn't be coming after them again. Put like that they had no option but to go along with the old Englishman's mad plan.

They made it to the ramp leading to the street unopposed. In turn it led to a service yard at street level and then via a gate into the road. The gate wasn't even closed.

Shaggy was just about to venture up the ramp when Fishman caught his arm and pointed. There were two guards outside.

Thankful to be dressed much like event security even if they were all much smaller men, they approached the guards outside as confidently as they could. Much of the confidence came from the planks of wood they tore from an old pallet. Hidden behind their backs, they proved to be surprisingly effective as non-lethal weapons.

Guards neutralised and disarmed, a single group text message mobilised the street racers, more than twenty of them setting off to converge on the venue. The next task was to call the police, but it was too soon for that. Go too early and the Koreans would see the police and withdraw. The police would confiscate the cars to leave Axel and his friends in the firing line of a professional criminal organisation. Axel had no idea what they were capable of and had no desire to find out.

Waiting nervously, Axel and the guys prayed Albert was having as much luck.

Chapter 62

"Come on!" Rex begged. He was overwhelmed with happiness to be back with the old man, but he needed him to see the cages. Albert clearly wanted to go the other way, but Rex wasn't leaving until the dogs were free and Albert was just the man for the task. "*It's this way!*" he whined and huffed, dancing down the corridor and keeping out of reach to make Albert follow.

Albert didn't know what had gotten into his dog, but he knew Rex well enough to accept he was trying to tell him something.

"I'm coming, boy," Albert jogged to keep up. DCI Garfield was with him and that had slowed them down, but the local detective was coming out of his frozen state and it felt good to have an ally at his side.

"*It's just along here,*" Rex chuffed. He wanted to bark but was still trying to be stealthy. They needed to avoid the humans working here for just a few more minutes. Once the dogs were out, all bets were off.

He reached the door to the room with the cages where he checked inside. It was full of dogs, but devoid of people. Perfect.

Rex waited for Albert to get nearer, then danced through the door, his paws excited.

"*Guys! Kevin! I've found my human. He's going to get you all out!*"

His announcement drew barks of excitement from almost every cage though Rex was too distracted watching Albert to see what was missing.

The sight of the dogs in their cages shocked Albert. In his life he'd witnessed many examples of human cruelty and greed, but this was something different. Somehow, exploiting animals was worse than doing the same to people. It disgusted him and he was glad to be able to do something about it.

The keys were in the padlocks, the set of two each lock came with hanging from the hole with one key inside to make opening the cages easy. Albert and Garfield threw themselves into the task, ripping each cage open and moving on while making encouraging sounds at the nervous animals inside.

Seeing the dogs being freed, Rex ran to the end of the line where he wanted to reassure Kevin. It was only when he arrived at the Bullmastiff's cage that he realised he was yet to hear his friend's voice. Kevin's cage was empty.

Absorbing the sight even as he denied it was true, Rex turned to the next cage where a boxer dog stood waiting for his turn to be released.

"*Where's Kevin?*" Rex asked.

The boxer didn't even look his way when he replied. "*Went for his fight. They are using him to open the event. He's up against Brain Scar. I think they said something about a David and Goliath match to get the punters betting on the wrong horse. Now if you can pick that apart and make any sense out of it, you let me know.*" He turned his head to see what Rex had to say only to find the space where he'd stood now empty.

Peering around, he questioned, "*Rex?*"

Chapter 63

Axel allowed himself to believe they had not been spotted lurking by the ramp, but that was because it took a while for the subbasement team to bring enough security guys through to the back area.

They were seen sneaking around by a forklift driver called Frederick. Everyone at the event was part of Sylvia van Lidth's organisation, not that he'd ever met her, but he understood why he was paid so much for a single night's work and what would happen if the authorities showed up.

He wasn't about to tackle or even challenge the four men who clearly were not part of event security, but he did find someone who could. The person Frederick found was Vincent, one of the dog handlers who said he was trying to find an escaped dog. He had a radio which he used to alert the security team once he had Frederick show him the supposed intruders – he wasn't about to embarrass himself creating a drama for no good reason.

Eight members of event security gathered in the subbasement. Each felt they could probably take on the four ordinary sized men by themselves, but were sufficiently well trained to park their egos and wait to have overwhelming numbers.

They drew their weapons, an assortment of automatic handguns, and advanced. Coming from behind the four men, who were tucked into an alcove by the ramp, Jeroen took the lead.

"Show me hands now. All of you."

Axel spun around, startled by the sudden voice. His friends did likewise, all four of them with nowhere to go and no weapons with which they could hope to defend themselves.

"Lose the guns," Vincent barked. "Do it slowly."

"We don't have any guns," Axel replied, feeling foolish. They disarmed the two guards left at the back entrance but threw their guns into the trash. They didn't want them.

The guards grinned, finding the four intruders amusing now that they knew how little threat they posed. They would be interrogated to determine who they were and what they were up to. There would be pain related incentive to provide answers if they were crazy enough to resist, and then they would be made to vanish forever regardless of who they were.

Jeroen had four of his number holster their weapons. They would use their hands if the captives got out of hand, but as he called the intruders to come forward, his eyes were drawn to a flash of headlights coming in through the gate.

They angled down, descending the ramp, but where they ought to have slowed, they were going faster instead.

Jeroen got half a second to realise he was directly in the path of a speeding car before it hit his legs and flipped him over the bonnet. The same car took out two more of the guards, the rest managing to narrowly dive out of the way.

Evading the car saved them from injury but not for long as the next car in line swept past the first to clip another guard and the third car went after yet another. Axel and pals ran to get into the mix as more and more of their street racers' friends poured down the ramp and into the wide-open space beyond.

They spilled from their cars, joining the fight to overpower the guards because no one wanted to miss the action. They would be talking about this for years.

Eyes wide, Frederick watched the security guards lose and slipped away. He had to warn someone. He had to warn Sylvia van Lidth.

Chapter 64

R ex ran, following the dual scents of Brain Scar and Kevin. The Bullmastiff was five times the Pitbull's size, but he would lose anyway. It wasn't a fight where size provided an advantage. Kevin was gentle in nature. There wasn't an ounce of fight in him, whereas Brain Scar was imbued with natural aggression and the ability to lock his jaw once he had hold of something.

Not that Rex held Brain Scar responsible for what would happen when the fight started. He would fight because he was given no choice. Well, Rex intended to upset the way things were expected to be.

The scent led him to a door, but it was fitted with a handle, not a push bar like an emergency exit would be. It presented a challenge but not one he would allow to defeat him.

He jumped up at it, clawing the handle with his paws. He could push it down but not enough to make it open. Rex didn't know it, but the door hinged inward, so no matter how hard he tried, he was never going to get through it. So it was luck that the guard outside saw the handle moving, assumed there was someone on the other side with their hands full, and opened it himself.

Rex shot out, going through the startled guard's legs to promptly vanish into the mass of people.

The guard grabbed for his radio, the message reaching the ears of Sylvia van Lidth just a moment later. She was supposed to be sipping champagne and watching proceedings from a raised dais ringed off from everyone else, but things were not as they should be. Ivan, one of her personal protection detail, had gone missing, the front desk had reported a phoney invitation – the invite itself was real, but the name on it was fake – and she'd just been informed of intruders in the subbasement. The last of those concerns was in hand – Jeroen had taken some men to deal with it – yet these were all things that did not happen at her events.

It all started with the inconceivable dog break out and was getting worse. The only items of good news were that the first fight was about to start so the guests would be entertained and never know the problems going on in the background, and that the takings had already hit a new record.

A few hours from now it would all be over, and her thoughts would turn to how they could make the next one less problematic. Right now, she just wanted to hear the sound of dogs tearing into each other. Sylvia looked up when startled screams and cries of surprise lit the air around the central pit.

Rex had needed a good run up to clear the fence around it, but yanked back to Earth by gravity, he hit the floor directly between Brain Scar and Kevin.

Brain Scar's back legs were bunched and he'd been about to attack. Goaded by the humans baying and yelling all around, he knew there was no way out other than to fight. Until Rex appeared from the sky as if by magic.

"*That's enough now,*" Rex commanded. "*It's time to get out of here and that means you too, Dodger.*"

"*Dodger?*" Brain Scar questioned.

"*Brain Scar is the stupid name your human handler gave you for the fighting circuit. Well, I'm giving you a new name. One that a human child might give to the puppy they got to grow up with.*"

Brain Scar sat back on his haunches.

"What the heck is this?" asked one of the punters. "Why aren't they fighting?"

"Yeah," chipped in another. "And what's with the German Shepherd? What's his part in this?"

Dodger? Brain Scar liked it. He also liked the idea of a human to live with or a child that would love him as a best pal. Getting back to his feet, he puffed out his chest.

"*What do you need me to do?*"

The level of complaint around the pit rose to a new level and one of the handlers stepped forward with a prod. It would deliver an electric shock of pain that would get the Pitbull going. The Mastiff was going to get one too.

Except when he jabbed it through the fence, the Pitbull took off. He ran at the Bullmastiff to make everyone think he was finally getting on with the fight. Kevin watched him coming and spat out his little teddy so he would be ready.

At the last moment, Kevin dropped his head, presenting the newly named Dodger with a ramp. The Pitbull leapt, landed on Kevin's back, and kicked off to sail over the top of the pit's upper edge. In the air with his tongue flapping from the side of his mouth, his choice of aiming mark was a woman with a snack in her hand. It was halfway to her mouth when she registered what was happening.

She fell backward with a scream of terror, Dodger riding her down to the floor like she was a magic carpet wearing a cocktail dress. A magic carpet with in-flight snacks. Her head hit the floor with a crack, Dodger snatched the snack from her hand, and vanished through the crowd with a triumphant bark.

Kevin laughed a gleeful, rueful sigh. He was glad to see another dog claim his freedom, but could see no way that he and Rex were going to do the same.

Turning to his friend, he asked, *"Got any other tricks up your sleeve?"*

Chapter 65

Albert couldn't believe that he'd lost Rex again. Reunited for five minutes, his best friend had wandered off once more.

There were two dozen dogs milling around his legs. The breeds varied but apart from a Staffordshire bull terrier they were all large animals, some of which reached his waist.

There were no leads or collars for the dogs, and too many of the brutes for the two men to hope to control even if they had them. Albert didn't care though. It was time to leave. DCI Garfield insisted it was time to call for reinforcements.

"I've got SWAT waiting," he told Albert. "They just need to know where to go."

"I have to find my dog," Albert replied though he was already heading for the door.

"I promise I will give you officers to help find him when we secure the place. You can stay here and look, but I have to find a phone. Nothing is more important right now than bringing in the cavalry."

Albert pursed his lips and nodded.

"I'm coming with you and so are the dogs."

"What are you going to do with them all?"

Albert grinned. "Cause utter bedlam."

It was a fight to get the door open, the dogs were pressing against it in their haste to get away from their cages, but once it was open they ran through it like a canine tide. Straight into his fake bodyguards.

"Albert!" cheered Axel. "I see you found your dog!"

"And lost him again."

"Huh?"

Albert waved the question away, hastening after the dogs. "This is DCI Garfield. He was being held captive."

"Who are these guys?" Garfield wanted to know, eyeing the black suits dubiously.

"Some friends of mine," Albert said over one shoulder as he puffed along the corridor after the dogs. "Did you call the police?" he asked Axel.

"Yup. About two minutes ago. We ran into a little ... local resistance," he found a phrase that worked. "But the um ... goods are here, and we know the fish took the bait ..." In deference to the DCI, Axel selected his words carefully, talking in code in the hope they could avoid being associated with the stolen cars now parked at the bottom of the ramp. "Everyone already left via the back entrance. We should head that way too."

"I can't," Albert apologised. "I have to find Rex. He's here somewhere and we already checked all around. I think he's in the event room."

Axel frowned. "What would he be doing in there?"

The dogs reached a door leading through to the party and unable to open it found themselves temporarily trapped. The humans arrived behind them, the street racers just about equalling the number of dogs as they filled the narrow space between the walls.

At the head, Pixie had to battle to get through the sea of excited fur, but before he could get there, the screams could be heard coming from the other side. Bedlam had already ensued and Albert could guess why.

Allowing himself a smile, he said, "Rex."

Chapter 66

Rex and Kevin ran at the side of the pit. Rex had been able to jump in, but there wasn't enough run up room to perform the same stunt from the inside. They needed a different way out, and Rex was willing to bet the temporary structure would yield if they hit it hard enough. He wouldn't be able to pull it off by himself, but Kevin's fighting name of 'Dreadnought' could not have been more apt.

They hit the fence, shunting one side back an inch. The feet were secured not with bolts into the floor, but with heavy plates that pinned them down. A few more hits and the feet would all be displaced.

The handler jabbed the electric prod into Rex's flank drawing a yelp of pain. He didn't know what else to do. The dogs were going mad.

He pulled back to aim another jab only to find it stopped dead. The Bullmastiff had the shaft clamped in his jaws. His eyes were locked on the man holding it.

In a deeply dangerous voice, he growled, "*Leave my friend alone,*" before spitting it out again.

The handler was giving it a yank when it came free, landing him painfully on his rump with a shocked look on his face.

The scene was already one of chaos, but it was mostly down to guests demanding their bets be refunded. The booths by the bar were twenty deep with irate rich people shouting to be heard.

Sylvia van Lidth watched it all with panic etched into her eyes. Her biggest concern running up to the event was getting hold of the right dogs and staging fights her guests would talk about for months to come. Never in her wildest dreams could she have imagined a debacle of this scale.

Chelsea and the rest of Sylvia's senior team were looking for direction, but she had none to give. Thinking things couldn't possibly get any worse, she regretted the errant thought when the first shots were fired.

All eyes turned to the direction of the elevator as a dozen armed thugs with Korean features emerged from it toting machine guns. To have made it that far they had to have gone through the security team at the entrance.

The nearest of Sylvia's men went for his gun only to be cut down before it cleared the holster. After that, and amid wails of panic from both men and women, hands went into the air.

Lee Yoo stepped into the room.

"I want Axel Janssen and I want him now."

Like everyone else in the room except Kerstin and Caprice, who had been nervously keeping out of the way, Sylvia had not the first idea who that was, but she didn't get to raise her question.

A voice rang out to silence everyone.

"Nephew? What are you doing here?"

The presence of Uncle Kim rooted Lee Yoo to the spot, but only for a second. He was too angry to be scared any longer, too full of the need to balance the scales to back down meekly as he always had before.

Uncle Kim was coming his way, passing through the crowd with displeasure etched on his face.

"What is the meaning of this? Weapons on display so blatantly. Have you lost your mind?"

"No, Uncle," Lee spat. "I think I am finally seeing things clearly. Perhaps for the first time. The cars are gone, Uncle. Taken from me while I chased after the final model missing from your order. Your impossible order! No one could have found all those cars. No one, and you knew it. So I got the last one and while I did someone broke into the lockup and took half of the order." He had his machine gun pointed at his uncle, but his elder relative acted as though it was unimportant.

"The cars? Half the cars are gone? Tell me this is some kind of elaborate joke." They were already filled with product, the high-grade drug hidden in the door panels, under the seats, and tucked anywhere they could possibly stow it.

The room was almost silent. The sound of the two men talking interrupted only by the sound from the central pit where Rex and Kevin were still trying to break free. Lee Yoo's men had spread out, each man aiming his weapon roughly into the crowd. Around the periphery, more of Sylvia's guards were slowly moving into positions where they were hard to see, but could open fire if a response could be coordinated.

The problem with hired henchmen in all situations where leadership is needed to unify their effort, stems from the simple fact that they have no hierarchy or rank structure. With such constructs, the moment the situation exceeds the bounds of the instructions provided, no one is in charge.

However, that does not mean they are not capable of individual thought. Having picked himself off the floor after the German Shepherd ran through his legs barely more than a minute ago, Hans Lunstrum, a German Norwegian travelling Europe for work, thought it wise to take command.

Whispering into his radio, he told everyone with a weapon to be ready to step out and fire at the latest intruders upon his count.

"Three, two ..."

Chapter 67

"O..."

Albert yanked the door open with all the force he could muster. The dogs exploded forth, sweeping into the room like a storm tide breaking through a levee's weak point.

A man stood just outside the door, he had his right arm up and extended to point a handgun. His mouth was open, forming an 'O' though Albert never got to learn what he might have been about to say because he was very suddenly lost beneath the dogs who took his legs out like bowling pins.

Garfield came through the door at Albert's side. He had Axel's phone in his hand and Captain Verbeek at the other end as he coordinated the police response. Seeing the felled gunman struggling to get up, he relieved him of his weapon.

Rex and Kevin burst free of the pit just in time for the pack of dogs to find them. Yelps and barks and general excitement filled the function room with noise. They were out of their cages and so far as the now enlarged pack was concerned, there was nothing to stop them escaping into the city.

Lee Yoo couldn't believe what he was seeing. The venue was madness. There were dogs all over the place, surrounding the quivering humans in their elegant evening wear. His uncle was heading straight for him, his mannerisms that of a person who believes they are in charge and will be obeyed.

Lee shot him.

The bullet passed through Uncle Kim's left shoulder and continued across the room where it found the ice sculpture which elected to explode in spectacular fashion. Shards of ice burst into the air, showering those nearest to it, and crashed to the floor in a barrage of noise. It acted as the catalyst to a stampede.

The sea of over-privileged, highly panicked humanity trapped inside the venue ran for the doors. There were emergency exits in the walls along with the doors leading to the kitchen, stores, and the parking garage.

Lee Yoo looked up to watch them go, a hate-filled grimace pulling his features into an ugly leer.

Caprice and Kerstin had to fight to get across the room to Axel, dodging party guests constantly.

"Rex!" Albert bellowed.

"*Old man!*" Rex barked in reply. It was difficult to separate one human from another with so many of them running and screaming, but when a gap appeared, Rex found Albert. He was holding a door open and calling that he should move his rear end.

Rex charged through the pack of dogs. "*This way! Everyone with me! It's time to get out of here!*"

Albert's plan to lure the gang of Korean car thieves in had worked a treat, but no one expected them to arrive carrying machine guns. The police were coming, but until they arrived the Koreans had the upper hand and they looked murderous.

Accentuating that point, Lee Yoo raised his machine gun and fired a burst into the wall above everyone's heads.

The room was beginning to empty, and those still pushing to get through a door ducked instinctively. Except for an old man guiding the pack of dogs back out of the room and the man next to him.

"Axel Janssen!" Lee Yoo bellowed.

Axel swore. Lee was bringing his gun around, swinging it in their direction with a clear intention to fire.

Seeing it, DCI Garfield threw himself at the open doorway, arms wide to tackle Albert and Axel. The machine gun spat bullets, chewing the wall where their heads had just been. Hitting the floor in the corridor, the trio of men wasted no time scrambling to get their feet beneath their bodies.

Kerstin and Caprice were ahead of them beckoning for the guys to hurry up. Staying low, they all ran, Garfield helping Albert along as the last of the dogs whipped around their legs.

They heard Lee's cry of outrage and knew he would be following. Garfield had the gun he'd confiscated, but it was all too little against a gang of armed men.

Lee Yoo saw his quarry leave and set off after him.

Stepping over a blood trail he remembered his uncle. He had gone too, ducking out with everyone else while Lee's attention was split.

"Did anyone see where my uncle went?"

Song Bin, Park Ji Hoon, and the rest of Lee's men shook their heads. It was long past time they were somewhere else.

"We need to get out of here, Lee!" shouted Song, the words a worried plea. "The police will be coming. Let's get the cars and go!"

Showing his agreement with action, Lee started across the floor to the door Axel went through.

"My uncle has Sookie! If you see him, shoot him, but don't kill him. I want to do that myself."

Chapter 68

With Rex in the lead, the pack of dogs swarmed through the subbasement. They could smell the outside air spilling in through the parking garage entrance, but the smell was everywhere. Confused by the labyrinth of passageways, the air swirled and formed pockets.

"*Which way is it?*" someone called from within the pack.

Rex didn't know the answer, but believed they would find their way out if they just kept moving. Due to that policy they found themselves running back into the fleeing guests they'd overtaken thirty seconds earlier. The pack had completed three sides of a square and were coming back the way they'd already gone, albeit along a different corridor.

"Turn around!" yelled Albert. He was at the back of the group of guests and out of breath, but buoyed along by those around him and the threat of machine gun toting car thieves, he was moving as fast as he could.

Rex and the pack skidded to a stop in the narrow space where they created a complete roadblock until the message got to those at the back and they were able to reverse direction.

Running again, the dogs found the parking garage. However, there was no jubilation. Facing them as they burst into the open space and could smell the succulent fresh air of the night drifting down the ramp, were a dozen armed Korean men. They were a couple of metres up the ramp itself, the elevation giving them a clear view over the heads of the fleeing guests who were pinned in place by the threat of death.

Positioned in their centre was Uncle Kim. Blood dripped from his left arm, but he showed no sign the wound bothered him. In his right hand he held an ugly, black machine pistol, the kind that spits the contents of its magazine in a fraction of a second.

The dogs found themselves trapped once more. Between the haphazardly parked cars and the impenetrable wall of legs, they were a handful of metres from freedom and just couldn't get there.

Albert, DCI Garfield, Axel, his pals, and the girls came into view moving too fast to duck back out of the way. Inertia and the hurried pace of the party guests following them pushed the front of their mob into the open space of the parking garage.

"Please, join us," called Uncle Kim, his voice far from friendly. "I am looking for some volunteers to drive my cars. I failed to bring enough of my own people with me. The volunteers will live. Everyone else is about to die."

Hands shot up, the guests all shouting at once to be picked as a volunteer. That went sideways when Lee Yoo appeared. He wasted no time opening fire, a volley of bullets spewing from his gun. It should have instigated a deadly firefight in which dozens of people would have died, but the police chose that moment to finally make an appearance.

Using a combination of firearms and nonlethal weapons, they took out Lee Yoo before he could properly aim his gun and overpowered both sides of the Korean gang in a clinical demonstration of tactical superiority.

The police swarmed into the parking garage from both directions, sweeping down the ramp and in through the maze of corridors to pin armed thugs, illegal event guests, street racers, and dogs in the middle of the parking garage. They bellowed commands, getting everyone's hands up and then down on their knees so they could control the area and dominate it.

Albert complied, groaning a little when his aching knees complained. He, at least, understood the strategy. The police had no idea who was who at this point. Anyone could be armed so the only way to keep the officers safe was to overwhelm everyone. Then they could sift the criminal from the innocent, but given the nature of the event there would be very few of the latter.

DCI Garfield remained standing when everyone else got down on the floor, calling to identify himself.

"These are with me," he added, encouraging Albert to get up again.

"Get down. Get up," Albert moaned. "I wish they could make up their minds." He used Axel's hand to help him back to his feet with a thankful nod. Garfield made his way around the event guests, heading for Captain Verbeek and the SWAT commander on the ramp.

At least, Captain Verbeek thought Garfield was heading his way, but realised his mistake when DCI Danielle Hoeks ran past him.

Garfield had done it all for her. The risk of undercover work and almost freezing to death when he was caught. It was time to reveal his feelings and he could see her running to get to him. She felt the same, he knew she did and now they would get back together and never let work drive them apart again.

He stopped at the bottom of the ramp and opened his arms to receive her embrace.

She ran straight past him.

"Kevin! Kevin are you here, my darling? Bark for mummy!" Danielle Hoeks cupped her hands around her mouth and shouted for her dog, praying he was here among the ocean of fur and tails and bright, shining eyes all now looking her way.

A deep booming bark rang out.

Rex nudged his pal's shoulder. "*That's your human? Go get her.*"

Head and shoulders above almost every other dog present, Kevin was easy to spot once you knew where to look. He bounded through the pack, shunting other dogs aside when they failed to clear his path swiftly enough. With a leap to clear the last few dogs, Kevin rose onto his back legs to land his front paws on Danielle's shoulders.

Lavished with wet kisses from her dog's dinner plate of a tongue, Danielle could not have been happier. She was going to quit police work and pursue her dream of being a writer. She had a couple of manuscripts completed already and some money in the bank to keep her head above water for the next few months. She had always been about her career in the police, but as though glimpsing an epiphany, being reunited with Kevin changed all her priorities. Spending time with the ones she loved, that was going to be her new focus and that included Garfield.

Struggling to support Kevin's weight, she twisted at the waist to find her ex and wave him over. They were going to be one big, happy family.

Rex watched for a few seconds, revelling in seeing his friend reunited with his human. Kevin's tail was wagging so hard it became a near invisible blur. The sight made Rex want to find Albert. He'd not been separated from the old man for more than a couple of hours in many months and the last two days had been hard.

He hadn't worried too much about him, his human was generally safe to be left alone, but he also had a worrying habit for attracting trouble.

Rex forced his way through the pack to get to Albert where he nuzzled into his embrace. It was good to be back together.

All around them, the police were disarming thugs, searching guests, and making arrests. They couldn't go anywhere, not until the officers were satisfied they had Albert's statement and knew how to contact him, so they waited.

Albert introduced the street racers to his dog, showing him off proudly to his new friends. Axel and his merry band started out as a tool he would use to achieve his goal, but they were more than that now. They might disregard almost every road and highway regulation known to man, but they were salt of the earth people. Albert's kind of people.

Chapter 69

The police provided sandwiches and bottles of water, or rather they made the hotel above provide them. The hotel manager was arrested despite protesting he had no knowledge of the event's illegal nature.

Paramedics dealt with the injured persons including Uncle Kim and Lee Yoo. Albert watched them be loaded into separate ambulances for the trip to the hospital, each with police officers riding along and a squad car escort. The guests at the event were all arrested too though Albert doubted any would be charged. There had been no dog fights; it all came to a crashing end before the first bite could be delivered, and that meant the guests' lawyers would find ways to wriggle them off the hook.

Animal services arrived en masse to deal with the dogs and were promptly arrested. Albert had already explained about his dog's supposed euthanasia, and DCI Hoeks already suspected they were part of the chain of people supplying dogs to the fights.

Yet more officers were at the city's various animal services shelters to arrest more of the staff and seize all records. They would figure out how deep the rot went and stamp it out once and for all.

The police arrested Sylvia van Lidth in her penthouse apartment. Having slipped out of the venue during the bedlam, she was fleeing the country and stopped only to grab her passport and a bag.

Ivan was found in the freezer, cold, angry, but still very much alive despite the teeth marks Rex left in his butt. He wouldn't want to sit down for a while but could stay standing in his cell for all anyone cared.

Once the subbasement was clear of criminals, attention turned to the street racers and the glut of stolen cars.

"We found another twenty-three in a lockup at the port," DCI Hoeks told Captain Verbeek. "We got an anonymous tipoff earlier this evening."

"Who from?" Verbeek asked without stopping to think.

"Um, it was anonymous," said Hoeks though she noted neither Albert Smith nor any of the street racers wanted to meet her gaze. "They are being recovered now. The rightful owners will be informed once the forensic team have been over them."

Verbeek nodded along, satisfied that he would be getting a call from the commissioner once his report had been submitted. It was a very good night. Except Garfield appeared to be back with Hoeks. He doubted there was anything he could do about that, but he could embarrass the man for his failings.

"I got a call from your boss on the cross-border drug smuggling ring," Verbeek announced. "He's not very happy with you."

Garfield didn't give a hoot. "I'm sure I'll get over it."

"Will you? On my advice he is raising a complaint with the higher-ups. This will be a big black mark on your report, Garfield. You ditched your duties to go after DCI Hoeks' dog. What do you think they will say about that?"

Garfield was about to shrug his indifference though in truth he didn't feel it. He was in line for promotion so a bad mark at this point would ruin his chances. However, before he could do anything, Rex shot away from Albert's side with a bark.

"*It's here!*" he told them, sniffing at the cars. The smell first got him when they reached the subbasement only to find their way blocked by armed men. Trained as a police dog, sniffing for drugs wasn't his primary task, but it was one of those things they were all taught. Nothing has the same distinctive scent, but faced with guns, finally reunited with his human, and trying to get the pack out of harm's way, he noted the presence of heroin and dismissed it as unimportant.

Now the humans were talking about it, he had to show them where it was.

At the driver's door of a Maclaren, he whined and pawed the handle.

Albert went to him. "What have you got there, boy?"

He opened the door and swung it wide, expecting Rex to clamber inside, but Rex started to nudge at the door card with his nose. The smell coming from inside was driving him nuts.

Albert wanted to pull Rex away before his dog did any damage to the expensive car, but Garfield got there first.

It felt like a crazy guess, but it also made perfect sense. Drugs were leaving Holland, they knew that much; police in other countries had been able to trace it back, but no one knew how it was getting out of the country. If they could find the export route, they could trace it back to the manufacturer and close the whole production system down. That is how you tackle the global drug problem.

Asking for a knife from one of the SWAT officers, Garfield carefully levered the door card away from the steel frame, a wide grin spreading when he saw the plastic bound packs stuffed neatly inside.

Danielle crouched next to him, sharing his smile with her arm around his shoulders.

Verbeek came in behind, standing on his tiptoes and dodging this way and that to see what was in the door.

"What is it? Stand aside. Let me see."

Garfield rose, placed a hand on the captain's chest and pushed him back.

"No, sir. This comes under the jurisdiction of the cross-border taskforce. I'll be taking things from here." Verbeek opened his mouth to argue, and Garfield shot him down. "What was it you told me earlier? Oh, yes. Drugs take priority over missing dogs every day of the week and I believe DCI Hoeks has been trying to instigate an investigation into the dog fight ring case for some time." He looked around at the SWAT team and the other officers at the scene. "I believe that makes you um, what's the word? Redundant."

Not bothering to suppress his smile, Garfield took Danielle's hand and walked away, leaving Verbeek to shout and fume.

Left in the captain's presence, Albert allowed himself a wry smile. He'd travelled hundreds of miles, but the captain here was little different from DCI Quinn back home.

"If you'll excuse me," he edged around the car door to get away from Verbeek. "I've spent enough time around pompous, tiny men."

Rex trotted along at his human's side, happy that everything was as it should be. The only task remaining, so far as he could see, was reuniting the kidnapped dogs with their families. He and Kevin were back with their humans, but that left more than twenty dogs with nowhere to go.

The same thought had occurred to Albert, and it was time to propose a solution.

Chapter 70

It took almost no effort to get the TV cameras involved; it was an animals-in-crisis storyline and with so many press crews lining up outside the Grand Hotel, Albert knew it wasn't a case of whether one would jump at the chance, but which one would shout first.

He stayed in the background, content to oversee with Rex at his side. He didn't know how canine friendships worked, but this was not the first time he'd witnessed Rex forming deep bonds with the dogs they met on their travels.

The police were kind enough to provide a place where they could house the dogs, and when the appeal asked for donations, beds, blankets, food, treats, and even doggy grooming services appeared in greater numbers than they could hope to use.

It took two days for the last of the owners to see the appeal and come forward, but just fifty-seven hours after the press agreed to help, the final dog, was reunited with their tearful owner. It was Brain Scar, recently renamed Dodger, whose owner hadn't seen him in more than a year.

His real name was Cadans, Dutch for Cadence, which suited him. Rex watched the Pitbull being carried from the room high on his human's shoulder, his expression happy and his tongue lolling.

The room felt suddenly empty. Rex had never yearned to be a pack alpha; his place was with Albert and there would never be anywhere else he would rather be. Yet leading the dogs, doing what was right, and seeing them all returned to happy homes filled him with a kind of satisfaction spending time with a human could never replicate.

His train of thought broke when Albert clicked his tongue. It was time to get moving again.

Albert's planned stay in Amsterdam was supposed to be two nights. They were now on their fifth and if he didn't get moving soon he would miss his rendezvous with Roy and Beverly. Germany awaited, Wing Commander Roy Hope's old stomping ground. His neighbours from across the street hadn't been back to the European mainland in years and he knew it would be good to have some familiar company.

Leading Rex back to their hotel to retrieve Albert's small suitcase and backpack – all they needed for the meagre belongings he carried – he thought about what they might eat for dinner that night.

"You know what, Rex. I don't think I've ever eaten a Bratwurst."

Rex licked his lips. The next stage of their travels sounded good already.

The End

Book 4 is waiting for you. Scan the QR code with your phone to find your copy of Old Testament.

What's Next for Albert and Rex?

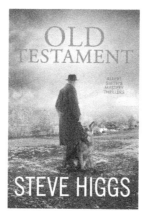

Be careful which stones you look under ...

An innocent walk through the woods turns sinister when Albert and Rex hear a cry for help. A desperate woman is trapped on the wrong side of a high fence ... and she is being pursued.

What follows is a situation more deadly than any they have faced before.

Author's Notes:

Hello, Dear Reader,

Thank you for reading all the way to the end of the book and beyond. This is the section where I get to talk a little about how the story came about and explain a few of the pieces that might have stood out.

When I first started to think in terms of the books I would write, many years before I finally put pen to paper, I had dog stories in my head. One was about a dog called Candle who found himself dumped at an animal shelter when his human, a soldier, was sent on an overseas operation, and his human's girlfriend decided to move on with someone new.

I guess I have always liked stories involving dogs and believe there is a lot of fun to be had imagining how they think and rationalise.

The story was about dogs in a shelter waiting to be rehomed or destroyed. Candle was going to arrive and through his spirit was going to change the entire culture before organising an escape that would result in all the dogs being rehomed.

I doubt I will ever get around to penning the original concept unless it appears in one of my short story collections.

I hope I didn't scare you too much with the Rex 'event'. I needed to create that moment for Albert and for the story but did so with serious concern that a chunk of my readership might close the book and refuse to ever pick it up again. I guess that doesn't apply to you since you are here, so maybe they will simply peek at the next chapter to be sure everything is going to be all right.

When Albert recruits Axel and the street racers I could see the cast of *Fast and Furious* in my head and when he starts to talk their language, I lifted the terms he uses directly from a piece of the first film when a character called Jesse says grace before they all tuck into dinner.

I also refer to a previous encounter with a car modification expert which occurred in *Bakewell Tart Bludgeoning*, the second book in the first series of adventures I wrote for Albert and Rex. The character in question is Asim, a young, Asian, British man who comes to Albert's rescue in *The Gastrothief* many books after his initial appearance.

Fishman is the nickname of a man I met in the army. He was and still is heavily invested in the modified car scene and it was fun to include him.

I employ the term clutterments in this book. It is a subject with which I annoy my wife, though that was never my intention. People buy ornaments and then put them on a shelf or a windowsill or the mantlepiece. What for?

They gather dust and often people have to buy the shelf or some kind of dresser so they can display the strange, inanimate objects they thought it would be fun to have instead of money in the bank.

I will admit there is a vintage Millenium Falcon on a shelf in my writing studio, but that serves as a reminder of my father and the childhood he gave me.

Stroopwafels appear in the story. If you have not come across these before I can tell you they are a pair of wafers used to sandwich a layer of caramel. I believe they make them with chocolate too. For research purposes only I bought a box and proceeded to devour them. They can be microwaved because they are better warm, but the trick is to sit them above the rising steam from your cup of coffee or tea.

It is a glorious summer day at the very end of July. My kids are in the garden playing in an inflatable pool with some other children who live in the village. My wife is chatting with another mum as they relax on the garden furniture. I am slaving away in my studio.

Only joking. I am in my studio, but my work is a joy. In three days I have a week of vacation with my family and some friends on England's famed Jurassic coast where my eight-year-old son will gleefully search for fossils.

I believe this is my tenth book this year, but whatever the number, there will be more. I need to wrap this note up and get it away to the proof readers so I might turn my attention to the next story.

Take care.

Steve Higgs

History of the Stroopwafel

According to Dutch culinary folklore, *stroopwafels* were first made in Gouda either during the late 18th century or the early 19th century by bakers re-purposing scraps and crumbs by sweetening them with syrup. One story ascribes the invention of the *stroopwafel* to the baker Gerard Kamphuisen, which would date the first stroopwafels from somewhere between 1810, the year he opened his bakery, and 1840, the year of the oldest known recipe.

After 1870, *stroopwafels* began to appear in other cities, and in the 20th century, factory-made stroopwafels were introduced. By 1960, there were 17 factories in Gouda alone, of which four are still open. Today, *stroopwafels* are sold at markets, by street vendors, and in supermarkets worldwide; are served as a breakfast snack by United Airlines; and have been used as a technical challenge on a 2017 episode of the *Great British Bake Off*.

Recipe

Ingredients

All purpose flour – 4 ½ cups

Unsalted butter (melted) – 1 cup

Sugar – 1 ¼ cups

Active dry yeast – 4 ½ teaspoons

Lukewarm milk – ½ cup

1 Egg

Vanilla Extract – 3 teaspoons

Cinnamon – 2 teaspoons

Sale – ½ teaspoon

Water – 2 tablespoons

Instructions

Combine all the ingredients for the waffles in a stand mixer.

After kneading the dough, allow to rest for 45 minutes.

Boil the ingredients for the syrup in a small saucepan over medium heat.

After the dough has finished resting, preheat and grease a waffle cone iron or pizzelle iron.

Knead the dough and divide it into small balls.

Cook the waffle until steam no longer escapes, and it has turned a golden brown.

Use a round cookie cutter to cut off the edges of the cooked waffle.

While the waffle is still hot, gently split the waffle with a serrated knife.

Spread 1 to 2 tablespoons of the caramel filling on one of the waffles and top with another waffle.

Repeat with the rest of the waffles.

Free Books and More

Want to see what else I have written? Go to my website.

https://stevehiggsbooks.com/

Or sign up to my newsletter where you will get sneak peeks, exclusive giveaways, behind the scenes content, and more. Plus, you'll be notified of Fan Pricing events when they occur and get exclusive offers from other authors because all UF writers are automatically friends.

Click the link or copy it carefully into your web browser.

https://stevehiggsbooks.com/newsletter/

Prefer social media? Join my thriving Facebook community.

Want to join the inner circle where you can keep up to date with everything? This is a free group on Facebook where you can hang out with likeminded individuals and enjoy discussing my books. There is cake too (but only if you bring it).

https://www.facebook.com/groups/1151907108277718

Made in the USA
Monee, IL
08 June 2025

19076224R00146